Bang to Rights

Helen Black

CONSTABLE

CONSTABLE

First published in Great Britain in 2018 by Constable

1 3 5 7 9 10 8 6 4 2

Copyright © Helen Black, 2018

A CIP catalogue record for this book
is available from the British Library.

ISBN: 978-1-47212-421-0

Typeset in Bembo by Photoprint, Torquay
Printed and bound in Great Britain by
CPI Group (UK), Croydon CRO 4YY

Papers used by Constable are from well-managed forests and other
responsible sources.

Constable
An imprint of
Little, Brown Book Group
Carmelite House
50 Victoria Embankment
London EC4Y 0DZ

An Hachette UK Company
www.hachette.co.uk

www.littlebrown.co.uk

The truth is rarely pure and never simple
— Oscar Wilde

Chapter 1

23 November 1989

I try to concentrate on my homework but there's ructions going on next door.

Imbo's kicking off again and that new key worker, Carl, is trying to calm him down. He's using the voice they put on in the beginning, all low and quiet. Probably something they teach them at Social Services. He should save his breath. When Imbo's in one of these moods, the only thing that will settle him is a two-litre bottle of cider and half an hour with his favourite issue of Knave.

'I can see you're upset, Ian,' says Carl.

I suck in a breath. If there's one thing guaranteed to send Imbo into one, it's anyone calling him that.

There's a bang, which might be Imbo's fist hitting the wall. Or Carl's head.

'What did you just call me?' Imbo screams. 'Say it one more time and I'll rip your arms off.'

'Please don't threaten me,' says Carl.

'It's not a threat, you twat, it's a fucking promise.'

I glance over at Vicky's bed, where she's buried herself beneath a pile of blankets and clothes, and then reread the essay question for the millionth time. How does Chaucer explore the Wife of Bath's attitude to sex and sexual attraction? I'm already two days late handing it in. If I don't get it to Mr Morris tomorrow, I'm bound to get a detention.

There's another bang and Vicky sits bolt upright. 'Shut up, Imbo.' She thumps the wall. 'Shut the fuck up.'

'Shut the fuck up yourself,' Imbo roars back.

I sigh as Vicky jumps out of bed and races next door in her denim shirt and knickers. Imbo might be nearly six foot and built like the Terminator, but nobody talks to Vicky like that. I close my textbook and follow her.

'Could you girls go back to your room?' says Carl, fiddling with his earring.

I feel a bit sorry for him. I expect he thought he'd help people in this job. I give him what I hope is an encouraging smile, but Vicky just pushes past and gets right up into Imbo's face.

'Listen to me, you ugly little prick,' she shouts at him. 'I'm trying to get some kip and she,' Vicky jabs a thumb behind her in my vague direction, 'is trying to do her chuffing homework. How do you think either of us can do that with you losing the plot like you're on a mental ward?'

'Carl says I can't watch the telly tonight,' screams Imbo.

Vicky spins on her bare heel and glares at the social worker. To be honest, the bed hair and smudged eye liner make her look like she's the one just stepped out of an asylum.

'Ian lost his privileges when he was caught vandalizing the staff toilets,' says Carl.

Last Saturday, off his head on Merrydown, Imbo spray-painted a knob on the wall of the staff toilets. And shat in the sink.

Imbo launches a flying kick at the wall. 'Stop calling me that.'

'And if you girls don't go back to your room right now, you'll lose your privileges too,' says Carl. I'll give it to him, he's still got the voice down pat even in these circumstances. 'Elizabeth? Victoria? Are you hearing me?'

'Do you think I give a shit?' Vicky steps towards Carl. The nail varnish on her toes is red and chipped and there's a yellow bruise on her shin. 'Do you think I'm actually bothered about watching the poxy telly?'

The thing is, Vicky does give a shit. We all do. It's Thursday so it's

2

Top of the Pops. And tonight's not just any Top of the Pops. Tonight, the Stone Roses and the Happy Mondays are on.

'Vic,' I say. 'Let's just go back next door.'

She doesn't look at me, but claws her hands as if she's about to scratch Carl's face off. I've seen her do it before. Not to Carl, but some boy up on the Crosshills Estate that she said called her a slag. That night I had to pick out the bits of skin from under her nails with a cocktail stick.

'Vic, come on. It's nearly time and I'm not missing it.'

She sniffs at Carl, pulls her knickers out from the crack of her arse and stalks from the room as Imbo lands another blow on the wall.

Present day

The waiting was always the killer. Once things got started, the adrenalin would kick in and the team would move on auto-pilot. Everyone would know where to be and what they needed to do. Clear heads, light limbs.

But now, squashed into the back of the van, watching the commander obsessively check her phone for the go-signal, Sol's mind jumped around. He needed a fag, a black coffee, to stretch his legs.

Outside, the pre-dawn morning was cool and still, but eight officers crammed in like sardines, all wearing Kevlar, filled the van with heat and sweat.

'Just so you know, Connolly,' Hassani leaned against him and whispered, 'you are minging.'

Sol gave her the finger.

The commander frowned and held up a hand, eyes glued to her phone. The timing of this raid was imperative. All over Yorkshire, other teams were also in place, ready to act as one. They needed to hit the top brass of the Delaney clan simultaneously so they couldn't tip one another off.

'Premature ejaculation by any team will be more than a

frustration,' the DCI had warned them. 'It will be an absolute disaster for which I will personally be slicing off bollocks.'

C Team's commander might not technically have any bollocks to lose but she was taking no chances.

At last she took a sharp breath and blinked. 'Unit, go.'

Her words were decisive, their impact immediate. Every officer including Sol braced themselves as the van sprang forward.

'Ready,' the driver shouted over the intercom.

A second later there was a jolt as the impact bars on the front of the van hit the gates and a metal clang ricocheted through Sol's bone structure. Then the back doors to the van were thrown open and they streamed out.

'Left, left, right,' Sol hissed at Hassani.

Exit by the left-hand side of the vehicle. Move around it to the left, then down the right-hand side of the house to the back.

He didn't *need* to say a word. Hassani already knew the drill. She'd gone over it with the team a hundred times, then another hundred alone with Sol in the Three Feathers.

Their boots crunched on gravel as they ran past the mangled security gates to the back of the house, arriving next to the vast lawn and swimming pool at the same moment as officers who had come around the other side with the ram.

'Clear,' Sol shouted and stepped back as the ram battered its way through the back door, splintering wood and smashing glass.

'Yeah, baby,' Hassani muttered, under her breath.

A faint smile flashed across Sol's face. It was her first raid. Better than sex, drugs and rock and roll. Welcome to the dark side.

They ploughed into the house, through the opulent dining room, heels dragging shards of glass with them, and down the hallway lined with antique tables and *objets d'art*. Sol had to hand it to Delaney. He might have started out selling nicked batteries and jars of coffee to housewives on the Crosshills but his house was bloody lovely.

When they reached the bottom of the stairs, Sol saw a figure leaning over the walkway that spanned the entire upper floor. Short and square, mouth drawn into an almost smile, it was Jackson Delaney himself.

'What is it with you lot?' Delaney shouted down to them in his deep-fried Mars Bar Glaswegian accent. 'You never write. You never call. Then here you are with not so much as a bunch of flowers.'

'Come on down, Jacko,' Sol said. 'Let's make this easy.'

Delaney laughed and headed for the top of the stairs.

'Put your hands where we can see them,' Sol called up.

'Have a word with yourself, Connolly,' Delaney replied. 'I'm packing nothing but my tackle.'

True enough, when Delaney began to saunter casually downstairs, Sol could see his hands were empty and that the head of one of the country's biggest crime families was wearing only a pair of boxer shorts and his ink.

When he was at the bottom, Delaney smiled at Sol and put his hands out to Hassani.

'Why don't you do the honours, hen?' he said. 'It's a long time since I've been tied up by someone as young and pretty as yourself.'

Hassani glanced sideways at Sol. He'd told her time and time again that Jackson Delaney was a clever bastard who would mess with them any way he could. This was all part of how he ran his business.

'Cuff him,' Sol told her.

Delaney watched Hassani intently as she secured his wrists. Nose bent from a thousand beatings. Knuckles raised and scarred from giving out two thousand. 'Tight as you like, sweetheart.'

She ignored him as Sol had advised.

'Right then,' said Delaney. 'Let's get this over with. I need to be back in time for the midday kick-off.'

'Not today, Jacko,' said Sol.

'Do you not think that every time, pal?'

Sol shook his head. He'd been involved in several attempts over the years to bring down Delaney. Some had fallen apart through lack of evidence. At least two from lack of budget. The one time they had actually managed to get a case to court, none of the main witnesses had turned up at the trial.

But this was different. Computers were being seized, bank accounts frozen and a couple of girls trafficked from Montenegro were already in a safe house.

'Everything that rises has to fall in the end, Jacko,' said Sol.

Jay cranked up the sound system and 'Get Lucky' by Daft Punk bounced across his garden, mingling with smoke from the barbecue and the chatter of a hundred guests. He grabbed Liberty's hand and spun her round, then planted a kiss on her cheek.

'You're drunk.'

'Yup.'

He danced off towards his wife, Rebecca, who was helping the caterers put countless bowls of salad onto an already groaning table.

'He always was a grade-A show-off,' said Crystal, mouth full of Juicy Fruit.

Liberty smiled as she watched her brother tell a passing waiter to refill glasses more quickly. 'He just wants everyone to have a good time,' she said.

'He just wants everyone to have a good look at how well he's done for himself,' Crystal replied.

Liberty shrugged. Not long ago she'd worked in a prestigious law firm in London where her partners routinely threw dinner parties with the sole intention of parading their latest extension, their children's exam grades and their sizeable bonus. At least Jay's guests were actually enjoying themselves.

As the chorus belted out from the speakers, Liberty hummed along.

'Please don't tell me you're going to dance,' said Crystal. 'Or I might have to kill myself.'

'Every cloud,' said Liberty, and tapped her feet.

Crystal turned her head as she always did when she didn't want Liberty to know that she'd made her laugh, but suddenly her shoulders stiffened.

'Crystal?' Liberty followed her sister's eye line to the patio, where a couple who had just arrived accepted flutes of prosecco. They were flanked on either side by men in dark suits, their heads shaved. 'Who the hell are they?'

But her sister was already striding across the lawn. She grabbed her husband, Harry, and together they approached the new arrivals.

Liberty moved to the table of food, partly because the smell of searing steaks was making her stomach growl and partly to distract herself from whatever was going on at the other side of the garden. Her family's business included several strip clubs, websites selling sex toys and a whole host of other endeavours that she preferred not to think about. She knew from past experience that the hidden safe in the Black Cherry contained used banknotes and a loaded gun.

'Should have known I'd find you near the grub.'

Liberty turned to find Raj grinning at her.

'You made it,' she said, and hugged him. His back was slightly damp under a polyester shirt and his belly jiggled against hers.

'I'm too nosy not to,' he replied.

When Jay had told Liberty she should invite whoever she liked to the party, the only person she could think of was Raj. 'Have you eaten?' she asked.

The look on Raj's face said he had. It also said he wasn't about to refuse a burger or three.

A young woman helped them pile their plates, her ponytail sprayed so hard it looked like a croissant. They'd barely stepped away from the table when Raj took his first bite, ketchup and meat juices running down his chin. 'I've been thinking.'

Liberty looked over her shoulder. 'Someone call a doctor.'

'Have you thought about a career on the stage?'

'At the Black Cherry?' Liberty looked down at her chest. 'I don't think my assets are up to it.'

'I think the assets are more than up to it.' Raj took another huge mouthful and Liberty did the same, both of them laughing.

'Seriously, though, I've been wondering if you're staying round here permanently.'

Liberty rubbed at a splodge of mayonnaise that had landed on Raj's cuff with a paper napkin but made matters worse. 'I don't have any firm plans one way or the other.'

'You must have been here, what, a year?' he asked. 'Thing is, I'm rushed off my feet at work. The missus helps out when she can but she's not a solicitor.'

'Are you offering me a job, Raj?'

'I suppose I am.' He sucked each finger in turn. 'The money won't be what you're used to, mind.' He told her the figure. It was a tenth of what she'd earned at her firm in London. In a bad year.

'That's kind of you, Raj,' she said. 'But you do know that my family . . .' She let the sentence trail away.

'That's them.' He attacked the second burger. 'Not you.'

Amira Hassani moved through the cars parked outside Jay Greenwood's house. Beemers, Jags, Mercs. Evidence, if ever it were needed, that crime did indeed pay.

She whipped out her mobile and took pictures of the registration plates. Not all of them would belong to villains, but she'd lay odds that a good proportion would. The Greenwoods might give out that they were legit, but Amira didn't believe it for a second. With enough spadework she would find something on them, she was sure of it.

Up ahead a younger leaned against a Porsche Cayenne with blacked-out windows. Amira could smell the weed he was smoking, hot and herbal, hanging in the early-evening air.

He made his finger and thumb into the shape of a C. Cop. And the other C-word. With her thumb and index finger she made an O and moved it up and down. He didn't scare her. She could tell just by looking at him that he wasn't packing.

He pulled out his phone and raised it to photograph her, so she turned away.

Her own mobile rang and she saw Sol was calling. 'Boss man.'

'Hey. You did good this morning.'

Amira smiled. 'Is Mr Delaney still enjoying our hospitality?'

'Yep. And half a dozen members of his family,' Sol replied. 'Plus at least ten of his top men.'

'Will anyone talk?'

Sol snorted. 'Not if they value their arseholes. But we've got enough to charge him.'

Amira pumped her fist and got into her car. 'We should clean this area up properly.'

'Oh, yeah?'

'Definitely. What's the point of shutting down Delaney if another clan just takes his place? We should bring them all down, one by one.'

'I don't suppose you have another family in mind?' asked Sol.

Amira looked over her shoulder at Jay Greenwood's house and heard the music floating towards her on the wind. Inside the perimeter, he'd be there, all white teeth and sunglasses on top of his head. His sister Crystal, pretty as a picture but as poisonous as a snake bite. Frankie was in rehab, but it was only a matter of time until he got out and returned to his favourite pastimes: smoking crack and beating women. And last of all Liberty. The eldest. Liberty My-shit-doesn't-smell Chapman. So squeaky clean she didn't even use the family name. Amira's mouth filled with acid bile at the thought of her.

'No family in particular,' she said.

Liberty found Dax on the drive. When he clocked her, he threw away his roach and blew smoke out of the corner of his mouth. Liberty rolled her eyes. 'What are you doing out here?' she asked.

'Jay asked me to keep an eye, innit,' Dax replied. 'Five-oh been sniffing around.'

Liberty pressed her lips together. She'd repeatedly asked Jay not to involve Dax in his affairs. The kid was sixteen. He should be in school worrying about his GCSEs and whether the girls thought he was fit, not acting as lookout for the local faces. 'Got the munchies?' she asked.

'Don't know what you're talking about,' Dax replied.

'There's some really good burgers on the grill.' Liberty nudged him with her elbow. 'I've already had two.'

He allowed her to lead him back to the garden. 'How come you ain't fat? I already seen you eating a bacon roll at breakfast.'

'Fast metabolism,' she said. 'Runs in the family.'

She had no idea if that was true. Both her parents had lived on pints of lager and Embassy Regal, from what she could remember. As for her siblings, Jay spent at least a couple of hours each day at the gym and Frankie smoked enough crack to keep a sumo wrestler thin. As for Crystal, Liberty had never seen her put anything in her mouth except a stick of gum.

Back at the party, Liberty noticed that Jay had now joined

Crystal and was chatting to the couple with the guards. 'Who are they?' she asked Dax.

He wrinkled his nose. He'd only been in Yorkshire twelve months but he already had an encyclopaedic knowledge of the area's gangsters. 'Paul and Bunny Hill,' he said.

'Bunny?'

'I doubt it's her real name,' said Dax.

'You think?' It never ceased to amaze her how little effort some women made to be taken seriously. Liberty had spent more than half her life creating a persona with gravitas. Everything from her accent to her wardrobe was carefully chosen to reflect what she wanted people to see.

Jay caught her eye and beckoned to her. Shit. The last thing she wanted was to meet Yorkshire's answer to Tony and Carmela Soprano. But Jay's grin had her, as it always did.

'No use trying to fight it,' said Dax, as he moved off to the barbecue.

'Fight what?'

'These are your people.' Dax laughed at her. 'Your bredrin.'

She shooed him away, plastered on a smile and walked over to her brother.

'Lib.' Jay swayed gently. He'd had a hell of a lot to drink. 'Let me introduce you to the Hills. Good friends of mine.'

Liberty thrust out her hand and Paul Hill pumped it. 'Heard all about you. The legal arm of the family business.'

She raised an eyebrow at Jay. 'I'm having a bit of a sabbatical from work, actually.'

'Trouble down in the Big Smoke?' asked Hill.

'Nothing like that,' Liberty replied. 'I just needed a change of scene.'

Bunny grabbed her hand. The fingernails were black claws, pointed and shiny. 'I get what you mean. Sometimes I'm so exhausted by everything I just have to take off to our place in

11

Majorca.' Her grip was surprisingly tight. 'Do you know Majorca at all?'

Liberty shook her head.

'To die for,' trilled Bunny. 'Like a little slice of paradise.' She turned to Crystal. 'What about you? Fond of the beach?'

Liberty swallowed a snort and avoided eye contact with Harry. Her sister was as allergic to sunshine as your average vampire. An English spring morning sent Crystal scurrying for the factor fifty to ward off her freckles.

'Another drink, Bun?' Jay snapped his fingers at a waiter, without waiting for her answer. 'Can't beat a few bubbles.'

When everyone's glass was refilled and the waiter had wandered off to the next group of guests, Paul Hill leaned in towards Jay. 'You hear about Jacko Delaney?'

'It's not bullshit, then?' asked Jay.

'Nope. I've half a dozen coppers on my payroll and they all say the same thing.' Hill took a glug from his glass. 'Still in custody. Him and half his crew.'

'Shame,' said Jay.

'It is,' Hill replied. 'Although of course it does mean that their patch is up for grabs.'

'Bit early for talk like that, Paul,' said Jay.

Hill shrugged and drained his glass. 'Nature abhors a vacuum. If someone doesn't step up the Russians will be all over it, like flies on the brown stuff.'

'And who's going to be doing the stepping up?' Crystal raised her drink to her mouth, but Liberty noticed that she didn't take a sip, didn't even wet her lips. 'You, Paul?'

'I was thinking we might do it together,' said Hill. 'Two families.'

Crystal eyed him over the rim of her glass but didn't answer.

'A fifty-fifty investment,' said Hill. 'Split the takings right down the middle.'

Bunny threw out her arms and expelled a theatrical sigh. 'For the love of God, give it a rest. This is supposed to be a party not a business meeting.'

'Can't argue with you there,' said Jay, grabbing her hand and pulling her towards a group of guests who were dancing. Bunny squealed and began shimmying in her skin-tight white jeans.

Frankie stumbled out of the taxi and swore as he lurched towards the party. He hadn't meant to get this caned. A few lines to take the edge off had been the plan.

'The trouble with you, Frankie, is you've got no off button,' Daisy kept telling him.

Frankie ground his teeth. Being lectured to by Daisy the Dog didn't sit well. Daisy, who had used class As for over ten years. Daisy who had sold everything from her kettle to her arse to pay for them. But once in rehab she'd given herself over to getting clean with as much energy as she'd put into being an addict. Frankie had tried to do the same, of course he had, but attending group sessions to make snot-stained confessions about how much you'd hurt those around you was never going to be as much fun as getting fucked on drugs, was it?

'And the trouble with you is you're so boring these days,' he'd spat back at her.

Daisy had just shrugged. She wouldn't even come to this frigging party with him. Said she had to go to work at the call centre. A fucking call centre! Eight-hour shifts on the phone trying to convince old biddies to switch their energy provider. He'd rather slit his wrists.

She'd point-blank refused to go back to work for Jay at the Black Cherry. Too much temptation, she said. The ironic thing was that when she had worked there she'd looked like shit and hardly made any money. These days, with a bit more meat on her bones, she'd have had the punters queuing up for private dances. Still, it was her funeral.

He scanned the crowd for his brother and sisters and spotted Jay twirling around with Paul Hill's latest wife. By the look of things, Jay was pissed. Thank God. He'd be a lot less likely to notice what state Frankie was in. Crystal was looking on, the usual black cloud hovering over her head.

Where was Lib? It was funny, but even though there'd been all those years when he hadn't seen or heard from her, he still felt closer to his eldest sister than the other two. She was always so pleased to see him. And she didn't judge.

He caught sight of her over by the food and smiled. However, the smile soon slipped off his face when he saw who she was with. That bloody kid from Brixton she'd all but adopted. Dax. What sort of name was that when it was at home? Had to be moody. Frankie didn't like or trust him. The sooner he slung his hook back down south, the better for all of them.

A trickle of sweat ran down his neck.

'Frankie.' Liberty bounded over to him and kissed his damp cheek. 'Great to see you.'

He kissed her back, scowling at Dax over his sister's shoulder. The little shit scowled at him, cocky as you please.

'Christ.' Liberty laughed. 'You're sweating like a fat lass at the bingo.'

Frankie stepped back. 'It's close, don't you think?'

'A bit,' she replied, casting a glance at the cloudless sky.

'Definite,' said Dax, looking Frankie up and down. 'There's a storm coming, bruv.'

Chapter 2

14 December 1989

When I come out of school, Vicky's waiting for me.

'All right?'

She's wearing this massive hoodie that says 'Feed Your Head' on it and some blue eyeliner she nicked from Boots last weekend.

'What's up?' I ask.

'Nice to chuffing see you as well.'

I laugh. I never really see Vicky outside Orchard Grove. For a start, she goes to the PRU. Or she's meant to. Mostly she skives off. Whereas I'm still in mainstream school. We get on well enough, me and Vicky. We leave each other to it. She hardly ever asks me anything. Actually, that's one of the things I like best about her. When I first moved into her room she said, 'Why're you here?'

'My dad killed my mam,' I said.

'Shit,' she replied.

'And then he died in the nick,' I said.

'Double shit.'

And that was it. No more questions.

I gathered from some of the other kids that Vicky had been chucked out by her mam when she accused her stepdad of trying to finger her. But I've never brought it up.

'Do us a favour, Lib,' she says.

'What?'

She fishes in her bag and pulls out a record. 'Take this into the Galaxy and see what you can get for it.'

I take it from her: 90 by 808 State. I love this album and run a finger across the blue and pink lettering. It looks like a new copy. 'Why can't you do it?' I ask her.

She pulls a face. 'Fat Rob banned us.'

To be fair, Vicky nicks anything not nailed down so it's no great surprise.

'Come on,' she says. 'Bat them big brown eyes at him and ask him how much. If it's more than three quid sell it to the tight arsehole.'

Half an hour later I'm being pushed out of the frosty afternoon into the Galaxy record shop. I've never been in before. Well, I've never got any money, have I? But I've peered in the window and watched lads in baggy jeans rifling through stacks of records, bobbing their heads in time to whatever EP Fat Rob's playing inside.

I feel utterly stupid in my school uniform.

'It makes you look more honest,' said Vicky. 'Plus, Fat Rob's a right perv.'

Thank God the shop's nearly empty. There's just one lad walking his fingers through the compartment marked A to C, humming along to the Inspiral Carpets. He looks up at me and clocks my navy blazer. I almost die, but then he notices 90, which I'm gripping in sweaty fingers.

'Class, that,' he says.

I take a deep breath and shuffle to the counter. No one there. I look around. Why isn't anyone on the till? I should take it as a sign that this is A Bad Idea.

The lad stops humming for a second and shouts, 'Rob, you fat fuck. Customer.'

Out of the back room comes another lad, Fat Rob, fag hanging out of the corner of his mouth, his hair a mess of dirty curls. 'Yeah?'

He's not actually that fat. Just a bit chunky, really. What Mam would have called well built.

'I want to sell this,' I say, and thrust the record at him. 'It's new.'

He gives me a stare through a plume of smoke. 'Did you nick it?'

'No.'

'So why don't you want it?'

My throat goes dry. What if he calls the police? They'll never believe me. They never believe any of us lot about anything. And when they find out about my caution, that'll be it. Arrested, charged, convicted. Criminal record. It doesn't matter how much Stacey Lamb deserved the pasting I gave her, there'll be no more second chances.

I pull at my frayed cuffs. 'I've already got a copy of it. I don't need two.'

Fat Rob snorts so hard the ash falls off his cig onto a pile of fliers for a club night. He brushes it away half-heartedly. 'What's your favourite track?'

'"Cobra Bora",' I answer, quick as a flash. I might not have been able to afford 90 myself but I've borrowed Imbo's like a million times. 'Then "Magical Dream".'

'Fair play.' Fat Rob squints at me. 'I'll give you two quid for it.'

For a second my outrage outweighs my fear of getting done. 'That's daylight robbery,' I say. 'It's bloody new, you can see it is.'

'Take it back to the shop it came from, then.' He folds his arms. 'You must have the receipt.'

I blush so much I'm radiating heat. I bet I'm bright pink. Why did I let Vicky talk me into this? The fact is she probably did nick it. Maybe even from in here. I should have told her to bugger off.

'I haven't got a receipt,' I mutter.

'Why not?'

'It was a present,' I reply. 'For my birthday.'

Fat Rob takes the cig from his mouth and grinds it out in an ashtray already overflowing with dog ends. I can't see a phone on the counter, so if he does want to call the police he'll have to go into the back room. I've got enough time to leg it.

'Never mind,' I say, and grab 90 from him.

When I spin round I almost bump into the other lad because he's now blocking my way out. Shit. If I'm going to get past him I'll have to push him out of the road.

'Don't be a twat,' he says. At first, I think he's talking to me, but then I realize he's looking over my shoulder at Fat Rob. 'Just buy the thing.'

'Four quid,' says Fat Rob.

I turn to face him. 'What?'

'Four quid.' He holds out podgy fingers stained yellow from too many fags. 'And that's your lot.'

I don't speak, couldn't even if I wanted to, so I just hand the record back and let him plonk the money into my palm without even looking him in the eye. I mumble a thank you and am about to hurry away when he picks up one of the fliers that are still covered with ash.

'You should go to this,' he says. 'You'll like the sounds.'

I shove it into my pocket and virtually run out of the shop.

Present day

Liberty parked the Porsche outside the Black Cherry and approached Jay, who was opening up the club. His hands were shaking so badly, he dropped the fob of keys.

Liberty bent to retrieve them. 'Good party.'

'Yup,' he replied, his words escaping in a cloud of ethanol that made Liberty wince.

She unlocked the door as Crystal arrived in a taxi with Frankie, who looked about as healthy as his older brother.

They entered in silence, pushing the velvet drape out of the way and moving into the main room. Liberty always thought there was something forlorn about the club in the early mornings. Not that the Black Cherry was a place of cheer and harmony later in the day, but at least it had an energy about it.

Liberty slipped around the back of the bar to the fridge and pulled out four bottles of Coke, avoiding a discarded black lace thong that Mel must have found when she locked up the previous night.

Right on cue, Mel waltzed in, thinning hair teased into a freshly bleached halo, bunions pressed into a pair of purple suede shoe-boots with six-inch heels. She looked Jay up and down. 'I've seen folk more lively on ketamine.'

Liberty leaned back into the fridge for the last cold Coke and held it out to Mel.

'Whereas you,' she pointed at Liberty, 'you look as fresh as a fairy's fart. I don't know how you do it.'

'Evil magic,' said Crystal.

They sat at a table and drank in silence. Jay had asked them to come over, away from Rebecca and the boys. He had something to say.

'No easy way to do this, sunshine.' He looked at Frankie over the rim of his bottle. 'But we all know you're using again.'

Frankie looked shocked.

'Don't,' said Crystal.

Frankie twisted in his seat to face Liberty for support. There were dark circles under his eyes and a sheen of grease across his forehead. She loved him so much it hurt. 'You were doing so well in rehab,' she said, and his face fell in betrayal. 'Your key worker told me you'd made tons of progress. She was convinced you could do this.'

'I can, Lib.' His eyes darted around the room. 'The days are just . . .'

'Just what, Frankie?'

He furrowed his brow trying to search for the right way to express himself.

'Just what, Frankie?' Liberty repeated. 'Hard? Painful?'

'Boring,' Frankie replied.

Jay slammed his bottle onto the table, making Liberty jump. 'Boring? Are you shitting me?'

Mel let out a cackle, and Frankie threw her a venomous glance. 'Well, what do you lot think I do all day?' he shouted. 'I can't see any of my old mates and you don't let me do anything in the business.'

Now, Frankie had a point right there. His key worker had made it plain that those fighting addictions needed to stay busy once they left rehab. Empty time and space were the enemies. What the hell did Frankie do all day except think about the stuff he'd like to be doing?

'Couldn't he work here?' Liberty asked.

'No,' Jay, Crystal and Mel replied as one.

'Because?'

'Because we tried that once before,' said Mel.

'And?'

Jay, Crystal and Mel exchanged a look. Frankie slumped in his seat, eyes on the floor.

'It ended up with one of the girls going to the police.' Mel sniffed. 'Cost a lot to sort that little mess out and Frankie had to be sent away to Marbella. And we all know how that turned out.'

Liberty gulped. Frankie had got in with the wrong crowd in Spain, especially a petty criminal calling himself Brixton Dave, who had convinced Frankie to get involved in a drug deal. Only there was no deal, just a ruse to snatch him and demand money from the Greenwoods. To say it had not been an easy thing to sort out was the understatement of the century.

'How about that new club you've just bought?' Liberty asked.

'It's not even open yet,' answered Jay.

'Exactly,' said Liberty. 'Stuff must need doing before the girls start working.'

Frankie lifted his head, eyes more alive than Liberty had seen in a while. 'I could do it, Jay. I could help get it set up.'

Jay looked unconvinced. Crystal just shrugged.

'I'm saying nowt,' said Mel, which would be a first.

Liberty held her hands up to Jay in a gesture of prayer.

'Oh, fine,' he said. 'But even a sniff of trouble and there'll be hell to pay.'

When a delivery arrived, Frankie jumped up with uncharacteristic helpfulness. 'Office?' he asked Jay, who nodded.

If the driver was embarrassed at having to cart boxes of nipple drops from his van to the back room, he didn't show it. 'How do, ladies?' he said to Liberty, Crystal and Mel, who were finishing their Coke.

Liberty scanned a label as he passed. 'Mustard flavour?'

'Custard,' Mel replied.

'That would make more sense,' said Crystal.

It made no sense at all to Liberty. But, then, the way her family made their money was a world away from what she'd been used to.

'You don't need to look quite so disgusted,' said Crystal. 'It'll probably come as a shock to you, but most people do actually like sex.'

Liberty stared. Crystal routinely made crack after crack at her expense, but she'd never mentioned her personal life before.

'What?' Crystal made a smacking noise as she chewed her gum. 'Touched a nerve, have I?'

'Pack it in, you two,' said Mel, collecting the empty bottles. 'Do you know how tedious it gets listening to your endless bickering?' She slung the bottles into a recycling bin, the glass making a loud clank. 'Were the Hills at the party yesterday?'

'Yeah,' Crystal replied.

'They make any suggestions?' asked Mel.

'One or two.'

'And?'

Crystal shrugged and stretched out her long legs, pale skin showing through the rips in her jeans. 'And I don't know if I trust them.'

'What do you think, Lib?' Mel asked.

'Don't ask me.' Liberty held up her hands in surrender. 'I stay well out of all that stuff.'

'Stuff?' Crystal asked.

'You know what I mean.'

'It's our business. How we put food on the table.'

Liberty sighed. 'I know that. But I can't get involved. I'm a solicitor, for God's sake.'

'You resigned from all that,' Crystal replied. 'You said you wanted to be a proper part of this family again.'

'I do,' said Liberty. 'I am.'

Crystal shook her head, making her red curls dance. 'It's not a part-time job, Lib. You can't dip in and out when it suits you.'

'What are you saying? That if I don't work with you and Jay, I don't count?'

Crystal pushed a stray tendril behind her ear. 'I'm saying that you're either on the bus or off it.'

'Fine.' Liberty scraped back her chair and stood. 'Let me off then because I've already agreed to take a job with Raj.'

'Raj Singh? That one-man band?'

Liberty had assumed she wouldn't take the job until that very second. But standing on the sticky floor of the Black Cherry, breathing in last night's beer, sweat and sex, she knew she would.

'He's a good man.' Liberty grabbed her bag. 'And at least he likes me.'

Crystal sneered. 'Fill your boots, then.'

'I will,' Liberty replied, and marched away, letting the drape fall between her and the rest of the Greenwood clan.

★ ★ ★

22

The door to the custody suite opened with a buzz and Sol stepped inside.

The sergeant was bent over his desk, reading through a bail sheet, while a skag head on the bench in front shivered in a puke-stained T-shirt.

Sol checked the whiteboard for the list of suspects currently sweating and swearing in the cells. A regular who sometimes went by Carlo Gaddioli was in for theft. Sol had also nicked him under the names Paulo Goldoni and Lucca Silvio (if the aliases were meant to put the police off the scent, you had to wonder why not pick something less Italian). Two working girls had been lifted for soliciting, which the custody sarge would not be happy about, and someone called Tomas Janowski was in for a GBH.

But there, right at the bottom of the roster, was the name Sol wanted to see. Jackson Delaney. Under the offence someone had scribbled SAO. Serious arrestable offence. Sol grabbed the marker pen and added an *s*. SAOs. Offences, plural.

'How happy does that make you, Connolly?' the sergeant asked.

'I haven't enjoyed myself this much since my wedding night,' Sol replied.

'Which wedding?'

Sol wagged a finger and wandered towards the cells. He opened the hatch on the second door and peered inside. Delaney was lying on the bed, staring at the ceiling, shredding a polystyrene cup onto his chest.

'Morning, Jacko,' said Sol.

'Connolly,' Delaney replied, without looking over.

'Treating you okay?'

'Can't complain,' said Delaney. 'Just waiting on my brief to get here.'

Sol nodded. Delaney used some big firm from Manchester. Probably had the partners on speed-dial. 'Will they get their arses over here for fifty quid an hour?' Sol asked.

'They charge a lot more than that, pal.'

'But they'll have to sign you up for legal aid,' said Sol. 'What with all your cash being frozen.'

Delaney sat up, causing a polystyrene snow shower, and shot Sol a look of pure hatred. The cool character was feeling the heat. Men like him expected to be arrested from time to time. They could do bang-up no problem. But put your hands on their money? That was another matter.

'How's Officer Hassani going? Pretty wee thing, no?' Delaney brushed away a few stray pieces of white confetti. 'I might see if she'd like to go somewhere when I get out of here.'

Sol gave a quiet laugh and shook his head. 'You're not getting out, Jacko.'

'You need to be very sure about that.'

'I am,' said Sol, and slammed the hatch shut.

Dax was sprawled across the sofa wearing only boxer shorts.

Liberty snatched up the remote control and flicked off whatever daytime crap he was watching. 'Would you put some clothes on?'

He scratched his six-pack with lazy fingers. 'Who pissed on your chips?'

She stalked past him into the kitchen and smacked the tap to hot. When the water began to steam she filled the washing-up bowl.

'We've got a dishwasher,' said Dax.

She ignored him and angrily squirted Fairy Liquid before dunking cups and a cereal bowl. The water burned her hands but Liberty didn't care.

'You gonna tell me why you're raging or do I have to guess?' asked Dax.

Liberty grabbed a blue J-cloth from the counter and ran it around the inside of one of the cups. Then she thrust it under a jet of cold water and banged it onto the draining-board.

'Crystal been vexing you, is it?'

Liberty spun around, fingers covered in suds. 'She is never going to let me move on from what happened when we were kids.'

'She's angry.'

'Well, duh.'

Dax kissed his teeth. 'Don't be getting all sarcastic on my arse, woman.'

Liberty plunged her hands back into the bowl. Christ, the water was *really* hot. Her skin was already bright pink and stinging. 'I'm trying to make things right, you know?' Her shoulders sagged. 'I did a lot of things I shouldn't have done to help my family but it'll never be enough.'

Dax nudged her out of the way with his bare hip, the skin smooth and caramel. He added cold water to the bowl and finished the washing-up. 'What do you think Crystal wants?' he asked.

Liberty sucked her burned thumb. 'I don't know. She says I need to join the family business, but I can't believe she'd ever want me to do that. I mean, what use would I be?'

'I wish I could join the family business,' said Dax.

'No.'

'I need to earn some peas.'

'I give you *peas*,' said Liberty.

'I ain't a charity.'

Liberty grabbed a tea-towel and dried the crockery. She knew how horrible it was to have no money of your own. Hadn't she battled long and hard to ensure that she would never feel that way again? 'We had a deal, Dax,' she said.

'And what if I don't want to stick to that deal no more?'

Liberty dried her hands, the edge of the tea-towel scraping her cuticle, which was now raw. She winced. 'When I was your age . . .'

'For fuck's sake,' Dax muttered.

Liberty grabbed his arms. 'When I was your age I had no one.'

'Yeah, yeah, both your mum and dad got killed.' Dax shrugged her off. 'You told me this story like a zillion times.'

'It's not a story.'

He stormed out of the kitchen and flopped back onto the sofa, this time on his stomach. Across his back was a ten-inch scar. He would never tell Liberty what had happened other than to confirm he'd been 'shanked'. Liberty sat on the floor next to him. 'I know how easy it is for people like us to get sucked into the wrong life, Dax,' she said.

He rolled over onto his side, eyes no longer angry. He was such a handsome kid. Liberty wondered if he looked like his mum or his dad.

'But who gets to decide what the wrong life is?' he asked.

Liberty reached over and rubbed his finger with her own. 'The wrong life is the one where you end up in prison or dead.' He didn't move away from her touch. 'Look, you're seventeen in six months and officially no one's problem,' she said. 'Social services will be only too glad to chuck you off their books. Then you can do whatever you want. Go to college, maybe.' Dax looked horrified. 'Or get a job. And I mean a proper job, not working for Jay watching out for the po-po, or whatever it is he gets you to do.'

Dax burst out laughing. 'The *po-po*? Man, you are beyond help.'

'True dat,' said Liberty. 'Now get down to the corner shop for some Savlon, would you? My bloody thumb's killing me.'

Amira sat in her car and waited. In the front passenger foot well there were two empty Tango cans and half a packet of Hula Hoops.

Without doubt, surveillance was the most boring part of police work, but often the most valuable. A numb arse regularly brought the best intel.

She yawned as she watched Liberty Chapman's front door. A quick search of the electoral register had confirmed that Chapman still owned her flat in London and was renting this property on Empire Rise.

A couple of days ago, when Chapman was safely out of the way, Amira had chatted to the neighbours on either side under the guise of Neighbourhood Watch. The old lady at number thirty-two had spent twenty minutes complaining about NHS waiting lists, then another twenty detailing the various operations and treatments she'd had in the last year. On the subject of Chapman she'd had little to offer, other than to confirm she was quiet and lived with her son. The man at number thirty-six had thought Chapman might be foreign.

Amira sighed. Chapman was most definitely not foreign and did not have a son. What was wrong with people that they paid so little attention to what was happening right under their noses?

When the front door opened, Amira snatched up her phone to film Chapman as she came out, but was surprised to see a lad close behind her, baseball cap perched high on his crown. Perhaps that was who the old woman at thirty-two had thought was Chapman's son. As he passed the car he flicked a glance inside, but turned away, uninterested, when Amira drew her hijab across her mouth. Who would have thought her headscarf would prove so useful for detective work? It was like an invisibility cloak.

She recorded the boy moving down the street, something familiar in his heel-bouncing steps, until he turned the corner.

It wasn't Chapman's son, she was sure of that. But he must be living there for a neighbour to make that mistake. Amira played back the recording, pausing when she reached a good shot of the boy's face, enlarging it with her fingers.

'Well, look at you,' she said, with a smile.

It was the younger she'd seen outside Jay Greenwood's party. A gangster in training. And he was holed up with the woman Amira was determined to put away.

Liberty sucked her thumb and waited for Dax. He was a good kid at heart. A kid who had just had a bad start in life. But that didn't mean his life had to go a certain way. All she had to do was keep him on the straight and narrow until he found something he wanted to do more than make easy money.

The front-door bell rang. Dax must have forgotten his key. Again.

'I'm going to get it soldered to your finger,' she said, opening the door wide.

But it wasn't Dax outside, it was Jay.

'Can I come in?'

She nodded and stepped aside.

'Crystal said you took your bat home.' Jay sauntered down the hallway. 'God knows why you let her rile you up.'

'She hates me.'

Jay plonked himself down on the sofa. 'Any chance of some hair of the dog?'

Liberty made a show of checking her watch but grabbed two cold beers from the kitchen and handed one to her brother. They clinked and each took a swig.

'She tells me you're going to work for that Singh bloke.'

Liberty nodded.

'A bit of a come-down for you.'

Liberty pictured her old offices, all glass atriums and wide wooden desks. The air-conditioning set to exactly the temperature she liked best, a secretary who knew how she took her coffee.

'Frankie's not the only one who needs something to do,' she answered.

'Crystal would rather you worked with us,' said Jay.

'So she can spend the rest of her life torturing me on a minute-by-minute basis?'

Jay laughed and wiped froth from his mouth with the back of his hand. 'Because you're family.'

'She even made a dig about my bloody sex life.'

'What sex life?'

Liberty's mouth fell open but Jay just roared with laughter. She slapped his thigh, and when he still didn't shut up, she slapped him harder.

'What?' Jay's shoulders rattled. 'There are nuns getting more action.'

'You cannot possibly know what I do in my spare time.' Liberty went to smack him again, but he used a cushion to defend himself. 'And, frankly, if one of our sex lives was up for inspection, it wouldn't be mine.'

Jay rubbed his thigh, still chuckling. 'That's below the belt.'

'Which is precisely where your wife will kick you if she ever finds out even half of what you get up to.' Liberty made a fist but this time only threatened him with it. 'Seriously, though, Jay, you need to pack it in with the girls at the club.'

He grabbed her hand, forced it open and entwined his fingers between hers. 'Seriously, though, Lib, you should come and work with us. We need you.' He snorted a giggle through his nose. 'Even Crystal.'

Chapter 3

23 December 1989
Carl the new key worker is helping the even newer key worker decorate the Christmas tree.

Her name's Hemma. That's like Emma with an H. Weird or what? She uses the Social Services voice but Carl's already put his to bed.

'Do you want to help, Elizabeth?' she asks.

I walk past them. She's only trying to be nice, but I'm not in the mood. I go up to our room and find Vicky and Imbo in bed together, huffing on a can of lighter fuel.

'I wish you wouldn't do that in here,' I shout.

'We're not shagging,' says Imbo, his voice slack and slurry.

'Well, I know that.'

Vicky laughs. She doesn't shag any of the lads here, no matter how hard they try. Imbo can beg all he likes and nick as much Merrydown for her as he can fit down his jacket, but he's wasting his time. The only men Vicky goes with live up the Crosshills. There's one at the moment she's keen on, called Sean. I don't know why, he looks like an albino to me, his eyes are so chuffing pink all the time.

'It makes the room stink,' I yell. 'And one of you will probably throw up.'

Vicky pushes her hair from her face. She's doing too much gas and glue lately and is getting all these nasty yellow heads round her mouth. 'You're just mardy 'cos of your Jay,' she says.

'I'm not cleaning up after you,' I tell her, and storm out.

When I get to the shopping centre, I sit on a bench and watch all the folk out last-minute Christmas shopping. That sodding song by Slade is playing again. I bend forward and cover my ears.

Vicky's right. I am upset about Jay. I was supposed to see him this afternoon. I had a travel voucher and everything. But he rang this morning to say he wasn't allowed any visitors because he's been nicked again for thieving. A Madonna single he was going to give me as a Christmas present. I don't even like Madonna but Jay doesn't know that. I mean, we hardly ever get to see each other so how could he?

He was nearly in tears on the phone, which isn't like him at all. Life and soul, our Jay, always cracking jokes. But today he just sounded sad.

I rang our solicitor straight away. She's called Miss Chapman and I saw her when I got my caution. She was just a student then but now she's fully qualified.

'It's a punishment,' she told me.

'But they're punishing me as well and I've done nothing wrong,' I said. 'Do they even think about that?'

'I tried to explain to Jay's social worker,' she said.

'Well, not hard enough,' I wailed, and hung up.

I feel guilty now because she's lovely and she'll have done her absolute best to sort it out. It's not her fault that me and my brother are so fucking stupid, is it? I should ring her back before the office closes and apologize. There's a pay phone over at the other side of the centre outside Chelsea Girl. When I get there, someone's using it so I hang around and wait. It's a girl in a cropped leather jacket, or fake leather anyway. It makes her arse look massive in a pair of white leggings that do her no favours. When she finally finishes her call and turns around my heart sinks.

Stacey Lamb. The last time I spoke to her was years ago. We were at the fair, her flat on her back, face like minced meat where I'd knocked ten bells of shit out of her. I've seen her about since but I've steered well clear.

When she sees me, she looks around wildly.

'I just want to use the phone,' I say.

At last she finds what she's looking for: Mark Johnson. Jonno. The lad I went to the fair with. She grabs his hand.

'She's staring at me,' she tells him.

'I'm not. I just want to use the phone,' I say.

'And it had to be this one?' she asks.

I sigh. The other nearest one is by Woolies. If I have to get myself over there, I won't catch Miss Chapman in time. I look at Jonno. He used to be nice. He used to be nice to me.

'You should get off, Lib,' he says.

I'm almost in tears when I find myself outside the Galaxy, music bleeding out of the open door, not one of the endless Christmas songs, but the steady bleep of acid house music. I press my forehead against the window and close my eyes. The glass is cold, the drum beat hypnotizing.

'You all right?'

Fat Rob's in the doorway. His hair doesn't look like it's been washed since the last time I was here. I punch my tears away with my knuckles.

'Do you wanna come in?' he asks.

I shake my head. 'I haven't got any money to buy anything.'

The other lad that was here before sticks his head out. He's wearing a black cagoule that rustles when he moves. 'Nobody comes in here to buy anything,' he says.

'Ain't that the fucking truth,' says Fat Rob.

And they both burst out laughing.

'Well, you can come in and listen to a new twelve-inch I've just got hold of,' says Fat Rob. 'Or you can freeze your arse off out here. Up to you.'

I don't really know why, but I follow them inside the shop. There are two other people in there. A lad dancing up and down the aisle, shoulders bobbing to the rhythm, and a lass with jet black hair that you can tell is natural because it hasn't got that blue tinge all the girls at school get with the tubes of Harmony.

'Customer?' she asks.

'Hardly,' says Fat Rob. 'Last time she was in here I ended up giving her money.'

'I sold you a record,' I say quickly, in case she thinks I was begging or something.

Fat Rob reaches for a packet of Embassy Regal on the counter. 'And I paid well over the odds for it.' He offers everybody a cig, including me. 'I must've been feeling generous.'

The girl laughs. 'Funny how you always come over that way if there's a pretty lass around.'

'When the rest of the time you're a tight arse,' says the lad in the cagoule.

This sort of thing regularly kicks off at Orchard Grove. Slag anyone off and they're likely to smack you one. But Fat Rob just chuckles and rubs his knuckle over the other lad's head.

'Christ, don't mess up the hair,' says the girl, and everybody laughs.

'What's your name then?' asks the lad in the cagoule.

'Lib.'

'Well, Lib, Fat Rob you know and this is Tiny.' He nods at the girl who gives a curtsy. 'That mental case is Danny, our answer to Sean Ryder, only with more drugs inside him.' The dancing boy waves at me, still dipping up and down in the aisle. 'And I'm Connor. Don't ask. My mam's Irish.'

Tiny and Fat Rob burst into a rendition of 'No surrender to the IRA'.

'I'd say this lot were my mates, but to be honest, I can't stand any of 'em.'

I blink. It's obvious that they're all close. Like I used to be with the kids. I concentrate hard on not crying again.

'Right,' says Fat Rob. 'It's officially Christmas.'

He goes to the door and turns the open sign to closed. Then he grabs a couple of carrier bags and plonks them on the counter. Tiny empties them. Two boxes of mince pies, four bags of cheese and onion crisps and a six-pack of lager. She hands me a mince pie while Fat Rob puts on a new record.

'Where you from?' asks Tiny.

Sometimes I'm vague. Sometimes I don't want to tell people that I'm in care. Today I couldn't give a shit.

'Orchard Grove,' I say.

They know what that means but don't seem to mind.

Rob lowers the needle onto the vinyl. 'You're gonna bloody love this one,' he shouts over to me.

'How d'you know?' I ask.

He taps the side of his nose, but as soon as the first bars kick in, I know he's right. A fast, high-pitched beat, followed by another, then another. Layers on layers.

'Tune,' sings Danny, and dances round me. Not taking the piss, just enjoying himself.

Tiny joins him, stepping from side to side, elbows tight to her waist. Connor begins tapping out the drum beat on the counter and Fat Rob hands me the record cover. 'Chime' by Orbital.

'It's . . .' I try to find the right word '. . . magic.'

Fat Rob bobs his face towards me and for a second I think he's going to kiss me, but instead he just starts dancing. So I join in, my mince pie still in my hand. And we're all dancing. We don't stop until the end of the track.

'Got any draw, Connor?' asks Fat Rob.

Connor nods and fishes into the front pocket of his cagoule, bringing out Rizla, fags and a piece of black resin wrapped in clingfilm.

Kids at Orchard Grove smoke it and worse. I don't very often. Mostly because I've never got any money and the rules are clear: if you want a share of anything, be it booze or drugs or glue, you pay. Nobody gets anything for nothing.

Connor licks the glue of three papers, pressing them together, then ripping open a cig and letting the tobacco fall. He burns the black and crumbles a bit on top. When he's finished, he lights up, takes a long drag and offers it to me.

'I haven't got any money.'

He blows smoke towards the ceiling. 'Lucky I'm not trying to sell it, then.'

'I mean I haven't got owt at all.' There's no point not telling the truth. 'I can't club in.'

'Me neither,' says Tiny, and takes the spliff out of Connor's hand.

Connor smiles at me, a bit puzzled but still friendly. I search his face. I can usually read people, me. I can spot the difference between what they're saying and what they actually think. I can't read Connor. But what I do know is that I'm in a closed shop with four strangers who are offering me mince pies and beer and drugs. Nobody gets anything for nothing.

'I've got to go,' I say.

Present day

Raj led Liberty through the reception of Singh & Co to the kitchen at the back. He found two empty cups in a grimy cupboard and made tea. Then he ferreted in the fridge for a Tupperware box. 'The missus made *gulab jamun*,' he said. 'She spends half her life telling me to lose weight and the other half making the best food this side of the Punjab. I can't win.'

They took a seat in his office, balanced their cups on towers of papers and case files as Raj propelled two empty cans of Red Bull into the overflowing bin. They bounced off the rim and landed on a small Red Bull mountain to the side. Then he removed the Tupperware lid with a flourish. Liberty took one of the golden balls and bit into it. Buttery and spongy, steeped in a rose-scented syrup, she knew they would polish off the lot. One of life's pleasures was finding a mate as greedy as yourself.

'Does Mrs Singh want a wife?' asked Liberty. 'She could dump you and move me in.'

Raj chuckled and licked his lips. 'I'm made up you've decided to work for me.'

'And I'm made up that you're made up.' Liberty took a second *gulab jamun*. 'But I can't help noticing that you've avoided showing me where I'll be working and what I'll be working on.' She waggled a sticky finger at him. 'All these calories are diversion tactics.'

'Fine.' He got up and tiptoed through the debris on his floor. 'Just try to see the bigger picture, eh?'

Liberty followed him up some stairs that she hadn't noticed on previous visits and discovered a huge store room on the second floor. He flicked on a strip light that buzzed and popped to reveal shelf upon shelf of files liberally sprinkled with dead flies. Liberty could taste the dust as it hit the back of her throat. 'When did Miss Havisham move out?' she asked.

Raj threw open a window. 'Could do with a bit of fresh air, I'll admit.' He moved across to a space in the corner. 'We'll put a desk here, get you set up with a phone and internet access.'

'All mod cons.'

He wandered over to the shelves and picked up a file, blowing away the carcass of a bluebottle. 'Most of this lot can be shredded or crated up and put in the cellar.' A cellar? Liberty could only imagine the state of it. 'I've been meaning to do it for years.'

Liberty took the file from Raj and read the name. 'Wayne Corbett. Aggravated burglary.'

'Now there's a blast from the past,' said Raj. 'I made my first bail application for Wayne Corbett. Crapping myself in the magistrates' court all kitted out in a new suit from Next.'

Liberty rubbed his lapel. 'And look how well it's lasted. What happened to him, then?'

'Who?'

Liberty rolled her eyes. 'Wayne Corbett.'

'Oh, he died of an overdose seven or eight years ago.' He shoved the file back on the shelf. 'Shame. Good client, Wayne was, always in bother, never used anyone else.'

Liberty could well understand the loyalty Raj inspired. He would give his all for his clients but take no nonsense from them.

Downstairs, the telephone rang. There was no one else in the office to pick up.

'You need someone working on reception,' said Liberty.

'I had a young lass called Lois, but she got pregnant,' said Raj.

'You'll miss cases,' said Liberty.

Raj reached under his turban to poke inside his ear. 'What usually happens is—' His mobile sprang to life and he answered. 'Raj Singh.' He patted himself down, presumably for a biro. 'What's he in for?' Liberty reached into her bag and handed Raj a leather-bound notebook and fountain pen. 'Worth my while? I'll tell you what, Bucky, you shouldn't make promises you can't keep.'

He hung up, chuckling.

'New job?'

Raj nodded. 'Got to get to court. Bucky's got someone in the cells for me.'

The local prosecutor was larger than life and twice as loud. Liberty had met her a few times and liked her.

'Will you be all right?' Raj asked.

'Course.' She waved at the files. 'I'll make a start here.'

'Most of it can be put to bed.' Raj made for the stairs. 'Ancient history.'

Sol used his thumbnail to scratch at a bit of egg yolk stuck to his tie. Natasha had bought the tie for his last birthday. She said he needed more than one. The old one was black nylon and could be slung in the washing machine. The new one was blue silk with white polka dots and had to be dry-cleaned (why anyone made clothes that couldn't survive a bit of soap and water was a mystery).

'Very sexy,' said Bucky, with a laugh dirtier than Viagra. 'Wife choose it, did she?'

'What makes you say that?'

'Because I've known you ten years and only ever seen you in a polyester number that threatened to spontaneously combust every time you wore it.' She winked and touched her hair, recently changed from pure white to pillar-box red. Only Bucky could get away with it. 'I suppose a move to the OCU will do that to a man. Ideas above his station and all that. It'll be skinny suits and a waistcoat next.'

Sol laughed. 'Fuck off, Bucky.'

The CPS office was busy as the prosecutors prepared for a morning in court. A temp was slumped over a cup of coffee and sixty traffic cases.

Bucky's assistant, Fazeel, was putting files in order and dealing with the stream of defence lawyers that came in to discuss them.

Sol checked the time on his mobile. 'Where is he?'

'Give him a chance,' said Bucky. 'He's coming in a knackered Five Series not a Harrier jump jet.'

Sol nodded but he felt edgy. Today was meant to be straight-forward. Get Delaney in front of the magistrate and transfer the case to the Crown Court. But his lawyer hadn't shown up.

The door opened and Raj Singh burst in.

'Now here's a man with enough sartorial elegance to make a woman forget her manners,' said Bucky.

'What manners?' shouted Fazeel, over his shoulder.

'Back to work, gorgeous,' she told him. 'Your reward will come in the next life. Seventy-two virgins and whatnot.'

Fazeel shook his head. 'That's only if I blow myself up.' He waved a file at her. 'Which I'm seriously considering.'

Singh eased himself down on the edge of Bucky's desk, puffing and sweating. 'Come on, then, tell me what's so important I had to race over here like Lewis Hamilton.'

'Do you know DI Connolly?' asked Bucky.

'We've met,' Singh replied.

They had. And that meeting had taught Sol not to under-estimate Raj Singh. His fingers might be covered with ink but his balls were made of steel.

'Then you'll know he moved from Vice to the Organized Crime Unit,' said Bucky. 'Two days ago, he arrested Jackson Delaney.' Singh's eyes opened. 'He's in the cells now and he needs a solicitor.'

Singh smoothed his own tie, which Sol couldn't help but notice also sported a small stain near the point.

'He usually uses some fancy outfit from Manchester,' said Bucky.

'But they won't rep him on legal aid,' said Singh.

'I called you, Raj, because while I know you won't do me any favours, you won't pull any fast ones either.' Bucky glanced at Sol. 'Basically, I know you're not bent.'

Sol eyed Singh. He was as sure as he could be that he wouldn't jump into Delaney's pocket for the offer of a few used notes and a holiday in Florida Keys. But would Delaney agree to instruct him?

'You'll need to chat him up,' said Sol. 'He's used to things being a bit more slick. No offence.'

'None taken.' Raj pulled out his mobile. 'I'm just going to call in some back-up that will make this Manchester lot look like a back-street outfit from Doncaster.'

Liberty had no idea what she was meant to be doing in court. She prayed to God that Raj wasn't harbouring any expectations that she was going to speak in front of a magistrate. She'd done that a year ago and the memories still kept her awake at night.

Raj had told her to meet him at the entrance to the cells. When he finally arrived, he was grinning from ear to ear. 'We've just landed a very big fish.' He rubbed his hands. 'Drug-dealing, money-laundering, people-trafficking.'

'And I'm here because?'

Raj stabbed the buzzer to be let in. 'You are going to reel this fish right in.'

'How?'

The heavy door to the cell area opened. 'Just be yourself.'

'Stop pissing about Raj.' Liberty refused to enter. 'What am I meant to be doing?'

Raj grabbed her sleeve and tugged her inside. 'Delaney wants slick. I'm going to give him slick.'

'I'm not slick,' said Liberty.

Raj looked her up and down. 'Have they not got mirrors in your house?'

The man in cell three looked like a baked potato. Squat, wrinkled, overly golden brown. He stared at Liberty through the hatch, eyes narrowed. He had the menacing air of someone working very hard to control his emotions. 'What sort of cases do you usually do?' he asked.

'Bigger than this,' said Liberty.

It was true. Sort of. Her corporate deals often had millions of pounds at stake.

'And you've experience of this type of thing?' he asked.

Liberty nodded at Raj. 'Singh & Co has been representing clients in criminal trials for twenty years.' She put her hand on the hatch, displaying her Cartier watch. 'I don't think there's a type of case we don't have a file on.'

Raj stood to the side so that most of him was out of Delaney's sight. What the man in the cell could see was Liberty in her black Prada suit. She felt ridiculous, like a girl in a beauty parade. Worse,

Delaney didn't seem impressed. He was too angry for that and desperate to contain it.

'Name?' he barked.

'Excuse me.'

He sighed, releasing a waft of unbrushed teeth. 'Do you have a name, hen?'

'Liberty Greenwood,' she said.

Delaney stepped back into his cell. 'Greenwood?'

Liberty cursed herself. She should have said Chapman. That was the name she'd always worked under.

'You're not related to Jay Greenwood?' he asked.

'Sister,' said Raj.

Liberty glared at him, but Raj shrugged.

Delaney's body language changed subtly. The frown melted a touch. 'A brief in the family?' He tapped his bottom lip. 'Now that's smart. Tell him thanks for sending you.'

'I can assure you, Mr Delaney, that my brother was not involved in my attendance here today.'

Delaney sniffed as Raj passed the legal-aid application forms through the hatch for him to sign and gave a tight smile as he handed back the Mont Blanc pen she'd lent to Raj earlier.

'How much longer is he going to be?' Sol asked Bucky.

'Will you calm down?' she said. 'You're like a lad on a promise.' She flapped a hand at him. 'Go and have a fag or something, will you?'

'I've given up,' said Sol.

'Again?' she asked. 'Vaping, are you?'

Sol shook his head.

'Patches?'

'Nope. Willpower and self-loathing.' Sol changed the subject. 'You've reviewed the evidence, yeah? It's bloody tight.'

Bucky raised an eyebrow. 'It is, but we've been here before with Delaney and he's walked.'

'Not this time,' said Sol.

When Singh re-entered the CPS room with a smile on his face, Sol's shoulders relaxed. 'You signed him up, I take it,' he said.

Singh gave a nod. 'I had my secret weapon.'

Sol's mouth opened when Liberty Chapman followed Singh into the room. He hadn't seen her in almost a year. Dark brown hair and darker eyes. Ice cold – or, at least, that was what she wanted you to think.

If she'd noticed him, she didn't acknowledge it. Instead she began asking Bucky and Fazeel a barrage of questions about the case.

'Hold up,' said Bucky. 'You're working for Raj now?'

Chapman nodded.

'Fuck a duck. Are you making amends for sins of a past life?'

Chapman blushed but no one except Sol seemed to notice.

They prepared to get the show on the road in Court One, Fazeel laden with files, Bucky sashaying ahead, Singh trotting alongside, like a terrier.

At the top of the stairs, Sol caught up with Chapman. She smelt delicious. 'This is a surprise.'

'Yeah.'

She was well spoken with a hint of Yorkshire in the back-ground. A hint that spilled over when she got pissed or pissed off.

'When did you join Singh & Co?'

'This morning,' she answered.

'Bit of a coincidence,' said Sol. 'On the very day a local gang-ster needs representing.'

She looked him right in the eye. 'You can be suspicious, if you want, but until I got to court, I'd never even heard of Jackson Delaney.'

'I'm pretty sure your family know him.'

'I expect they do,' she said. She reached into a handbag that looked as if it had cost more than a month of Sol's wages. With decent overtime. Then she smiled. 'How have you been? I heard you left Vice.'

'Who told you that?'

She exhaled loudly. Her family would have made it their business to keep tabs on him. Still, he couldn't help but be pleased that she paid attention to his movements.

'The last time I saw you I said you should call me if you ever got bored,' he said.

'You know what they say? Only boring people get bored.'

Amira bought herself a Diet Coke and sat opposite Sol. It was a quiet lunchtime in the Three Feathers, only a few coppers nursing pints and chip butties. 'How did it go?' she asked.

Sol took a swig of his lager. 'Fine. Case transferred to the Crown Court.'

'Delaney didn't go for bail?'

Sol snorted. 'No point in the mags, is there? They might make an application to chambers. We'll see.'

'He wouldn't actually get it, would he?' asked Amira.

'Can't see it.'

She nodded, gulped her drink, letting an ice cube slip into her mouth. She knew she should take a leaf out of Sol's book and relax, but it was hard. People like Delaney had ruled the roost for too long. They needed to be brought down.

'Guess who he's got representing him,' said Sol. Amira crunched her ice cube and shrugged. 'Raj Singh.' Amira's mouth fell open and she had to catch a sliver of ice in her hand. 'And that's not all.' Sol put down his pint, but kept his fingers around the glass. 'He's got Liberty Chapman helping him.'

Amira spat out the remnants of the ice cube. He'd got to be

joking. But one look at Sol told her he wasn't. 'We can't let that happen.' She flicked the shards of ice onto the floor. 'That woman cannot be allowed anywhere near this case.'

'What do you propose we do about it, Amira?'

'We go to the DCI and tell him that she's as bent as a fifteen-pound note.' Sol didn't answer. 'C'mon. You know it and I know it.'

He took a long drink. 'You have your suspicions.'

Amira couldn't believe her ears. The Greenwoods were criminals, and Chapman might have changed her name but she was still one of them. Allowing her to be involved in Delaney's defence was suicide. 'Why are you so reluctant to admit what Chapman is, Sol?'

Sol frowned, the scar beneath his eye refusing to crinkle. Amira loved Sol. When he'd moved from Vice to OCU he'd convinced the powers that be to take her too. He'd taught her so much, not only about building cases but about playing the game. Lately, though, she was increasingly tired of the game.

'It doesn't matter what I think of Chapman,' he said. 'It matters what I can prove. We're not on the telly, Amira. We don't work on our hunches.' He drained his pint and stood to leave. 'I'm not going to the top brass to make accusations against a lawyer without solid evidence because in this job you don't get to make a twat of yourself without there being serious repercussions.'

Chapter 4

31 December 1989
I eat my sandwich and try to read my book.

Vicky and Imbo throw their crusts at each other. One lands not far from the new girl. She doesn't speak. Carl says her name's Leanne and she won't be here long. She doesn't look up from her bowl of cereal, which is all she'll eat.

Hemma hovers in the kitchen doorway. Everyone ignores her. 'Elizabeth,' she says, applying the second rule they teach them all: use our proper names. 'You've got a visitor.'

I jump up. Jay. Miss Chapman must have convinced his social worker. God, I bloody love that woman.

But when Hemma moves to one side, I see it's not my brother. It's Connor, cagoule zipped right up to his chin. My heart sinks and my face follows it.

'Sorry to be such a disappointment,' he says.

'I thought you might be my brother,' I tell him.

'You know that can't happen at the moment, Elizabeth.' Hemma uses the low, calm voice. 'It's all been explained.'

Vicky stands up and stares at Hemma. 'Doesn't make it any nicer, though, does it?'

Hemma's cheeks blaze and she buggers off. Vicky and Imbo cheer. Even Silent Leanne smiles into her cornflakes.

'Lib won't shag you,' Vicky suddenly tells Connor. 'Just so you know.'

'*And there was me thinking we might get down to it right now on the table.*' *He laughs and looks at me.* '*I'll get off. I just wanted to see if you were all right.*'

I nod and watch him leave. I don't know what he thought he was doing by turning up here. I try to get back to Return of the Native but Hemma appears again, holding something wrapped in Christmas paper. '*Your friend said this was a belated present.*'

I run my fingernail under the Sellotape and open it. It's a copy of '*Chime*'. I stare at it for a second and race after Connor.

He's got as far as the park when I catch up. I grab his arm, making him jump.

'*You scared the shit out of me,*' he says.

I wave the twelve-inch at him. '*What's this for?*'

'*I thought you liked it.*'

I did.

'*I don't want it,*' I say.

'*Fine.*' *He holds out his hands.* '*I'll sell it back to Fat Rob.*' I push it towards him so that we're both holding a side each. '*But you know how tight he is so you might as well just keep it.*'

'*I won't shag you,*' I say.

He shakes his head, laughing into the nylon funnel of his cagoule. '*That has been made perfectly clear.*' *He lets go of the record.* '*It's a relief, to be honest.*'

A couple walk past with a toddler in a buggy. He's kicked off his blanket and it's trailing under the back wheel. The woman frowns and yanks it out, tucking it back round his fat little legs.

'*Why won't they let you see your brother?*' *Connor asks.*

I sigh. '*He's in trouble. He won't behave and they think they can force him by not letting him see me. But they won't break him.*'

'*What did he do?*' *Connor asks.*

'*He nicked a Madonna single,*' I say.

'*They should just make him listen to it.*' *Connor nudges me with his elbow.* '*That'd be like a real punishment.*'

I turn my head so he won't see my laugh.

'Look, I've got to go,' he says. 'Mam's asked us to get round to the Co-op for some sausages before it closes. If I go back empty-handed I'll never hear the end of it. It's their version of the death penalty in Cork, repeating something in a disappointed tone until the perpetrator just stops breathing.'

I press my fingers into the edge of the sleeve of 'Chime'. 'Thank you.'

'You're very welcome, Elizabeth,*' he mimics Hemma. I kick his shin. 'Ow.' He pretends to limp. 'Are you doing much tonight?'*

I shake my head.

'There's a party at the Cube. Should be good.' He raises both hands. 'And before you start going on about money, Fat Rob's doing a set so he's putting us all on the guest list.' Connor's eyes sparkle. 'And I promise no one will try to shag you.'

Present day

The Trap smelt of burning fish. The electrician said the whole place needed rewiring, but Jay didn't want to fork out that kind of cash to get the club up and running. 'A good clean and a lick of paint,' he told Frankie. 'Then get the stage sorted.'

Frankie could see what he was saying. The punters didn't much care about the state of things once the girls started getting their kit off. But the stink was making his stomach roll. He went into the bogs and retched into a bowl. Trying to lay off the gear was easier said than done. He'd do a couple more hours' work here, then head back home for something to make himself feel better. Not a rock. Though he could really go for one. But the fact was that one always led to two, more often than not three. Then a bit of brown for the come-down. Better to get a few jellies down him and grab some kip.

When he made his way back into the club, two men were

hovering at the bar. One thin with white hair, the other bald and built like a brick shithouse.

'We're not open yet, lads,' Frankie called, wiping his mouth with his sleeve.

The men turned to him and Frankie clocked it was Paul Hill and his security. Frankie was pretty certain that Paul Hill didn't need a bodyguard twenty-four seven. All for show.

'All right, Frankie?' said Hill.

'Not bad, Paul.'

Hill opened his arms. 'The new club's coming along.'

'A fair way to go yet.'

What did Hill want? He hadn't dropped by to pass the time of day. 'I'd offer you a drink, Paul, but the bar's not wired up yet.'

Hill shook his head as if a cold beer was the last thing on his mind. 'You've heard about Jacko Delaney?'

Was there anyone in Yorkshire who didn't know that Delaney had been nicked? 'Bad business, that.' Frankie's stomach lurched again. 'Have you heard what they've charged him with?'

'I'd have thought you'd have the inside track on that,' said Hill, and his sidekick chortled.

At the far end of the club, the electrician turned on his radio and Britney Spears warbled across to Frankie's already pounding head. He put up a finger to Hill and marched over to where the electrician, on all fours, arse crack on display, was ripping at a socket with a claw hammer. Frankie snapped off the radio. 'Can't hear myself fucking think,' he said. The sparky scowled but didn't answer back. 'And do something about that smell, would you?'

Frankie returned to Hill.

'Like I was saying, Frankie, I assumed you'd know what gives with Jacko,' said Hill. 'What with your sister representing him.'

Shit. Crystal had mumbled something about Liberty going to work for Raj Singh. To be honest, Frankie hadn't paid much attention. Crystal was always bitching about Lib and it got on his wick.

'You didn't know she was his brief?' asked Hill.

Frankie laughed. 'Course I did, Paul. She's family, for fuck's sake.' Hill crossed his arms. It was impossible to tell if he believed Frankie or not. 'You know how it is, though, loose lips and all that.'

Hill stared at Frankie. Frankie stared back. At last Hill smiled and gestured to the man mountain at his side that they were leaving.

'Ask Jay to call me,' he said. 'We need another discussion about what I suggested at his party.'

Frankie had no idea what had been suggested. 'He's thinking it over.'

Hill nodded and began to walk away. 'Tell him not to take too long.'

Liberty watched the workman install new telephone lines in her office. He had sleeve tattoos on both arms, ear extenders and a baseball cap that read 'I Can't Adult Today'. He'd told Liberty at least three times that his name was Bam, which seemed highly unlikely.

He yawned loudly.

'Keeping you up?' Liberty asked.

'Sorry,' Bam said. 'Late night.' He burped. 'The girlfriend's birthday so we went for a curry. Cost me a fortune.'

Liberty gave a vague smile. Bucky had emailed half a dozen files on the Delaney case but Liberty hadn't yet been able to look at them. She couldn't even use Raj's desktop, as he'd been holed up all afternoon with a kid called Bella who'd been nicked for robbing a punter on Carter Street.

Liberty had already made her well-inked workman two cups of tea. She wasn't going to offer another.

'What is it with you women?' Bam said.

'Excuse me?'

Bam waved at Liberty. 'You say you want equality and all that, but you still expect us blokes to do all the running.' Liberty didn't know what to say. 'I mean look at you, a career woman and everything.' Liberty glanced around her dusty workspace. She was hardly at the top of her game. 'But I bet you still expect your old man to pay when you go out.'

'I'm not married.'

Bam shrugged. 'Boyfriend, then. Or partner.' He made quotation marks with one finger and a screwdriver around the last word. 'But I'm guessing he still gets the bill, including the bloody tip.'

'How long do you think this is going to take?' Liberty asked.

'God knows,' Bam answered, and went back to his telephone sockets.

Liberty was relieved when her mobile rang. 'Frankie?'

'All right, Lib?'

He sounded okay. No slurred speech, no heavy breathing. 'Where are you?'

'Work,' he said. 'Listen, I've just had Paul Hill in here asking questions.'

'Who?'

'Local face,' said Frankie. 'Married to an ex-glamour model called Bunny.'

'Oh, him. What did he want?'

Bam let out a long sigh as if he'd never come across such a complex job. Fearing she might kill him, Liberty left the room and stood at the top of the stairs.

'He said you were representing Jackson Delaney.'

'What?'

Frankie laughed. 'It's true, then?'

'How the hell would Paul Hill know that?'

'C'mon, Lib, he pays people to tell him this shit.' Liberty heard the click of a lighter and Frankie exhaling. She had long since stopped nagging him about smoking. 'So what's the deal? Is Jacko going down?'

She opened her mouth but clamped it shut. She shouldn't discuss the case, not even with her brother. Especially not with her brother. Not that she could anyway, seeing as she hadn't actually set eyes on any of the evidence yet. Behind the door, Bam called for her.

'Gotta go, Frankie,' she said. 'The world's most incompetent workman wants to give me his views on feminism.'

Sol scanned his inbox but didn't open any mail. He hadn't seen the sender he was looking for.

He knew he shouldn't be checking but couldn't help himself. A couple of hours earlier he'd emailed Singh & Co to introduce himself as the day-to-day liaison officer in the Delaney case. The DCI had overall responsibility but any questions on evidence and such could be addressed to him. It was routine and he wouldn't normally expect a reply, maybe an acknowledgement at most.

Time to go home. Natasha had already texted to ask what time she could expect him back.

On his way out of the nick, his mobile rang. 'Half an hour,' he snapped. 'Please tell me we're not having salad for tea.'

There was a laugh. Not Natasha. 'I can absolutely assure you, I'm not having a salad.'

Shit. 'Miss Chapman?' he said. 'Or should I call you Miss Greenwood?'

'I think I told you once before that I don't care,' she said, her voice still soft with humour. 'I'm sorry to call you directly, but I currently don't have internet at work.' She hadn't ignored his email, then. 'I just wondered if I could get a copy of Mr Delaney's interview from you while I'm waiting to get access to the files Bucky sent.'

He should tell her to piss off, that she'd receive them in due course.

'I thought I could at least crack on and watch it after I've had my fry-up,' she said.

He crossed the car park. 'A fry-up?'

She laughed again. 'Yeah. I've spent all bloody day with someone calling himself Bam, so I'm having my tea in Scottish Tony's as consolation.'

'I'll meet you in there with the interview,' said Sol.

'You don't have to do that.'

Sol unlocked his car. 'No, I don't, but right now there's nothing I would like more than a sausage, bacon and egg butty.'

When Sol arrived, Chapman was already polishing off one of Tony's all-day breakfast specials. It looked as if she'd ordered extra bacon.

'Usual?' Tony shouted from the counter.

Sol gave a thumbs-up and took the seat opposite her. The working girls in Carter Street were not yet out in numbers, but a couple were at a table by the window nursing milkshakes as they kept an eye on the road for any early birds.

Sol brought a Jiffy-bag out of his pocket and slid it across to Chapman. 'Not a very exciting viewing, I'm afraid.'

'No comment?'

Sol nodded. A pro like Delaney would never answer a police question.

Chapman put down a greasy fork and wiped her mouth with a paper napkin. 'I know you won't believe me, and I know I shouldn't care one way or the other, but me being on this case *is* just a coincidence.' Sol blew under his fringe, making the hair lift from his eyes. 'And I know you won't believe me and I know I shouldn't care but I did think about calling you, like you asked.'

Scottish Tony arrived with Sol's food, yolk running from the fried egg over the crust on the bread. 'You know he's polis?' Tony asked Chapman.

'I do.'

'Nice enough, considering.'

'Now there's a compliment,' said Sol.

He lifted the top slice of bread and spread brown sauce over the dark-skinned sausages as Tony went to harass the toms at the window into getting another drink. He didn't expect them to buy food when it was quiet, but a seat indoors didn't come for free.

'Go on, then.' Sol pressed the top slice back down and felt the squelch under his fingers. 'Why didn't you call?' He took a bite. 'Bear in mind that over the years most men have heard every excuse under the sun.'

Chapman smiled and took a sip of tea. 'Last summer my life was very complicated.' She paused, as if waiting for him to agree. 'And I kept hoping things would settle down.'

'Did they?'

'Not really.' She was still smiling but there was a hint of something else in her eyes. 'I think I'm coming to the conclusion that things might never settle down and that this is just how life is for me.' She grabbed the Jiffy-bag and stood. 'Thanks for this.'

'Enjoy the show,' said Sol.

As he watched her go to the counter and pay, his mobile bleeped. Another text from Natasha. He should reply. Send some of her favourite emojis. She was always sending them, especially the cat with the heart eyes. And the volcano (did anyone know what it actually meant?). He wondered what face Liberty Chapman would pull if he sent her a volcano. The very thought made him laugh as she left the café with a wave in his direction.

His thumbs danced across his mobile as he composed a text. He reread it, deleted it, then typed it out again. Fuck it. He pressed send. *Embrace the chaos Miss Chapman/Greenwood.*

He was swallowing the last of his sandwich when she replied: *Not fucking likely.*

That really made him laugh. He typed again: *You once told me that control is an illusion. That we're all just a bunch of needs, wants and urges.*

There was a long pause and Sol thought that might be the end of their conversation, but no.

And what is it you want Officer Connolly?

He gulped. This was just banter and he should make a joke about wanting to send Delaney to prison or buying a retirement home in Barbados. No line would be crossed and the next time they saw each other they could crack on as normal (not that normal had ever featured very heavily in their interactions to date). *Good question Miss Chapman/Greenwood. I think I just want to forget about all the complications and focus on the needs and urges.*

Amira had never had a one-to-one with the DCI before. She'd been on the receiving end of group pep talks and bollockings as part of the Delaney operation, but he had never spoken to her directly.

'Why hasn't Sol come to me about this?' the DCI asked.

'He likes me to use my own initiative,' she answered. 'He's not one for spoon-feeding.'

The DCI smiled and poured her a coffee from a cafetière. It looked thin and weak. At home her father usually made coffee on the stove in a *dallah*, more often than not adding a pinch of cinnamon to the grainy liquid.

Amira smiled and took the cup. 'But obviously I've discussed my thoughts on this with Sol.'

'It's not actually an offence to be related to a criminal,' said the DCI.

Amira took a sip. The coffee tasted of . . . nothing. 'All I'm proposing, sir, is that we put eyes and ears on Chapman,' she said.

'A week maximum. If my concerns are unwarranted then I'll be the first to admit I've made a mistake.'

The DCI tapped his knuckle on his desk. 'And what are your concerns here?'

She'd prepared what she was going to say, repeating it to herself a hundred times, like a kid doing times tables. It was important not to sound emotional in any way. She would not mention how she had joined the police to ensure that wrong things and people were punished. She would certainly not mention that she and her family, or what was left of it, had fled a country where the police could not be trusted, where the best advice they could give when her cousin was kidnapped was to pay in American dollars.

'My main concern is to ensure the conviction of Jackson Delaney,' she said. 'We've all worked too hard for that to be jeopardized.' She didn't mention the cost of the operation. The DCI would have that figure lasered on his brain. 'From my previous dealings with Liberty Greenwood, I suspect she will hinder the prosecution.'

The DCI smiled. 'It's the job of a defence brief to do that, Amira.'

'By legal means.' Amira put down her still-full cup. 'But this woman operates outside that.'

'Evidence?'

Amira leaned forward in her chair. 'She has only ever been involved in two cases here in Yorkshire. One collapsed, and although the other did end in a conviction, it was not of the original suspect, Jay Greenwood. That's some impressive hit rate in anyone's books.'

'And you don't think it's chance that she's ended up working for Delaney?'

'She hasn't done any legal work in a year, sir. Not one case. Then the day we finally get Delaney to court, she turns up suited and booted, ready for action.'

The DCI exhaled through his nose.

Amira could smell success. 'If we put eyes and ears on her we get to protect the Delaney case and build one against the Greenwoods at the same time,' she said. 'Serious value for money, sir.'

The DCI laughed at that. 'Fine.' Amira wanted to whoop, but just smiled back. 'But no ears. Wires and what-have-you are too expensive. 'Report back to me in a couple of days.' Amira stood to leave. 'And no bloody overtime, you hear me?'

Liberty reread Connolly's last text for the tenth time and dropped her mobile into her handbag. Then she kicked the bag under the coffee table in the sitting room. So many reasons not to go there. First, he was married. Second, he was a copper, and not just any copper but one taking a lead role in a case she was defending. In fact, she would do well to stop thinking about him and watch the Delaney interview tapes.

She slid the disk Connolly had burned for her into the slot at the side of her laptop and the screen sprang to life. There was her client with his meat-pie complexion and challenging eyes, flanked by a suit scribbling furiously on an A4 pad. It was the solicitor who had attended the station when Delaney was arrested but had now abandoned ship due, no doubt, to the lack of funds available. The suit shoved the pad onto Delaney's lap, and Delaney's eyes lowered as he took his time to read whatever message his lawyer was giving him. Then he nodded slowly and pushed the pad away.

On the opposite side of the table, an officer checked his phone, looking up only when the door of the interview room opened and Connolly entered. Even on film Connolly exuded a mass of contradictions: a suspicious tilt of the head on top of relaxed shoulders, a gruff nod at the prisoner as he handed him a bottle of water. He didn't even glance at the camera, yet brushed his hair over his eyes.

Liberty kicked off her shoes and forced herself to focus on her client as he answered each and every one of Connolly's questions with a slow and deliberate 'No comment.' Nothing in his voice gave anything away, all traces of anger or frustration banished.

Dax wandered into the sitting room in a towel.

'Do you ever wear clothes?' she asked, as she paused the interview.

'If you was in a shape as good as this, would you?'

'Are you calling me old and fat?' asked Liberty.

Dax laughed and melted into the sofa next to her. 'Don't ask me that, Lib.' She rubbed his shoulder, pleased he'd used the family's nickname for her. 'What's that?' He gestured to the laptop. 'Work?'

She nodded. 'Police interview.'

'He say anything interesting?'

'Only if the words "no" and "comment" set your heart racing,' she replied.

'Gotta be done,' he said, and leaned against her.

When she'd told her family that she was going to have Dax living with her, they'd been appalled. 'He'll be away on his toes inside a week,' Jay had said. 'With only your purse and your telly, if you're lucky.'

'How many times have you been nicked, then?' Liberty asked Dax.

'Ask me no questions, I'll tell you no lies.'

'Did you always give no comment?'

He looked at her sideways. 'Course. Ain't my job to help the feds bang me up. Same for your man.'

'But what about the trial?' Liberty waved at Delaney's face, frozen and pallid. 'Won't a jury think it's off that he didn't explain his innocence?'

Dax shrugged. 'Sometimes you gotta take a risk in life, Lib. You can play it safe and still get mugged off.'

Amira watched Chapman's front door. She'd been doing this on the QT, of course, but tonight was different. This time whatever she gathered together could be legitimately used against the lawyer. And she was certain she would find something.

She hadn't yet told Sol about her visit to the DCI. She'd gone behind his back and he wouldn't be impressed, even though the DCI had basically agreed with her about Chapman. Better to find something concrete on the lawyer first and show Sol the evidence. He might still be pissed at how Amira had gone about it, but his copper's instincts would kick in, like they always did, and he'd want to start building a case.

When Chapman left her house, Amira tracked the Porsche 911 across town to the Radisson Hotel, where Chapman parked up. Now, this was interesting. Who was she meeting? There was no reason to meet her brothers or sister here and the hotel was definitely not the sort of stomping ground she'd grab a drink with her scruffy colleague, Singh.

Chapman locked her car and strode inside, glossy hair swishing around her shoulders. She thought she was clever and special and above the law, but she was about to find out that she was not.

Amira needed to be careful now: Chapman knew her from their previous run-ins, and if she saw Amira, the game would be up. She'd let Chapman get settled in the bar or the restaurant, then do a very quick recce wearing her hijab, snatching a shot of whoever Chapman was meeting. Easy, these days, with a smartphone.

Five minutes later, Amira was fastening her headscarf, pins ready in her mouth, when a car appeared. Her lips parted and the pins dropped into her lap. It was Sol.

It must be a coincidence. Maybe he was bringing his wife here. The Radisson was just the sort of place she'd like, with its air-conditioned bar and overpriced vodka tonics. However, when Sol got out of his car, he was alone and he strode across the car park with the same purpose as Chapman had done minutes ago.

As Sol disappeared into the hotel, Amira fought back tears.

Chapter 5

31 December 1989
'Can I borrow your hoodie?' I ask Vicky.

She's in bed, staring at the ceiling. 'Why? Where you off to?'

I shrug as if it's no big deal. 'There's a thing on up at the Cube.'

Vicky sits up. No one here ever goes to anything like that. We just hang about mostly. Parks, streets, flats if we're lucky. 'With that lad?' she asks.

'And a few others.'

She jumps onto the floor. 'Can I come?'

'Dunno. He said I was on Fat Rob's guest list. Without that, you'd probably need a ticket.'

Vicky's already pulling on her jeans and trainers. 'Fuck that. We'll get Fat Rob to put me on it as well.' She grabs her coat.

'Where are you going now?' I ask.

'We'll need some ale before we go out, won't we?'

Three hours later she comes back with twenty quid, two bottles of Lambrini and a love bite. By the time we get to the Cube we're a bit pissed. Well, I'm a bit pissed, Vicky's well gone.

The girl checking tickets at the entrance looks us up and down as I try to stop Vicky swaying.

'I'm on the guest list,' I say.

The girl laughs. 'Course you are.'

'She is.' Vicky's immediately up in the girl's face. 'Are you calling her a liar?'

The girl sighs. 'Whose list?'

'Fat Rob,' I say.

'What's your name?'

'Lib Greenwood.'

She pulls out a tatty piece of paper covered in scribbles and runs her thumb down the names. She's wearing a silver ring on it. 'That you?'

I check the writing. It says, 'Pretty Lib'. I blush and nod.

Vicky grabs the paper and stabs the name below it. 'And that's me right there. Tony.'

'Tony?' The girl laughs and looks behind her. 'Tiny. Tiny, get over here.'

Tiny comes over, looking fantastic with her hair tucked in a bright red headband and her lips painted an even brighter red.

'Apparently this is you,' says the girl, nodding to Vicky.

I'm so embarrassed. Tiny's going to think I'm a right chancer. They won't let either of us in now, will they? Why did I bring bloody Vicky?

'Let 'em in, Mags,' Tiny says to the girl.

'We're full.'

'C'mon.' Tiny rubs her shoulder. 'Connor will see you right later.'

'Fine,' says the girl, and stamps our hands.

I know that I'm not going to wash mine off for days so that people will keep on asking me what it is. I doubt Vicky will either.

As Tiny leads us through to the dance-floor, we're hit by a wave of heat and sweat. Hundreds of people are dancing, faces drenched. Danny bounces towards us, grabs my hand and kisses it with sticky lips. Then he grabs Vicky's and does the same. There's a possibility she might lamp him and I hold my breath but she just giggles.

Then I spot Connor. He's sitting on a step to the side of the dance-floor, right up close to a girl, sparking up her fag for her with his lighter. My heart sinks a bit, which is daft because I've made it perfectly clear to him that I'm not interested. When he sees me, he whispers something in the girl's ear and comes over. 'All right, Elizabeth?' He uses the Hemma voice. 'And you too, gobby shite from the kitchen.' He winks at Vicky. 'And before you tell me again, I know Lib's not going to shag me.'

'No, she's not,' says Vicky. 'But I might.'

'Christ!' shouts Connor. 'I don't know whether to be flattered or terrified.'

Tiny nudges us and nods at the stage. Fat Rob's pulling a pair of giant headphones over his mucky hair. A few people slap the walls and Connor puts his fingers into his mouth and whistles. When Fat Rob lays down his first track anyone who wasn't dancing gets up and the place erupts.

A couple of hours later, my eyes are stinging from the sweat dripping into them and the smoke of a million fags. I need some fresh air. Through the door at the entrance a cool breeze rushes in and I step outside, still smiling. I stand with my back to the wall, trying to remember when I last had this much fun. The true answer is that I don't think I've ever had this much fun. Which is sad in a way.

Three men come around the corner. One of them is seriously worse for wear, being virtually carried by the other two.

'Happy New Year,' shout the two who can speak.

'Happy New Year,' I say back.

They stop by a lamppost and prop the drunk mate against it like a stick. 'On your own, love?'

'No,' I say. 'My mates are inside. I'm just having a breather.'

'How about a kiss for auld lang syne?' says one, his moustache covered in what looks like brown sauce.

'No chance,' I say, with a laugh.

The two of them are on either side of me now and I stop laughing.

'Don't be tight,' he says. 'It's New Year's Eve.'

I step away from them, but they move with me. The one with the moustache grips my arm and the other leans in so I can smell his breath, all whisky and bad teeth. I try to wriggle out but they spin me around. I struggle and manage to elbow one in the stomach.

'Little cunt,' he says, and pushes me into the lamppost. My mouth smacks it hard and I can taste blood. I feel dizzy and sick as someone's hands pull at the back of my jeans.

Then there's a scream behind me. 'What the fuck?' I think it might be Tiny who is shouting.

The men run away, leaving their drunk mate. Both him and me slump to the ground.

Present day
'Please tell me the internet's working,' said Liberty, and handed a cup of tea to Bam.

This morning's baseball cap read 'Sex Slave'. Apparently, there was no limit to the man's talents. He yawned, scratched his chin and replied, 'The internet's working.'

'It's not, though, is it?' Liberty asked.

Bam shook his head, swigged his tea and winced. 'Any chance of some sugar?'

'No,' said Liberty, and stamped out of the room, down the stairs to Raj's office.

A box of Frosties was perched on the desk and Raj absently reached inside with one hand, the other tapping a mouse.

'I need the Delaney files,' Liberty told him.

Raj stuffed a handful of dry cereal into his mouth. 'Still no joy upstairs?'

'Nope.' She waved away the offer of some pre-fingered Frosties. 'Can you print off a copy for me?'

'Think of the trees,' said Raj. Liberty folded her arms and stared. 'For every piece of paper wasted, a polar bear dies.'

'I can't stand around doing nothing all day, Raj.'

'An employee with a conscience,' he said. 'Wonders will never cease.' Liberty leaned against the door frame and gently banged her head on the wood. Laughing, Raj closed the box of cereal, grabbed his suit jacket and stood. 'I'm off to the mags,' he said. 'Use my computer.'

Liberty pushed past him and slid into his still-warm chair. 'Don't rush back.'

'I don't know why folk say you're a pain in the arse.'

'What people?' she called after him, but he just whistled and sauntered off to court.

Frankie really wished there was something the sparky could do about that frigging fish smell.

He'd kept his nose clean last night. No rocks. No brown. Just a couple of diazepam to help him sleep. When Daisy had called in on him, she'd been impressed. But even with a good night's kip under his belt, the stench made him queasy.

When Jay and Crystal arrived, they wrinkled their noses.

'It's like I told you,' said Frankie. 'The place needs rewiring.'

'And it's like I told you,' Jay replied. 'We're not spending that sort of money on it.'

Frankie shrugged. He hadn't asked them over here to argue about electrics. He wanted to dive right in with his news, but Crystal had already headed off across the room, inspecting the newly installed bar. Frankie had checked it and double-checked it against the paperwork. Everything was just as ordered. But that didn't stop Crystal bending from the waist to peer under the bloody thing. It was as if she wanted to catch her little brother out. Jay wasn't much better, running a finger across some fresh paintwork.

'Paul Hill was round here yesterday,' said Frankie.

He almost pissed himself laughing at the way that got their attention. Crystal virtually ran back to him.

'What did he want?' she demanded.

Frankie took a step away from them and ran his own finger across the new paint. It was still a bit tacky and he could see his dab in it. 'Just a chat,' he said.

'Frankie,' Jay growled.

Frankie rubbed his thumb and forefinger together to remove the white mark. 'He wanted to ask about Lib.'

Jay and Crystal exchanged a glance.

'In terms of Jacko Delaney,' Frankie added.

'Delaney?' asked Jay. They didn't know. Jesus Christ, this was like Christmas. 'What's Lib got to do with Jackson fucking Delaney?'

'I figured she'd told you.'

Jay balled his fist and Crystal stepped in front of him. 'Don't piss us about, Frankie.'

'I'm not.' Frankie hid his smile. He held up his hands, the finger still smeared with paint. 'Our Lib's representing him.'

Liberty cleaned Raj's keyboard with an anti-bacterial wipe. She couldn't fathom how he worked in this mess. Not just the piles of files and yellow Post-it notes dotted on every flat surface, but the tsunami of crumbs that washed over everything.

When she could bear to touch the keys, she scrolled down the prosecution files Bucky had sent on the Delaney job. There were at least thirty and that was just the first attachment. The CPS had prepped a rigorous case against him.

She found statements from the various officers who had raided her client's house. Goosebumps bubbled along her forearms when she found the name she was searching for. Solomon Connolly. She skim-read what he had to say: the time the team arrived, the method used to gain entry to the premises, what Delaney had said.

She pushed back the chair, let her head loll and sighed.

It had been stupid to meet Sol at the Radisson last night, not least because she had known exactly how it would end. Cold drinks, great sex, then an excruciating disentanglement in the early hours. At least he hadn't made up some lame excuse for leaving that she would have had to pretend to fall for.

She went back to the case. The next document was the statement of the arresting officer, and when Liberty opened it, her stomach lurched. Officer Amira Hassani had arrested Delaney. Amira Hassani. Liberty had hoped she would never come into contact with the woman ever again.

Her mobile pinged as a text came through from Sol: *You okay?*

Liberty rattled off a reply: *You failed to mention that your lovely colleague Hassani was involved in the Delaney case. Slipped your mind?*

He didn't respond and she tapped the edge of the phone against her lips. It was bad enough that Sol was involved, but Hassani too? She didn't wait but rattled out another text: *I think we both know that last night was a mistake.*

His reply was instant: *Is that what you think?*

'Do you want to know what I think, Connolly?' Liberty shouted at the screen of her phone. 'I think that you're married and that you're the main liaising officer, or whatever the fuck you call it, on Raj's biggest case this century. And now I discover that a copper who would love nothing better than to stab a cold knife into my heart is working for you on the same job.'

She typed: *Things are complicated right now.*

Again, Sol replied quickly: *I thought you said things were always going to be complicated with you.*

Liberty paused. Sol was the first man in a very long time that she'd wanted. She tapped out a reply: *There's complicated and then there's a car crash.*

She turned off her phone, went back to the computer and read the arresting officer's statement.

An hour later, Liberty yawned and tried to concentrate on her client's custody record, each cup of tea and sandwich he'd been given carefully noted. No one was taking any chances with getting the paperwork wrong on this one.

The office doorbell sounded. With no one working at reception, the front door had to remain locked, which was ludicrous. It would be one of Raj's clients, an arrest warrant held tightly in a sweaty hand. She ignored them and got on with her work, but the bell went again. Whoever was at the door obviously had no intention of leaving.

With a sigh, Liberty made her way down the corridor, but when she unlocked the door, she found not a defendant but Jay on the street. 'Lunch?' he asked.

'Sorry?'

'Lunch. Well, back in the day we used to call it dinner,' he said. 'Then we'd have tea later, but that's now dinner apparently. Tea's just something you get in a mug.'

'What are you on about, Jay?' Liberty asked.

He gave a smile. 'Come and get something to eat with me.'

'I'm working,' she replied.

He put a hand on his chest. 'I'm heartbroken that you can't spare your brother half an hour.'

She laughed, and her stomach rumbled on cue. 'Just so you know, you're buying.'

The Jade Garden wasn't busy. A couple sat in the far corner, whispering to one another over crab and sweetcorn soup. Something in their body language was secretive and made Liberty wonder if they were having an affair. She banished all thoughts of Sol from her mind and took a seat with Jay.

The owner came out to greet them, clapping Jay on the back. 'Usual?' he asked.

'Yes, please, Chen,' Jay replied. 'With extra chicken balls, mate.'

Chen snapped his fingers at a waitress who scurried over with a jug of water and glasses. He barked at her in Cantonese and she immediately raced off to the kitchen.

'No rush,' said Liberty.

'Time is money,' said Chen 'Am I right, Jay?'

'Bang on,' Jay replied.

Liberty rolled her eyes and watched Chen retreat.

'You know you complain about Crystal not letting go of the past, but you're as bad,' said Jay.

'How?'

'You still see me as the snotty-nosed kid in YOI.' Jay pointed at himself. 'A fuck-up who wouldn't amount to anything.'

'I never thought that.' The waitress arrived with a plate of spring rolls. Liberty picked one up in her fingers, dipped it into soy sauce and crunched, the contents escaping and burning her tongue. 'Not even once.'

Jay poured them both a glass of water. 'But you never thought it would all work out this well, did you?'

Liberty took another spring roll and stuffed it into her mouth so that she couldn't answer. Jay was proud of what he'd got and she wasn't going to rain on his parade.

'I bet you never imagined I'd be a happily married man either.'

Liberty snorted. 'Is that how you describe yourself to all the girls working at the Cherry?'

Jay tried to pick up a spring roll with a pair of chopsticks, dropped it twice, gave up and used his fingers. 'I didn't say I was perfect, Lib.' He mimed bringing a bottle to his mouth at the waitress, who brought over two Chinese beers. Back in London, Liberty had made it a rule never to drink during the day, but times had changed. 'Anyway, sex is good for you,' said Jay. 'You should try it.'

Liberty picked up a prawn cracker and threw it at him.

'What about internet dating?' Jay asked.

'Are you out of your mind?'

Jay pulled out his mobile. 'Nothing to be ashamed of, a lot of folk do it.'

'Well, I'm not.'

Jay pulled up Tinder on his phone. 'This is popular.'

'I don't care.'

'I'll set up your profile,' said Jay. 'My name is Liberty and I'm looking for hook-ups with men under seventy.'

'Don't you dare.'

'No one reads that stuff anyway. It's all about the picture.' Jay raised his mobile. 'Say cheese.'

Liberty screamed as the shutter clicked. Jay showed her the photo. Her eyes were wide in a mixture of horror and panic.

'Not your best smile, I'll be honest,' said Jay, 'but the puppies look amazing.'

Liberty picked up a chopstick. 'I'm going to spear you with this.'

'I think you'll be a lot less homicidal when you start getting some, Lib.'

'Maybe I am getting some.'

'Sex with yourself doesn't count.'

When the waitress placed a dish of greasy chicken balls in front of them, Jay and Liberty were both laughing so much they could barely speak.

Liberty heaped egg fried rice onto her plate and plopped a doughy ball on top. 'So, let's not pretend you brought me here to chat about my love life.' She slopped sweet and sour sauce on top of the ball. 'We both know you want to ask me about Jackson Delaney.'

'Am I that obvious?'

'Yup.'

Jay dunked his own chicken ball directly into the dish of orange sauce. 'It's true that you're representing him, then?' Liberty nodded. 'Is he going down?'

'I've only just got access to the papers,' she said. 'I haven't managed to read them yet.'

69

'But how's it looking?' Jay asked. 'Will it stick?'

Liberty eyed him coolly. 'Why do I get the impression that you're not asking out of friendly interest?'

The couple in the corner got up to leave. As they passed Liberty and Jay's table, the man patted the woman gently on the arse. There was a pink mark on the third finger of his left hand where his wedding ring should have been. It was probably nestling in the bottom of his pocket or in the glove compartment of his car.

'Someone's suggested that we might want to take over Delaney's business,' said Jay. 'But we'd only consider that if he was definitely out of the picture.'

'Like I say, I haven't even read the evidence.'

Jay leaned towards her. 'When you have, will you tell me?'

'I shouldn't discuss it with you, Jay.'

'I know,' he replied. 'But will you?'

Liberty stuffed the chicken ball into her mouth. It was like a salty doughnut filled with dry meat. Nevertheless, she shoved in another.

Sol pushed his flask to the other side of his desk.

About a month ago, Natasha had started sending him to work with soup. More often than not, she attached a little note in her neat handwriting, informing him what sort of soup the flask contained, with hand-drawn hearts and smiley faces. Apparently, today's offering was sweet potato, ginger and orange (since when did fruit have any business being in soup?), and from the number of kisses lined up under the ingredients, it had been made with a lot of love.

He wasn't hungry. Especially not for soup.

He had the Delaney papers in front of him, reading them in turn. Knowing that Liberty was doing the exact same thing didn't help.

She was right, of course: last night had been all kinds of wrong. Maybe that was why it had felt so good. There was some sort of natural law at play, where food that actively made you healthy tasted like shit and dirty sex with a woman who would cause nothing but trouble tasted like a gift from God.

When his phone rang, he scrambled for it, but was disappointed not to see Liberty's number.

'Sir,' he said.

'Come up to my office, Sol.'

No 'hello', no 'goodbye', no 'please'.

When Sol opened the DCI's door, he was surprised to find Hassani at the window, a cup of coffee in hand. The smile she gave him was forced and tight. Something was up.

'I'll get straight to the point, Sol,' said the DCI. 'I agreed to have Delaney's solicitor placed under surveillance.'

'Sir?'

'She's a Greenwood.'

Sol stared at Hassani. She stared right back. Going behind his back wasn't something she was ashamed of.

'Last night Amira followed her target to the Radisson Hotel,' said the DCI. 'But you know that's where she went.'

Sol's mouth went dry. Amira had been at the Radisson? Presumably she'd seen him with Liberty in the bar. He narrowed his eyes at the young woman he'd plucked from Vice. Without him she would still be stuck nicking kerb-crawlers on Carter Street.

'I do know that, sir.' Sol cleared his throat. 'I met Miss Chapman there.'

'Can I ask why?'

'To give her the interview tapes,' he said.

The DCI furrowed his brow. 'In person?'

'She'd requested the tapes, and when she said she'd be at the hotel, I agreed to hand them over. I was passing.' Sol shrugged. 'Unlike Officer Hassani, I hold no grudge against Miss Chapman.'

Hassani's coffee sloshed out of her cup. 'It's not a grudge.'

'Yes, it is,' said Sol. 'You hate her because you feel she got one over on you. Now it's payback time.'

Hassani slammed her cup down on the DCI's desk. 'All this time I've been wondering why you felt the need to defend that woman and now I know.'

'You know nothing,' said Sol, and whipped round to face the DCI. 'Sir, am I being accused of something here?'

Hassani pulled out her mobile, scrolled and thrust it in Sol's face. There was a picture on the screen of Sol and Liberty having a drink together. They were laughing. Liberty's eyes crinkled. She looked beautiful.

'She bought me a beer for doing her a favour. It's what normal people do.' Sol kept his voice casual. 'If I'd known you'd make such a fuss, I'd have got the round in myself, Amira.' He turned back to the DCI. 'Sir, you'll see I burned the interviews onto a disk and logged it all. I also confirmed by email to Singh & Co that they were in receipt. Nothing about any of this is remotely underhand.'

'You stayed at the hotel for hours, Sol,' said Hassani.

Sol shook his head. 'I left after a couple of drinks. Maybe your surveillance skills aren't up to the job.'

'Your car, Sol, it was still in the car park when I called it a day.' Hassani brandished the phone once more. 'The time recorded is after midnight.'

'I'd had a few so I left it there, walked for a bit while I had a fag, then flagged down a cab.' Sol sniffed. 'And before you show me a photo of Chapman's car in the car park, well, where else would it be? She stayed after I left. By the look of how she was dressed, I'd say she had a date, but, no, I didn't ask with whom, what with it not being any of my bloody business.'

The DCI stood, picked up Hassani's phone and handed it back to her. 'Could you leave us, Amira?'

'Sir . . .'

'Now,' he said.

The young woman growled into her chest and stalked from the room, slamming the door behind her.

'I have to tell you that your behaviour last night was far from ideal,' said the DCI. Sol nearly laughed out loud. 'If there is any hint that this lawyer isn't above board and that you've been socializing with her, I don't have to spell it out, do I?'

'Sir, the problem is not me or the lawyer,' said Sol. 'The problem is Amira. She's obsessed with Miss Chapman. I should have come to you with it, I can see that now, but I didn't want her to get into any bother.' Sol sighed. 'Back in the day that's how we used to handle these things. Maybe I'm getting too old for all this.'

The DCI gave Sol a penetrating look as Sol gripped the desk for support. His palms were sweating and his heart hammered in his chest. Did his superior believe him?

At last, the DCI broke eye contact and exhaled loudly. 'This had better not come back to bite us on the arse, Sol.'

'It won't.'

The DCI nodded. 'Fine.' Sol took a breath and turned to leave. 'Tell Amira that the surveillance stands until the end of the week.'

'Sir, I'm not convinced we should be pandering to Amira's feelings about this.'

The chief put up a hand. 'Until the end of the week. No more, no less.'

Amira rocked Rahim in her arms, fat tears pouring down her face. One dripped off her chin onto her son's flawless cheek. She bent and kissed it away. He was asleep and she should have put him in the cot beside her bed, but she clung to him.

Downstairs, she could hear her father and Zaid chatting in the kitchen as they cooked and laid the table. She needed to wash her face and help them, but she couldn't move.

Sol had been someone she'd looked up to. Not a saint, far from it, but a good copper. A man she trusted. Not any longer. Today in the chief's office, she'd seen him for what he really was; a man covering his back. A liar.

There was a tap on her bedroom door and it was opened by Zaid before she could dry her eyes. 'Sis?'

Amira buried her face in Rahim's shoulder.

'What's wrong?' Zaid padded across to her, sockless feet in a pair of slippers. At college, he was the epitome of cool in Nikes and snap caps, but under his own roof he dressed like Dad.

'I'm just tired,' said Amira.

Zaid took the baby from her and lowered him into his cot. Rahim blew a tiny spit bubble as his head touched the mattress. Zaid burst it with his thumb. 'Is it work?'

Amira rubbed her eyes with her knuckles. 'Have you ever been really disappointed in someone?'

'Yes,' Zaid replied. 'Omar.'

Amira was surprised to hear her ex-husband's name. 'I thought you liked him.'

'I did. That's why I was disappointed when he turned out to be a complete dick.'

Amira laughed.

'The important thing, sis, is that you didn't let Omar drag you down,' said Zaid. 'You did what you knew was right.' He stood and held out his hand. 'Now, come down and eat. Dad's made biryani.'

'Again?'

Zaid led her to the door. 'It's only the third time this week.'

Chapter 6

1 January 1990
'Sure, I think it might need stitches,' says Connor's mum. 'She should go to the hospital.'

'We've got to get back,' I say, and struggle to my feet, but my head spins and I fall to my right.

Connor catches me and pushes me back onto the settee.

He and Fat Rob took it in turns to carry me to Connor's house, with Tiny wiping the blood off my chin every two seconds, Vicky swearing and calling the men who'd attacked me every name under the sun. Danny mostly smoked weed.

I feel bad that we woke Connor's mum. She seems lovely. All flannel nightie and fresh perm.

'Well, we can't spend what's left of the night looking at this lip,' she says.

'Shall I call us a couple of taxis?' asks Tiny.

Connor's mum waves her hand. 'On New Year's Eve? Don't talk soft. No, you'll have to stay here tonight.'

'Cheers, Mrs O,' says Fat Rob.

'But I'm telling you now.' She wags a finger. 'There's to be no shenanigans of any type.' She turns to Connor. 'And this wee one is having your bed.'

'Yes, Mam,' he says.

'Well, show her where it is then. Sure, she can't guess, can she?'

'No, Mam.'

Connor's bedroom is rammed with stuff. Motorbike magazines, bits that look like they belong on motorbikes, records by the lorry load. The wall behind his bed is plastered with fliers from club nights and raves.

He goes to a set of drawers and pulls out a Stone Roses T-shirt. 'Sleep in this.'

I take it from him. It smells of fabric softener. 'I'm sorry,' *I say.* 'I ruined everyone's night.'

'Nah.' *He sits on the bed next to me.* 'I had a brilliant night. And you seem to have managed to keep all your teeth. Win-win.'

I laugh and immediately regret it as pain runs across my jaw. 'Did you get to tell your girlfriend what happened?' *I ask.*

'Well, I would have done if I had one,' *he says.*

'Sorry,' *I mumble.* 'I just saw you with a lass and I thought . . .'

Connor leans back on his elbows. 'What can I tell you? Chicks love me.'

I laugh again. Then there's a knock on the door and Connor's mum sticks her head round. 'Someone needs to get some rest now, Connor.' *She jabs her thumb over her head to signal he should leave.*

He gets up. 'Night, Lib.'

'Night, Connor.'

As the door closes behind them I hear Connor's mum say, 'And don't even think of sneaking up these stairs.'

'Mam,' *Connor says.* 'She's been knocked virtually unconscious and her lip's split in two. What do you take me for?'

'Hmm.'

'You're actually offending me now, Mam.'

'Sure, I know a pretty girl when I see one.'

They bicker all the way downstairs until they're out of earshot and I put on the T-shirt.

A few hours later, I wake from a terrible dream. Dad's cornered me in Orchard Grove and is demanding I tell Carl that he didn't chuck Mam off the balcony. He says he'll kill all the kids if I don't admit the truth.

Tears are running down my cheeks and my mouth is wet. I turn on the light and find my hands covered in blood. My lip must have opened up again.

I slip out of the bedroom and down the landing to the bathroom. In the mirror, I see the state of my face and Connor's T-shirt, which is now covered in blood. Shit. I run the cold tap and put a wad of toilet paper under it, then hold it to my mouth, trying not to scream.

'Lib?'

'Yeah.'

Connor comes in. He's wearing the shirt he had on last night and his pants. 'I thought I heard you shouting.'

'Sorry,' I say. 'Bad dreams.'

He lifts the paper and checks my lip. 'You're bound to be shook up.'

I don't tell him that I have them all the time. 'Can I swap you?'

'Swap what?'

'You have your bed back and I'll go downstairs,' I say.

'I'm on the chair under my cagoule, Lib,' he says. 'Tiny and Fat Rob are out for the count on the settee, you'll never move them. And Dan and Vicky are snuggled up under the table, doing God knows what. I think you need to be somewhere more comfy tonight.'

My eyes fill with tears and I turn away from him. How can I tell him that I'm too scared to be on my own?

'I'll come back to my room with you and sit for a bit, if you like,' he says. 'On the floor. Obviously.'

'Will you?'

He nods and we creep back to his bedroom. He lifts the continental quilt for me and I slip under it. He doesn't mention the blood on his pillow slip or his T-shirt.

'Shall I turn off the lamp?' he asks.

'Can we leave it on?' I ask. 'Just for five minutes?'

'Course.'

He sorts himself out a nest on his floor and drags a dressing-gown over him. Then he reaches up and puts his hand over mine.

I lace my fingers through his. 'You're nice, aren't you?'

'I am.' He yawns. 'And, yeah, I know, you're still not going to shag me.'

Present day

Dax emptied a can of Alphabetti pasta into a bowl and slid it into the microwave.

'Tell me that's not your breakfast,' said Liberty, looking up from a slice of toast. Dax kissed his teeth and rooted in the drawer for a fork. 'And what are you doing up at this time?' Liberty took in the jeans and hoodie. 'Dressed?'

'Thought I'd get some fresh air,' Dax replied.

Liberty watched him suspiciously. Dax rarely surfaced before ten, then spent several hours lolling on the sofa in his boxers.

When the microwave pinged, he wrapped his hand in a tea-towel and grabbed the bowl. Then he took a forkful of pasta and blew on it. An orange B fell off and flopped onto the table.

'Can I ask where you're planning on getting this fresh air?'

Dax raked a P and a W off the fork with his teeth and shrugged. Liberty was about to tell him to stop messing her about when the doorbell went. Dax jumped up to answer. He came back into the room with Crystal.

Liberty sighed. 'I already told Jay that I haven't even read the case files yet.'

'Who says I've come about that?'

'Well, haven't you?'

Dax shook his head, took his breakfast and sloped out of the kitchen. Alone now, the sisters stared at each other. Liberty ripped off a piece of toast with her fingers and ate it. Crystal pulled a packet of Juicy Fruit from her back pocket and shoved a stick into her mouth.

'Why are you and Jay so keen to take over Delaney's patch?' Liberty asked. 'It's just drugs and girls, right?'

'And?'

'And it's got him banged up in case you hadn't noticed.'

'I'm touched you care about us.'

Liberty scraped back her chair and tossed the left-over crusts into the bin. She didn't want to fight with Crystal again. 'Delaney's problem is that he pushed it for too long,' she said. 'There comes a point when it's time to clean up or face the music.'

'He's going down, then?'

Liberty slipped her dirty plate into the dishwasher. 'I didn't say that. But even if he walks, the police won't leave him be. He should have gone legit when he had the chance.'

'And that's what you think we should do?'

'Of course.' Liberty faced her sister. 'You and Jay did what you had to do in the past. I get it. But you're both half-decent business people with money now. You could do anything you wanted.'

Crystal glared at her. 'What right have you got to tell us how to live our lives?'

'I'm your sister.'

The slap came hard, knocking Liberty backwards. She was so shocked she barely felt the sting.

'I was eleven when you took off. Jay was inside and Frankie was still wetting the bed.' Crystal pointed at Liberty, her hand shaking. 'I looked for you everywhere.'

Liberty put a hand to her cheek. It was hot and she began to cry. She took a step towards Crystal, bracing herself for the second blow.

'You changed your fucking name to make sure I couldn't find you,' said Crystal.

Liberty took another step towards her sister, close enough now to smell the chewing gum. She reached out a hand, but Crystal batted it away. She lifted it again, held it inches from Crystal's shoulder. Then slowly she lowered it and stood like that, crying silently, feeling the furious rise and fall of her baby sister's body.

'I slept with someone the other night,' said Liberty.

'Shit.'

'He's married.'

'Double shit.'

Liberty burst out laughing.

'What's so funny?' Crystal asked.

'Someone said that to me years ago when I told her about Mam and Dad.'

Crystal spat the wad of gum into the empty packet and balled it up. 'Double shit about summed it up.'

'How have you and Harry managed to stay together so long?' Liberty asked.

'He knows I'll kneecap him if he tries to leave me,' Crystal replied. 'You think I'm joking?' She unwrapped another stick, split it and gave half to Liberty. 'Paul Hill wants us to take over the Delaney patch with him.'

'I figured as much.'

'If we don't, he'll just take it for himself.'

'And?

'And then he'll have twice as much local turf as us.'

Liberty chewed the gum thoughtfully. Gangs and businesses didn't behave very differently. If your rival swallowed up the competition, you could assume it was only a matter of time until they came, jaws open, for you.

'If Hill tried to make a move on our business, Jay would . . .' Crystal paused. 'I couldn't stop him.'

Liberty knew it was the truth.

The girls at the Black Cherry arrived in dribs and drabs. Frankie nodded at a Latvian as she came through the drape. She looked like

80

a kid without her make-up. Later, in PVC bra and hot pants, she'd move through the punters as sleek and hungry as a shark.

'Eyes on the road, sunshine,' said Mel, holding out a beer for him.

He sneered at her, but grabbed the bottle all the same. 'Where's Jay?' he asked.

'Out.'

Mel reached to replace some clean glasses on a high shelf. Her top rode up to reveal a red ring left by her too tight jeans. Frankie almost gagged. The woman should be riding into town with her bus pass, legs in support tights, not tottering around in a strip club. 'You said he wanted to see me.'

Mel smoothed down her top. 'I lied.'

Another girl arrived and waved at them. She'd had her lips done since Frankie had last seen her. They looked like swollen slugs.

'Why the fuck would you lie, Mel?'

'I wanted a word in your shell-like.'

Frankie pulled out his mobile. 'These were invented not long since.'

The girl with the new lips waddled over to them, despite Mel's efforts to shoo her away, and leaned in to whisper something in the old bag's ear. Mel let out a sigh that smelt worse than the wiring at the Trap, fished in her handbag and gave the girl a packet of paracetamol.

'There's always something wrong with them,' said Mel, watching the girl head to the stairs. 'I'd get less moaning if I worked in the local hospice.'

'Maybe you're getting too old for all this, Mel.'

'Maybe you should watch your fucking mouth.'

They stared at one another and Frankie imagined what it would be like to put his hands around her scraggy throat and squeeze until her eyes popped. 'Spit it out then,' he said. 'What have you dragged me over here for?'

She took the empty bottle from him and handed him another beer. The staff in rehab had gone on and on about avoiding booze. Didn't matter that you weren't an alkie, you needed to steer clear of any mind-altering substance. Mel obviously gave not one flying fuck whether Frankie started using again.

'Paul Hill came to see you yesterday,' she said. Frankie nodded and put the bottle rim to his lips to hide his smile. 'Doesn't that seem a bit odd to you?'

Frankie shrugged. 'He wanted to show us that he's got inside information on the Delaney case.'

'No doubt.' Mel fingered the gold M on the end of a chain that Jay had given her for Christmas. 'But why come to you?'

Frankie took a swallow of warm beer. He'd been so pleased at having one over on Jay and Crystal that he'd skated over why Hill had chosen to speak to him and not his brother. 'Does it matter which one of us he came to? We're family.'

Mel raised an eyebrow. They both knew that Frankie was not an equal when it came to business and money. Jesus, Liberty had had to fucking beg them to let him do the grunt work in the Trap.

'I know Paul Hill from way back,' Mel said. 'He doesn't do anything without good reason.'

Frankie drained the second beer. He didn't want to play guessing games with Mel. 'Why don't you ask him, seeing as how close you are?'

'You cause this family nothing but aggro,' she snarled. 'How about you try and do something useful for a change?'

'Like what?'

She tapped his forehead. 'For once in your life, use this, Frankie.' He jerked away from her touch. 'Paul Hill came to you because he wants to cause problems.' She circled a finger, weighed down with a sovereign ring. 'He knows how things are with you and Jay so why not ratchet up the tension, eh?'

Frankie shook his head. Paul Hill wanted to go in with the

Greenwoods fifty-fifty on the Delaney spot. Why would he want to needle any of them?

'There's one way to find out,' said Mel.

If there was, Frankie couldn't think of it. His brain was starting to hurt now and he needed a painkiller.

'Go back to Hill, tell him you've had enough of how things are here,' said Mel. 'See where that conversation leads.'

Frankie sighed. 'He won't buy that.'

'Well, you wouldn't just rock up and say it straight out.' Mel rolled her eyes. 'Get chatting to one of his chuffing gorillas. I hear the bald one's fond of the Bolivian marching powder so you should have plenty to talk about.'

Frankie cocked his head to one side. The way Mel put it was starting to make sense. Ease in gently with Hill's bodyguard, say he was sick and tired of being the family whipping boy. It shouldn't be too hard to be convincing because he *was* fucking sick and tired of it. Then when he found out what the deal was with Hill, he could bring it all back to Jay and Crystal.

'I wouldn't tell Jay what you're up to,' said Mel. 'Not until you've found something out worth knowing.'

Frankie laughed. Of course, he wouldn't tell Jay or Crystal. They'd just say no and make him go back to cleaning the Trap. He looked at Mel in a new light. He'd always resented the way Jay let her stick her oar in family affairs when her job, as far as he knew, was to keep the snatch in line, but now he could see that devious brain of hers was useful.

He got up and slid his mobile back into his pocket. 'I'll let you know how I get on.'

'You do that.'

Jackson Delaney sported an orange bib over a checked shirt. Being on remand meant he didn't have to wear prison uniform but even he couldn't avoid the bib.

Liberty held back from making a crack about netball.

He ignored Raj and gave Liberty a cool nod, finger inside his ear.

When a guard passed their table, he shook hands with Liberty's client, oblivious to where it had just been.

Delaney rubbed the other hand through his hair. 'Any chance of getting some clippers for me, Mr Lawson? I hear one of the lads on B wing has a pair I'm certain he'd give me.'

'I'll see what I can do, Jacko.'

When the guard had gone, Delaney placed his hands on the table near Liberty's. Surreptitiously, she inched hers away.

'Right then,' he said. 'Am I going down?'

Liberty had grilled Raj about this on the journey to the prison, as he'd fiddled with every knob and dial in the Porsche.

'The police have built a pretty comprehensive case,' she said. 'They've been watching you for months.'

'How long will I get?' Delaney snarled.

'If you're convicted on each offence on the indictment, probably more than ten years.'

He blinked slowly. With good behaviour he'd serve two-thirds. Still a long sentence for a man of his age.

'I think, though, that it's not a done deal yet,' she said. 'We can still make the prosecution sing for their supper.' Delaney opened his palms for her to continue. 'There's a lot of evidence collected by surveillance teams. Their statements are anonymous at the moment.'

Delaney stiffened. 'At the moment?'

'We can make an application to the court asking for their details,' she replied. 'The CPS will say it's not in the public interest but we can argue that, unless we can check those police officers out, we can't know if they're credible.' She opened a folder and pointed to a list Raj had typed, setting out which witness statements they could potentially challenge. 'That's quite a lot of coppers to take on trust, don't you think?'

'So, what?' asked Delaney. 'If you win we get a bunch of names.'

Liberty shook her head. 'The CPS probably won't hand over their details.'

'Why not?'

'It would compromise the officers, especially if they're on new operations.'

'Then what's the point?'

'No details.' Liberty pointed to the skylight, high above them on the ceiling. 'No statement.'

Delaney grabbed her hand before she was able to dodge him. 'You're bloody good, hen.'

Liberty reddened. She was just parroting what Raj had told her.

'A judge might chuck out our application.' She didn't look down for fear of seeing a wad of brown earwax. 'There are no guarantees.'

Delaney released her and stood, gesturing to a guard that he wanted to leave. 'You know what they say? There's only two things in life guaranteed and that's death and taxes. Well, I've never paid tax and I'm not dead yet.'

In the 911, Raj leaned back in his seat and buzzed the electronic windows up and down.

'The air-con won't work if you do that,' Liberty told him, locking his window from her side.

'Spoilsport,' Raj replied. She floored the accelerator and the car let out a roar. 'I could listen to that all day.'

He turned on the radio, scrolling through the stations until he found what he wanted and bhangra filled the car. 'Get in,' he said, and jiggled his shoulders in time, palms pointing to the roof.

★　★　★

Liberty pulled up outside the office and they hauled their bags and files back inside. 'This application for the names of the witnesses,' she asked. 'Will it work?'

Raj kicked aside that day's post with the toe of his slip-on. 'Depends. We'd need to show that, without knowing who those witnesses are, we can't properly defend our client.'

'How will their details help us do that?' Liberty scooped up the letters and placed them on yesterday's still unopened pile. God, they needed a receptionist.

Raj inspected a flier for pizza delivery: £8.99 for a fourteen-inch with cheese-filled crust. 'Maybe some of these anonymous witnesses are unreliable,' he said. 'They might have disciplinaries against them as long as their arm.'

'So, what do we do?'

'We get ourselves a shovel, my love, and we start digging.' He pulled out his mobile. 'Ham and pineapple or pepperoni?'

She grabbed the flier from him. 'We're not eating a pizza the size of a tyre for lunch.' She chucked it in the bin. 'Let's say we make our application and it actually succeeds. What then?'

'The CPS have a choice. Give us the details or withdraw those statements.'

'Is there still a case against Delaney without them?' Liberty asked.

'Yeah, but nowhere near as strong,' he said.

'He's probably guilty, though,' said Liberty.

Raj shrugged. 'Let's leave the judging to them that like it. Our job is to test the evidence. It's what they're paying us for.'

Liberty smiled. If Delaney got off or out of prison relatively soon, Paul Hill would have to keep his grubby mitts off her client's patch and he couldn't drag Jay along with him one way or the other.

She headed for the door, her shoulders more relaxed than she could remember. She had a plan and it felt great.

'Where are you off to?' Raj asked.

'I'm going to get us some brain food,' she answered. 'And a bloody great shovel.'

Chapter 7

3 January 1990
Vicky and me are two days into a week's gating, and she's furious. 'I can't fucking stand this,' she says, and throws open our bedroom window.

'Don't do it, Vic,' I say. 'There'll just be even more trouble.'

'Don't care,' she says, and slips out of the window onto the flat roof. Then she gives me a wave and shimmies down the drainpipe.

We tried to tell them what happened on New Year's Eve, but did they believe us? No, they chuffing well did not.

'Were the police called?' Carl asked, arms folded.

'What would have been the point?' Vicky yelled at him. 'The two what attacked Lib had run off, hadn't they? And the one left behind was paralytic and couldn't tell them anything.' She doesn't mention that she and Danny had given him a few kicks for good measure, which meant calling the police was not exactly on our agenda.

'You know the rules,' said Hemma. 'A night's unauthorized absence results in a seven-day gating.'

I expect they could hear Vicky screaming in Manchester.

I watch her troop off into the rainy afternoon and sigh. Next door, Imbo and Silent Leanne are shagging. She might not speak, but she bloody well groans and moans when she wants to. I grab Connor's now-washed Stone Roses T-shirt, stuff it into a carrier and step out onto the roof.

I'm not sure which house is Connor's. I was completely out of it when

88

we arrived on New Year's Eve, and the next morning his mum didn't stop yapping as she bundled us out with bacon rolls in our hands. I was so busy trying to keep up with what she was saying, I didn't pay much attention to where I was.

I think it's the one with a motorbike parked outside. That would make sense. So, I ring the bell. When no one comes, I ring again. I'm about to give up when I see a figure coming down the stairs through the frosted glass in the door.

Connor opens it in just his jeans. He's got a tattoo on his chest, just above his heart, that says 'Rave On'.

'Lib.' He looks shocked and doesn't ask me in. 'What are you doing here?'

I offer up the bag. 'Your T-shirt. All the blood's come out, I think.'

'Ta.' He looks behind him nervously. 'Your lip looks on the mend.'

I touch it. There's a scab now, which itches a bit.

Then I see her at the top of the stairs. The girl from the Cube. She's as pretty as anything with blonde hair and a nose-ring. All she's wearing is Connor's shirt and her knickers.

'Sorry,' I say, and leg it.

When I get to the bus stop a couple of streets away, I sink into one of the seats under the shelter. I shouldn't have come over here. I've embarrassed Connor, I've made a right tit of myself, and when I get back to Orchard Grove there'll be hell to pay.

Maybe I could go to the Galaxy for a bit and see Fat Rob. I check the timetable and try to work out the bus fare from here. I've only got fifty pence on me. I'll have to start nicking stuff like everyone else. It's impossible to live on what the social workers give us.

Suddenly Connor sprints past me, white trainers splashing in the puddles. He stops, turns and doubles back to the bus shelter, breath coming in jagged bursts. He puts his hands on his knees and pants.

'You need to stop smoking,' I tell him.

'Thank you, Dr Elizabeth.' He plonks himself down on the seat next to me. 'Why did you run off like that?'

'Because you were with your girlfriend,' I say.

'I told you before, I haven't got a girlfriend.'

'Does she know that?'

He laughs and rubs his face. 'It's just. You know.'

I nod. I do know. The kids at Orchard Grove have sex all the time. Imbo's slept with every girl except me and Vicky. He's worked out that most of them will spread their legs if he says he likes their nail varnish. But none of them is his girlfriend. He's actually secretly in love with Vicky. I mean it's not even that secret. Whenever they're on the glue he tells her he loves her and she strokes his head. I once heard her tell him that she wishes she could love him back, but she can't. Then they both cried.

'Look, do you fancy a cuppa back at mine?'

'I'm thinking that Mrs I-Need-To-Put-Some-Clothes-On won't be too happy about that,' I say.

'And I'm thinking that Mrs I-Need-To-Put-Some-Clothes-On won't still be there, seeing as how I ran out of the house after another lass.'

Present day

Amira watched Sol from the other side of the incident room. Most of the stuff from the Delaney operation had been removed. Boards wiped clean, papers filed, officers dispatched back to their own nicks.

A small team remained to oversee the trial, with Sol having day-to-day supervision. He was at his desk, a flask to one side. He took off the lid, sniffed the contents and pulled a face. There was some sort of note or label attached to the flask. Sol removed it, screwed it into a ball and aimed for the wastepaper basket. He missed.

A couple of uniforms walked past the open door, hooting with laughter, hands wrapped around steaming cups of tea. Their camaraderie jeered at Amira's solitude.

The pang of dread sat in her stomach. She knew she couldn't

ignore Sol much longer and that it would need to be her who broke the ice. She muttered a quick *hadith* under her breath and headed over. 'Sol?'

'Fuck off, Amira.'

'We need to talk.'

'Which word do you not get?' he asked. 'The fuck or the off?'

Amira stood her ground. 'We work together, Sol.'

He turned to her and his face said it all. They had indeed worked together. They'd been a team. And she'd gone behind his back reporting him to the DCI.

'This is your doing, not mine, Sol,' she said. She could smell what was in the flask. Some sort of soup with onions and tomatoes. It made her feel a bit sick. 'We could use this situation to our advantage,' she said.

He acted like she hadn't spoken, getting to his feet, snapping the lid back on the flask and carrying it with him as he strode across the incident room. Amira followed him as he stalked along the corridor, throwing open the door that led outside to the car park.

'We could use your connection with Chapman as part of the surveillance.'

Sol didn't stop until he reached his car, when he fished in his coat pocket for his keys.

'Think about it,' Amira continued. 'You're in an ideal position to gather intel.' He stared at her now, features smeared with anger. 'On the Delaney case. On Chapman. And on the whole Greenwood enterprise.'

Sol might have let himself be led astray by the lawyer with her high heels and bouncy hair, he was just a bloke after all, but at heart he was first and last a copper.

'You always tell me that in this job there is more than one way to skin a cat, Sol.'

He unscrewed the lid of the flask once more and for a second she thought he was going to drink straight from its mouth, but instead he poured it out between them, the red liquid hitting the tarmac with a hiss.

Amira jumped away but not before a red lump hit her shoe. 'What the hell, Sol?'

'Like I said back in the nick.' He flicked away the last dregs of the soup. 'Fuck. Off.'

Liberty brushed a raisin from Raj's chair. At least, she hoped to God it was a raisin. Then she rubbed hand sanitizer into her palms, working it between her fingers, then took a seat and opened the Delaney case files on his PC.

As he'd left for court that morning, Liberty had suggested that she go through the anonymous witness statements, noting similarities and discrepancies. 'I'll make up two spreadsheets,' she'd told him.

'Can you do that?' he'd asked, balancing six files. The top one had the words 'Spencer Hopwell – indecent exposure', scribbled on top in felt tip. 'Make a spreadsheet?'

'Of course, Raj.' She flicked her hands, ushering him away. 'You go and do what you're good at.' All she could make out from the second file was the word 'weapon'. 'Whatever that is. And leave me in peace to do what I'm good at.'

She flexed her now bacteria-free hands and opened Excel. No previous files existed.

As she created her first spreadsheet, there was a thud from above and a shower of dust fluttered down. She growled and marched to the bottom of the stairs.

'Bam?' she yelled.

Bam appeared at the top. 'Yeah?' Today's cap read 'Don't Ask Me'.

'What are you doing up there?' Liberty asked. 'You're banging about like a bloody elephant.'

Bam scratched his neck, which appeared to be covered in tattoos of reindeer. Liberty thought about asking him if it was some sort of tribute to Christmas but decided she didn't actually care.

'Sorry about that,' said Bam. 'I fell over.'

'You fell over?'

Bam nodded slowly. 'Doing a bit of yoga. It's good for keeping calm.' He gave Liberty a meaningful look. 'I'm trying to get the missus into it.'

Liberty counted to ten in her head and walked back to Raj's office, shutting the door behind her. She returned to Excel and considered what to name her file. Her old boss, Ronald, had always said that the name a lawyer gave a file was important: 'It sets the tone, darling.' He was a twat, but he was right about file names. Her finger hovered over the keyboard when the doorbell rang. She ignored it and typed the first letters of her file name. The bell rang again and didn't stop. Whoever was out there kept their finger firmly on it.

'You've got to be shitting me,' Liberty shouted, and wondered when she had started to sound like Jay. It had better not be him at the door. Or Crystal. She was sick of them trying to pressure her and, anyway, she had a perfect plan to sort them out: get Delaney out of prison so that his patch would be well and truly off the radar.

With the bell ringing through the office she bounded to the front door and threw it open. Shocked, she found Sol outside. He pushed past her and slammed the door behind him.

'Come in, why don't you?'

He grabbed her arm above the elbow and pulled her through the reception area. 'Is your room down there?'

'Sort of.'

He nodded and dragged her to Raj's office, pushing her inside. Even then he didn't let go of her arm.

'You're actually hurting me now,' said Liberty. He looked at her, eyes wild. 'Sol?'

He gathered himself, looked down at his hand gripping her arm and let go. 'Sorry.'

Liberty rubbed her skin through her suit jacket. She should chuck him out. Who did he think he was, barging in here?

'You called me a car crash,' he said.

'No. I said this—'

'Well, I am a car crash.' He was up in her face. 'Guilty as charged.'

Liberty turned her head and could feel the gush of his breath on her cheek.

'At least I can say I know what I am,' Sol hissed. They stood like that for a long moment until at last he stepped away. 'Though I don't know why I'm here.'

Liberty swallowed, but something sharp was stuck in her throat. She closed the gap between them and put a hand on his chest. Under her palm his heart beat like a hammer.

'I don't even know what your fucking name is,' he said. 'Greenwood or Chapman?'

'Lib,' she answered. 'My name is Lib.'

The gorilla's name was Nathan Osborne, known as Ozzie around these parts. He balanced a pint of Stella on top of the fruit machine and fed it pound coins, slapping the buttons with an open palm. From time to time, an avalanche of shrapnel cascaded into the tray below. Ozzie scooped it up and rattled it straight back into the machine.

Frankie watched him over a bottle of Diet Coke and waited.

'Do you want sauce with that?'

He looked up to find the woman who had served him earlier, hand on her hips, hair scraped back from her face. He fingered his untouched burger. 'No, ta.' The woman nodded but didn't budge. 'What?' he asked.

'I was just wondering how Daisy Clarke's doing,' she said. 'Heard she got herself clean.'

'D'you know her, then?' Frankie asked.

'She went to school with my eldest.'

At the other side of the pub, Ozzie was out of change and draining his pint. 'She's all right,' said Frankie, wanting to get rid of the nosy cow. 'Got a job and that. When I see her later I'll tell her you were asking.'

The woman stood her ground, messing with a cheap earring. Behind her Ozzie was putting on his coat.

'It might be best all round if you stayed clear of Daisy,' said the woman.

Frankie snapped up his head. Who the fuck did she think she was? Just some sad old barmaid in a pub no one went in any more. 'And it might be best all round if you stayed clear of me,' he said.

She scowled but moved on at last, just as Ozzie passed Frankie's table. He thought he'd missed his chance but Ozzie laughed and said, 'Giving you earache, Frankie?'

'Story of my frigging life, Ozzie,' replied Frankie, and dipped his head for Ozzie to sit opposite. 'How's it going?'

Ozzie flopped into the seat. Up close, Frankie could see that his freshly shaved skull had razor nicks here and there.

'Not too bad,' he said. 'Yourself?'

Frankie shrugged.

'How was rehab?'

Frankie pushed away his plate. 'Fine. I only did it to please our Jay. He's like an old woman when it comes to a bit of Charlie, you know what I mean?'

Ozzie laughed. For such a big man he had surprisingly small teeth, like someone had filed them down by half. 'You still using, then?'

'I dabble here and there.' Frankie finished his Diet Coke. 'To be honest, I was on my way up to the Crosshills for a taste now.' He stood to leave. 'If you fancy it?'

Ozzie got up too. 'Your Jay's not gonna be too happy.'

'Ain't that the truth.' Frankie clapped his hand on Ozzie's shoulder. 'Thing is, mate, I'm past caring.'

Liberty moved a stack of tapes from the client chair in Raj's office and pushed Sol into it. Then she sat at the opposite side of the desk.

Sol glanced around the room, taking in the out-of-date Leeds United calendar and half-drunk cups of coffee, discs of congealed milk wobbling on top. 'I like what you've done to the place.'

'This is Raj's office,' she replied.

Sol nodded. 'I thought as much. Yours all chrome and polished wood, is it? Files in alphabetical order?'

Liberty looked up at the ceiling. Above them Bam was crashing around in a sea of dead flies and dust. 'Do you want to tell me what's wrong?' she asked.

He let his head roll back and laughed. 'If I got started on that one, you'd run a mile.'

'Have you met my family?'

He let out another bark of laughter, eyes closed behind his fringe. At last he looked at her. 'I'm sorry I didn't mention Hassani was on the Delaney case.'

'She hates me,' said Liberty.

'You're in good company.' He put his left hand on a pile of legal aid forms. There was no wedding ring. Had he taken it off before coming to see her? Had he been wearing it last night? Did it even matter? She knew he was married, after all.

'This,' Liberty moved her finger between them, 'is a stupid idea.'

'I know.'

'And we are very bad people.'

Sol shook his head. 'If I've learned anything in my job it's that most people aren't bad. They're just trying to survive the only way they know how.'

Liberty didn't know if she believed that. Most people hadn't done a tenth of the terrible things she'd done in her life and they never would. Most people would not be sitting here now with the lead copper in the case she was desperately trying to win.

She stood and held out her hand. 'Let's get out of here.'

Amira logged the time Greenwood and Sol left the office, then started her car to follow them.

Despite his fury with her, Sol must have taken on board what Amira had suggested about using the lawyer.

Sol Connolly was a lot of things, but stupid wasn't one of them.

Chapter 8

On the morning that my gating's finally lifted, Vicky refuses to get out of bed. She's got another three days for calling Carl a kiddie-fiddler.

I'm a bit worried about her, to be honest. She spends most of her time huffing under her blankets. I want to say something nice when the bedroom door opens.

'It's your brother on the office phone, Elizabeth,' says Hemma.

I push past her and take the stairs two at a time.

'Jay,' I'm virtually shouting down the phone, 'are you all right?'

He laughs. 'I'll live.'

'I've missed you,' I tell him.

'That's because I'm the coolest person you know. And the best-looking,' he says. 'Have you seen our Crystal and Frankie?'

'Not since before Christmas. They've moved them again and Frankie's wetting the bed.'

'Don't tell me,' says Jay. 'The new foster parents think it'll help him settle in if he has a break from seeing the rest of his family? Honestly, when will these people get it into their thick heads?' I know what he's going to say. He's said it hundreds of times before. 'We're all much better when we're together.'

'I know,' I say, though I'm not sure it's true. Would Jay stay out of trouble if he saw me regularly? He thinks so anyway.

Carl sidles into the office, pretending to look through a pile of papers. What he's really doing is earwigging my conversation.

'Thing is, Lib, I'm up in court tomorrow,' says Jay.

'Is Miss Chapman going with you?' I ask.

'Yeah. So I'm not too worried.'

Jay might not be, but I am. Miss Chapman's lovely and she's worked wonders before, but the last time Jay was nicked she told me he was in last-chance saloon.

'I just wondered if you could come,' he says. 'You always know how to explain stuff better than me.'

I glance at Carl. There's no way he'll agree to me taking a day off school or give me a travel voucher. 'I'll be there,' *I tell Jay.*

When I go into Imbo's room, he's in bed, a copy of Knave on his chest, his hand under the covers.

'You haven't got any money I can borrow, have you?' *I ask him.*

He shakes his head. 'How much do you need?'

'Train fare to court.'

'Nick some batteries,' he says. 'Eveready's best.' *He gives a little grunt.* 'I know a bloke who'll buy 'em off you.'

I go to Boots and find the shelf of batteries. I even pick some up, but then a woman walks past and looks at me over her shoulder. I know from what Vicky says that they have store detectives in here, so I put them all back.

Woolies is my next stop but I call in the Galaxy on my way. Tiny throws open her arms. 'Hiya, stranger.' *It seems the most natural thing in the world to let her give me a hug.* 'Let's see that lip.' *She lifts my chin with her finger.* 'Doesn't look like it's going to leave much of a scar.'

'Connor told us they had you on some sort of lockdown,' says Fat Rob.

'Gated,' I say. 'Can't leave Orchard Grove, can't make phone calls.'

'Sounds like prison.'

The door opens, and in walk Connor and Danny.

'All right, Mrs I-Always-Keep-My-Clothes-On,' says Connor. *He comes close and nudges me. He smells like the fabric softener on his*

Stone Roses T-shirt. Danny spins me around and laughs. 'Get some sounds on, Rob.'

'I can't stop,' I say. 'I need to get some batteries.'

'I'm pretty sure I've got a couple in the back,' says Fat Rob.

I laugh. 'I need more than a couple, Rob. I've got to nick enough to sell for a train fare to Sheffield.'

They all stop what they're doing. Fat Rob scratches his greasy head and even Connor can't think of a smart-arsed answer.

'Our Jay's in court tomorrow,' I say quickly. 'I need to be there for him.'

The look on their faces makes me see I've made a real mistake in telling them, and my cheeks burn.

Connor opens his mouth to speak when a customer walks in. I groan. It's only Stacey Lamb, looking like she spent her Christmas eating sausage rolls and selection boxes. Jonno stands behind her. They stop dead in their tracks when they see me.

'Are you following us?' She points at me. 'Because I'll report you, see if I don't.'

This is all I need. I'm about to go on the rob and I've got Stacey chuffing Lamb threatening to call the filth.

'How can she be following you when she was already in here?' Tiny asks.

Stacey shrugs as if how I operate is a mystery to anyone. 'You shouldn't let the likes of her hang about in your shop,' she says to Fat Rob. 'It'll stop decent people coming in.'

Fat Rob glances at me. Will he bar me now he knows what I'm really like? I want to punch Stacey in the face. I can remember the feel of her mouth on my knuckles and it was bloody ace.

'Decent people are overrated,' says Fat Rob, and lights a fag.

'They've never got enough money for one thing,' say Tiny. 'And they've always got shit taste in music.'

'You can laugh,' says Stacey. 'But she's not even normal. Did you know she's a lezza?'

The way my foot connected with her jelly belly and then her head *replays in my mind. I would do anything to be able to put the boot in right this second.*

'A lezza, eh?' Tiny looks Stacey up and down. 'Well, at least you've no need to worry yourself, love. Not with the size of that arse.'

As Jonno drags Stacey out of the shop, Fat Rob snorts a stream of smoke through his nose. 'Do you want to tell us what all that's about, Lib?'

I sigh. Today is turning out to be rubbish. 'A couple of years ago I beat her up.' Connor throws back his head and laughs. 'It weren't funny. I got cautioned and everything.'

Connor is still laughing so I thump his arm. 'Sorry,' he says, tears streaming down his face. 'I'm just trying to imagine how she came off the worst.'

'I was mad as hell,' I tell him. 'She said some horrible things about a foster carer that I really liked. Well, the only one I ever liked at all.'

'Let me give you a lift to Sheffield tomorrow on my new bike,' he says.

Tiny puts her chin on his shoulder. 'Which translates as "Let me show off my new Kawasaki, pretty lady."'

I look at Connor to check he's being serious. 'I need to set off dead early.'

'The sunrise is my alarm,' he says. 'And at least now it all makes sense. You won't shag me because you're a lezza.'

The next morning, Connor arrives at Orchard Grove around eight. I take the helmet he offers me and he helps me fasten it under my chin. Imbo and Vicky lean out of the bedroom window. Imbo grins and Vicky sticks out her tongue as we roar away.

At Sheffield Crown Court, I go through security and find Jay sitting next to his social worker. I throw my arms around his neck.

'You've grown,' I say, and check the spots on his chin. 'Tell me you're not glue-sniffing.'

'Shut up, Lib,' he says.

'I mean it,' I say. 'I will not be responsible for my actions if you're on the glue.'

Jay laughs and turns to Connor. 'God help you if you're the boy-friend, mate.'

'He's not,' I say. 'He just gave me a lift.'

'Well, at least I know my place,' says Connor.

They're both laughing when I spy Miss Chapman with a barrister in his wig and gown. I race over. 'You need to prepare yourself, Lib,' she says.

'You'll tell the judge everything that's gone on?'

'Of course.' Her face is so serious. 'But we've been here too many times now.'

When they go into court I can't be there. No one can because of Jay's age. Not even his sister. I suddenly feel like every bit of energy has been sucked out of me and tears spring into my eyes. Connor puts his arm around my shoulders and I soon nod off.

'I'm sorry.' I wake up, with Connor whispering gently into my ear, as Miss Chapman comes out of court alone. 'I really am sorry, Lib.'

Present day

Frankie snorted a nice fat line and handed Ozzie's credit card back to him.

'Good gear that,' said the gorilla.

Frankie took a dab with his finger and rubbed it into his gums. The coke was average at best. He opened the toilet door and went back into the dealer's kitchen, handed him a couple of twenties from the wedge Mel had provided him with that morning and headed to the door.

His throat felt numb when he tried to swallow the chemical taste and his ears were ringing.

Outside, Ozzie caught up with him on the walkway. 'Going back to the Trap now, Frankie?'

'Nah.' Frankie stopped to let some young girl pass with a toddler on her hip. The kid didn't have a pair of shoes and the soles of his socks were thick with muck. 'Can't be doing with all that.' He opened and closed his hand, like a beak. 'Don't get me wrong, Ozzie, I love my brother, but he's fucking hard work sometimes.'

The lift was bust so they took the stairs, stepping over a pile of cans that had been used as crack pipes.

'Right shithole this place,' said Ozzie.

Frankie sniffed, getting a fresh hit of coke. He'd been born round here and, although he could hardly remember it, it felt oddly like home. He'd spent loads of time at Daisy's when she used to have a flat a couple of blocks away, smoking rock after rock and shagging like rabbits before the come-down. Then a dig of brown and they'd stare at the damp patches on her ceiling for an hour or two. Good times.

'You think this is bad,' said Frankie. 'You ever been over to Jacko Delaney's patch?'

Ozzie shook his head and Frankie laughed.

'Don't get me wrong, there's good money to be made over there,' he said. 'Drugs, gambling, you name it. I can see why Paul's keen.'

When they came out of the stairwell a gang of lads were having a game of footie on the scrubby patch of grass next to the car park. Shirts versus skins, a half-deflated ball barrelling from one end of the pitch to the other.

'I've no idea why Jay's dragging his feet on the whole thing,' said Frankie. 'Well, I do, but I think he's wrong, you get me?'

Ozzie scratched his head, knocking off a small shaving scab. When he saw the fresh blood on his finger, he licked it off and pressed the wet pad to his skull. 'Don't suppose you fancy something a bit stronger, mate?'

Frankie raised an eyebrow. He was trying to lay off the rocks. Full evangelical conversion hadn't exactly happened to him in rehab, but he had to admit that things had got out of hand before he'd gone in. The football landed at his feet and the lads shouted for him to kick it back. He threw it into the air and headed it in their direction.

'You must know somewhere round here,' said Ozzie. Frankie knew loads of crack houses round the estate. 'Unless you're worried about it getting back to your Jay.'

Frankie nudged the gorilla with his elbow. 'Like I say, I don't give a flying fuck at the minute.' He set off to another block. 'There's a good place over this way. Always bang on it.'

Liberty fingered the tiny bottles of body wash and body lotion by the sink. She removed the lid of the lotion, sniffed and wrinkled her nose. There was more than a hint of air freshener about it.

She let the cold tap run, cupped her hand under it and drank, then looked in the bathroom mirror. Her hair was messy, mascara smudged, and she wore only Sol's shirt. She flicked water at the glass and rubbed it with the side of her fist, obliterating her reflection.

Sol was still in bed, reading the room-service menu. 'Hungry?' he asked.

Liberty picked up her suit trousers from the floor and shook them. 'I have to get back to work.' Sol flopped onto the pillows, hands behind his head. 'What about you? Don't you have criminals to fit up?'

He leaned over and pulled her back to the bed. 'Come on, then. What's so exciting you'd rather spend the afternoon doing that than this?'

'I didn't say I'd rather be doing it.' She smiled. 'But it's got to be done.'

'Like what exactly, Miss Important?'

'I'll have you know that before you rudely interrupted me I was creating two spreadsheets for the anonymous witness statements on the Delaney case.'

He opened a button on the shirt she was wearing. 'Spreadsheets, you say?'

'It's important stuff.' She watched him undo the last two buttons. 'Someone's got to record that officers A, B, C, D and E all say the raid took place at exactly six ten on the morning in question.' With the shirt now open he pulled her on top of him. 'Whereas officer F says six fifteen.'

He pushed off the shirt and kissed her throat. 'Sounds like vital legal work.'

'You won't be laughing when my client walks out of court.'

'I'm not going to let that happen, Lib,' he said.

Liberty pulled up outside Singh & Co. Raj's battered BMW was parked nearby. Obviously, he was back from court. Where the hell would she say she'd been all this time? Something told her that if she admitted she'd been shagging in the Radisson he wouldn't see the funny side.

Sol opened the passenger door to let himself out. 'You know you're not a bad person, right?'

'I think a lot of people might disagree.'

Sol cocked his head to one side, his left eye slightly closed. 'You were just a kid when you left.'

Liberty felt heat leap across her throat. She hadn't expected him to mention that particular sin.

He got out of the car, turned and leaned back inside, arm on top of the side window. 'Give yourself a break.'

Once inside, she called Raj, but the low murmur of his voice spilling from his office told Liberty that he was on a call. Good. She'd butter him up with a cup of tea. Maybe there'd be some food kicking about. She was sure she'd seen a packet of Maryland Cookies in the back of the cupboard.

She scooted past his open door, ignoring his beckoning hand, and filled the kettle. She pulled out two mugs. One chipped with a picture of Harry Kewell on the side, the other a replica of Gromit. His huge black nose was meant to turn red when you added boiling water but she'd never known it to work.

'Lib.' Raj stood in the doorway, his face grey.

She threw a teabag into each cup. 'Sorry I've been gone so long, Raj. I won't expect you to pay me for today.'

'Lib.'

Liberty sloshed water in and foraged in the fridge for milk. 'And I'll get those spreadsheets done tonight, I promise.'

'Lib.' Raj grabbed her arm. His eyes were very serious. 'Something's happened. Something bad.'

The plainness of his words told Liberty that she did not want to hear what he was about to tell her.

'Crystal just called me. She said she couldn't get you on the mobile.' His hand was still on her arm and her heart pulsated in her chest. 'It's your Frankie. He's not in a good way.'

Scottish Tony slid a coffee in front of Sol. 'Someone pish on your parade, pal?'

Sol grunted a reply without looking up. For a man who'd spent several hours having some of the best sex of his life with a woman who'd paid the hotel bill, he felt like shit.

It wasn't even because of Natasha, though it should be.

His first wife, Angie, had always called him a dog with two dicks and no conscience. The last he'd heard, she'd quit the force, married an actuary called Ewan. Apparently, actuaries worked out pension funds and what-have-you. It sounded pretty dull to Sol, but he supposed they earned a shit ton of dough. Funny thing was, Angie never gave a damn about money and status. She liked getting drunk and catching villains.

After one spectacular fight, when she'd put her fist through a cupboard door in the kitchen, she'd sunk to the floor in a puddle of cider and snot. 'Why do you keep cheating, Sol? It's not like we don't have enough sex.'

He didn't have an answer then and he didn't have one now.

He stirred his coffee in the bright wash of the café's overhead lights. When Hassani arrived, she was wearing a hijab. Sometimes she wore one and sometimes she didn't. People commented on that. Sol didn't see the issue. Sometimes you felt like one person and sometimes you felt like another. Right? Today's headscarf was sky blue and framed Hassani's face, emphasizing her eyes. She waited for Scottish Tony to bring her a mug of tea before speaking.

'I hope you've good news with you,' Tony said to her. 'This one's got a face like a slapped arse.'

'What's up, Sol?' she asked, when Tony was back behind his counter.

'Fuck off.'

She blew on her tea. 'We're back to that, are we?'

An envelope of anger opened wide in Sol's stomach and he leaned over the sticky table. 'What did you think was going to happen, Amira? That I was just going to laugh this off and we'd go back to playing nicely?'

Her face was calm in its silk wrapping. She took a sip of tea and placed her mug down gently. She was usually the fiery one, with Sol telling her to get a grip.

'Tell me then, what did Ms Greenwood have to say?' Hassani asked. 'Or were you banging her so hard you couldn't hear?'

Sol slapped the table, making her jump. 'Don't push me, Amira.'

Hassani put her hands in her lap and checked them intensely. Sol removed the spoon from his mug, tapping it against the rim, then dropping it on the table, suddenly wrung out.

'They're building their defence around the anonymous police officers,' he said.

Hassani frowned. 'What do you mean?'

'There's a ton of evidence from undercover officers whose details have been withheld.'

'Isn't that just standard?'

Sol shrugged. 'Doesn't mean the defence have to take it on the chin. If they can find some reason why they need to have that information, then . . .'

He let Hassani work it out for herself.

'And she told you that this is their next move?' she asked.

'She didn't need to spell it out.'

Hassani pulled out her mobile.

'Who are you calling?' Sol asked.

'Bucky.' She scrolled through her contacts. 'We need to make sure that Delaney's defence team can't get any traction.'

The inside of Raj's Five Series smelt of sausage rolls, and the greasy paper bag from Greggs in the footwell told its own story.

'It'll be an overdose,' Liberty said. 'He's using again. We could all see it.'

Raj patted her knee. 'Don't get ahead of yourself, love.'

When they arrived at the hospital he walked with her step for step, hand in the small of her back, the kindness making her cheeks prickle.

The last time Liberty had been in a hospital with Frankie had been when Dad had given Mam a pasting. Frankie had glued himself to Liberty, his shitty nappy stinking out the waiting room.

When they turned the corner to Intensive Care, they almost bumped into Jay. 'Lib.' He threw his arms around her. 'Thank God you're here.'

Liberty put her hands around his face and looked into his eyes. 'What's happened, Jay?'

'It's fucking bad, Lib.'

Behind him, his kids, Liam and Ben, sat on metal seats, swinging their legs and eating packets of Monster Munch.

'Watch your language,' Rebecca hissed.

Jay spun round. 'Are you shitting me?'

Rebecca glared at him, all sensible haircut and linen cropped trousers from Boden, arms around her boys.

'Pack it in, Jay,' Liberty said, and turned to Rebecca. 'Take the lads home. This is no place for them to be.'

'Jay needs—'

'I'm here now,' said Liberty. 'I'll call you as soon as there's anything to report.'

Rebecca nodded and ushered the boys to the door. At the last second, she veered back and kissed Jay's cheek. 'I love you.'

When she was gone, Liberty tilted Jay's chin so he was looking at her. 'You don't deserve her.'

'Tell me something I don't know.'

'Now, please, what's happened to Frankie? Is it an OD?' Liberty asked.

Jay stepped back, took the sunglasses from the top of his head and scratched his scalp. 'An OD? What made you think that?'

'Are you shitting me now?'

Jay gave a sad laugh. 'Fair dos. No, it's not an overdose, Lib.' He put a fingertip to the tear duct of each eye. 'He's been popped.'

'Popped?'

'Shot,' said Jay. 'Someone's shot our Frankie.'

Chapter 9

19 January 1990

'Test me again, Tiny,' I say. She drops her head and bangs it against the table. 'Please.'

'It's so chuffing boring,' she says. 'And I wouldn't mind but you get every question right.' She throws the book over her head. 'Can't I test you on something you're not good at?'

We're at Connor's. His mam's gone back home for a christening. 'It's a big deal,' Connor says. 'Welcoming little Siobhan into the fold.'

Connor and Fat Rob are on the settee, watching a documentary about giraffes. Danny's at work. No one seems to know what he does.

'Physics is my worst subject,' I tell her.

She shakes her head. 'I don't believe you. What's your predicted grade?'

'An A.'

She rubs the side of her head with her knuckle. 'Exactly.'

'I find it hard,' I say. 'All them equations.'

'You've got every single one spot on for the past hour,' she says.

I've got better at physics recently. Paul Lewis still beats me in tests, but his dad's a maths teacher, so he should.

'What are your predicted grades in your other subjects?' asks Fat Rob, over his shoulder.

I go quiet, but they all look at me.

'An A.'

'An A?' Connor stands up. 'In all four?'

*I don't answer. I don't need to because Fat Rob is on his feet as well.
'Are you some sort of genius?'*

*I pick up the physics book from the floor. I'm not a genius. Mr Morris
says I'm 'gifted' in English but I find other subjects a bit harder.*

*'What are you even revising for any road?' Connor asks. 'You took
your O levels last summer, didn't you?'*

'They're not called O levels any more.'

'What happened to O levels?' asks Fat Rob.

'They don't exist,' I say.

'What about CSEs?'

'Gone,' I say.

*'Fuck me,' says Fat Rob. 'I grafted for that CSE in woodwork and it
doesn't exist no more?'*

I laugh, but Connor grabs the physics books from me. 'We're off out.'

'I need to revise,' I say.

*'No.' He picks me up and spins me around. 'You need to have a bit
of fun.'*

*After a night at the Cube we're all back at Connor's. Fat Rob and
Tiny are spark out on the settee. Danny is under the table with some
girl he's picked up. There's some very slurpy kissing going on. Fat Rob
mumbles in his sleep and gives a massive fart, then Danny groans. Connor
and I exchange a glance and race to the stairs. I beat him and run up
them two at a time. When I'm in his room, I dive onto the bed.*

'No chance,' says Connor.

I pat the bed. 'There's plenty of room for both of us.'

*He rolls his eyes and lies next to me on his back. 'You'd better not
snore.'*

*I'm fast asleep when Connor shakes me with a disgruntled huff.
'What's up?' I ask.*

He sounds pissed off. 'Just go back downstairs, Lib.'

*'Did I have a bad dream?' I sit up and try to remember. 'Vicky says
I'm getting them all the time. I think it's cos I'm worried about our Jay
and my exams.'*

111

Connor pushes himself up. 'Why the hell are you worried about some exams that don't even count?'

It's all right for him. He's got his mam and this lovely house to live in. He can take each day as it comes. I can't do that, can I? It's not long until I'll have to leave Orchard Grove and, even though it's not the nicest place in the world, I don't actually have anywhere else I can go.

'I need to do well in my A levels,' I say. 'Then I can go to university.' His eyes go wide. 'And study to become a solicitor.'

'A solicitor?'

I nod. 'They earn good money and I'll be able to get my own house and have the kids come and visit whenever they like.' He exhales loudly and rubs the top of his head. 'Don't tell anyone else.'

'Why not?'

'I don't know.'

Connor frowns but his voice softens. 'It's not your bad dreams, Lib. I just want you to go back downstairs.'

'What have I done?'

He flicks his head with his finger. 'Look, Lib, you're a top girl. You're one of my best mates and I get that's what you want: for us to be mates.' I nod. I've never had proper friends, like Connor and Rob and Tiny. Even Danny. He might not say much but I know he cares about me. It's different with Vicky and Imbo. 'And I'm happy with that. Honestly, I am. But when we're like this.' He gestures to us sitting side by side. 'I'm less happy.'

'Why?'

He covers his face with his hands. 'Because friends don't have thoughts about the two hundred and sixty-three bad things that I want to do to you right now. Is that clear enough?' He twists so he's facing me. 'Will you do me a favour and bugger off now, Lib?'

I stare at him. He's talking about sex. I mean, I've kept the lads at Orchard Grove at bay but I'm not clueless. I've seen Imbo's copies of Knave.

'I'm sorry.'

'Don't apologize,' he says. 'That just makes me feel worse. It's fine that you don't fancy me. Just not in the same bed, okay?'

I'm still staring at him. 'I do fancy you, actually.'

He's staring back at me now. 'What?'

'And I think about doing things. With you,' I say. 'Though not two hundred and sixty-three things. What even is that? Different positions?'

'It doesn't matter, Lib.'

'Well, it does,' I say. 'Because that sounds time-consuming and I've got to revise.'

Connor laughs. A proper belly laugh. 'You are unbelievable. And that's why you need to go back downstairs because . . .'

I shut him up by kissing him. I didn't intend to. But I need to make him stop talking and I like him so much. He kisses me back and we stay like that a long time.

At last, he pulls away, licks his lips and smiles at me. 'Just to be clear. I'm not going to shag you if that's what you're after.'

Present day

Amira knocked on the door to Bucky's office and slid it open. The prosecutor was in her chair on her phone, bare feet on the desk, each toenail painted blood red. She waved at Amira and Sol, wafting her hand at two empty chairs and wrapped up her call.

'I hope this is urgent,' she said. 'I've sixteen cases to review, then there's a bottle of Pinot Grigio with my name on it.'

'You'll want to hear this,' said Amira.

Bucky swept her hair behind her ears. 'Go on.'

'Delaney's lawyers are planning an application for the details of the anonymous witnesses.' Amira looked at Sol for confirmation, but his eyes remained guarded. 'If they're successful and those details can't be given out, you'll have to withdraw their statements.'

Bucky lifted her feet from the desk and slid them back into a pair of leopard-print sling-backs. Amira had never owned a pair of shoes with heels higher than a centimetre and often wondered how women like Bucky could walk in them, let alone do their jobs.

'And you know this, how?' Bucky asked.

Amira heard Sol exhale. 'Can't really talk about that, Bucky, but trust me, it's true.'

Bucky got up, moved to her office door and kicked it shut with the pointed toe of her shoe. Then she went back to her chair, but didn't sit in it. Instead she stood behind it, hands gripping the top. The sound of workmen in the street outside bled through the open window: drills on hard concrete. 'Sol?' she asked.

'It's just a heads-up, Bucky,' he replied.

Bucky drummed her chair with her fingers. 'I personally asked Raj Singh to take the Delaney case because I trust him.'

'Singh isn't the problem,' said Amira.

Bucky didn't answer her, continuing to look at Sol. 'I hope you know what you're doing, mate.'

'We're just letting information flow up the stream, Bucky,' he replied. 'What you do with it is your call.'

Amira wanted to scream and knock their heads together. What she'd always taken for measured thoughtfulness was now looking like fear of rocking the boat. They both knew full well that this was the best chance they'd ever had to put Delaney away. 'If we lose this case, it won't look good for any of us,' she said.

Bucky smiled at Sol, which made something in Amira crackle. Then her mobile rang. Then Sol's rang too.

'Looks like the party's started,' said Bucky, with a laugh. 'And then there's me. NFI.'

Amira checked her phone. It was the nick. Sol had already answered, speaking low and quick. He hung up.

'There's been a shooting at the Crosshills.'

★ ★ ★

People thought that when someone got shot, they just fell on the ground unconscious. But that only really happened when someone was shot in the head or the heart. Take a bullet anywhere else and the victim would usually arrive at hospital in agony. Even if the wound was fatal, and a lot were, it could still take hours to die.

This was what the surgeon seemed to be telling Liberty. Not in so many words, of course, but she'd long ago learned to read between the lines.

'We've stopped what internal bleeding we can,' he said. 'And we've removed your brother's spleen.'

'Is he awake?' she asked.

'God, no,' the surgeon replied. 'We've given him a massive dose of morphine.'

Liberty squeezed her eyes shut. 'He's a drug addict. He's not meant to . . .'

The surgeon put his hand on hers. There was a mark around his wrist, presumably from latex gloves removed as he left theatre. 'That's the least of our concerns right now.'

Liberty nodded. Above them a strip light made a tiny popping sound. 'Is he going to die?'

'I hope not.' The surgeon smiled. 'He's as stable as we can get him at this moment. We might need to perform more surgery later, if that's possible.'

His pager bleeped and he excused himself, leaving Liberty to make her way back down the corridor to the others. Jay and Mel were huddled in metal chairs. Harry leaned against the wall, knee up, sole of his trainer flat against the plaster. He looked up when he heard Liberty's footsteps. 'How is he?'

'Stable,' she said.

Jay jumped to his feet. 'He's going to be all right?'

'They hope so.'

'What the fuck does that mean?'

Mel clamped a hand around his upper arm. 'It means we wait, Jay.'

'Crystal's popped out to the car,' said Harry. 'I'll get her.'

'I'll go,' said Liberty. 'I need a breath of fresh air.'

Jay and Mel slumped back in their seats and Harry took his place against the wall, blond hair falling in his face. Liberty almost ran for the exit.

Outside, it was dark. A breeze whooshed around, making a crisps packet dance. A man ran past her, face contorted with worry, throwing himself into the hospital as if it were a life-raft.

In the car park, a couple bickered next to the ticket machine, riffling through their pockets for the right change. Didn't it occur to the hospital that those arriving might not have six pounds fifty on them?

Liberty scanned the rows of cars for her sister's black Audi and spotted it in the far corner, internal light on, driver's door open. Crystal was sitting at the wheel, eyes closed, taking deep breaths. A foot away there was a pool of fresh vomit.

'Crystal?' Her sister's eyes snapped open and she jumped from the car. 'It's okay.' Liberty threw up her hands. 'I just came to check you were all right.'

'He's not dead?'

Liberty shook her head and shivered even though it wasn't cold. 'Shall we go inside and track down a vending machine? I expect everyone could do with a hot drink.' Liberty nodded at the puddle of congealed stomach contents. 'You especially.'

'I don't do hot drinks.'

'Fine. A cold drink.' Liberty slammed the car door. 'Just as long as it's got lots of sugar.'

'Do you remember how much pop our Frankie used to drink?'

Liberty snorted. He'd been permanently attached to a bottle of purple squash. 'It's a wonder he's got a tooth left in his head. I was constantly telling Mam about it.'

'You were a bloody know-it-all even then,' said Crystal.

Sol watched the monitor. The heart rate was steady, hovering at around sixty. Frankie Greenwood had been lucky. The bullet had missed his chest, hitting the top of his stomach and passing through the lower part of his spleen. It had made a mess of him, but there was at least a chance he would survive.

The door opened and Jay Greenwood caught sight of Sol. 'What are you doing here?' He looked a lot like Liberty. Same thick dark hair and molten brown eyes.

'I need to ask a few questions,' said Sol.

'Get out.'

Sol glanced at Frankie on the hospital bed, bloodless and life-less. 'You surely want to get to the bottom of this?'

Jay stepped to one side, leaving enough space for Sol to leave. Old habits obviously died hard. Sol shrugged and moved from the room into the corridor where he received dead-eyed stares from Mel and Harry. He gave them both a two-finger salute and headed to the lift.

When it opened, he put his hand against the right-hand door to stop it closing and called back up the corridor. 'If any of you are interested in finding out who shot Frankie, feel free to get in touch.'

'Oh, don't you worry,' said Mel. 'We'll find out who did this.'

Liberty and Crystal turned the corner, a drink in each hand, and almost bumped into Sol.

'What do *you* want?' Crystal asked.

'There's been a shooting and I'm a copper,' Sol replied. 'It's traditional for me to turn up.'

'Do you know who did it?' Liberty asked.

Crystal sighed. 'Of course he doesn't.' She skirted around Sol towards the lifts. When Liberty didn't follow she gave an impatient groan. 'There's nothing he can tell us, Lib.'

When Liberty still didn't move, she jabbed the lift button with her elbow and stomped inside as it arrived. When the doors closed on her sister, Liberty handed Sol one of the plastic cups of coffee she was carrying. 'You might as well have this.'

He took a sip and winced when the liquid burned his lips. 'Are you okay?'

'Not really,' she replied.

'What was Frankie doing at the Crosshills?'

'He's using again.'

In front of them, the lift doors reopened and Mel stepped out. She didn't approach but watched.

'You're being summoned,' said Sol.

Liberty could feel Mel's eyes on her. She was so very tired. She wished Sol would just take her hand and tell her what to do next. But, of course, he didn't. She spun on her heel and walked towards Mel.

'Hey, Lib.' The clarity of Sol's voice surprised her. 'Thanks for the coffee.'

She stepped into the lift and let the doors shut between them. Mel stared at her. As they rose three floors, Liberty tried her best to ignore her. 'What?' she asked at last.

'He called you Lib?'

'It's my name.'

There was blood over the carpet, the sofa, the walls. The room would have been a hell-hole beforehand, knee-deep in syringes and crack pipes, but splattered in blood it was like a scene from a Saw movie.

Amira trod carefully, as much for her own safety as to preserve evidence. SOCO had already arrived and were bagging up the overflowing ashtrays and empty plastic supermarket cider bottles. A woman in full forensic suit, the hood pulled tightly around her face, took photographs. 'Did he die?' she asked Amira.

'Not yet.'

Amira ducked out of the flat into the fresh air on the walkway. By now, uniform had released the people they'd found in the flat, but a few were hanging around in the small garden below. Amira recognized a couple and made her way down.

A teenage girl called Tia Rainsford sat on a patch of grass, expertly rolling a fag. She was a runner for one of the dealers on this part of the estate. Amira had nicked her a few times, but had only ever been able to get a conviction for possession. And she'd never had anything useful from her.

'Tia,' she said.

The girl nodded and rubbed a pinch of tobacco into a cigarette paper laid on her open palm. 'It's not weed before you start,' she said. She moved her thumbs to shape the fag, then ran the pink end of her tongue against the glue on the paper.

Francine, a transgender prostitute, scuttled over. 'Give us one of them, Tia babes.'

Tia scowled but held it up. Francine took it gratefully and tried to light it but her hands were shaking too much. Tia waggled her own hand – she would do it – and Francine bent, holding her wig away from the flame.

'I've never seen anything like it,' Francine said, taking a puff. 'And I had a front-row seat when Debbie Dallas chucked herself off the roof of Aldi.'

Tia began building another smoke. She had her hair in a

ponytail but the fringe was pushed back into a little quiff held in a hump by spray.

'Did you see who did it?' Amira asked.

Francine shook her head, the red glow of her fag moving from side to side. 'I'll be honest, I was nodding until I heard the bang. I thought a bomb had gone off or something.'

'A bomb?' Tia laughed and took a long drag, picking a stray string of tobacco from her lip with the nail of her ring finger. 'On the Crosshills?'

Francine blew a column of smoke into the night sky above her and held up her hands, as if she had no clue what to say. 'I didn't even know it was Frankie until one of the coppers told me.'

Amira crouched next to Tia. 'What about you? Anything to tell me?'

Tia laughed again and rummaged in the pocket of her tracksuit bottoms for her phone, checked it and pocketed it again.

'Did you know Frankie Greenwood?' Amira asked. Tia leaned back as if it were the stupidest question she'd ever heard. 'Okay, everyone round here knows him. But what do you know about him?'

Francine flicked away her dog-end and said. 'On that note, I'm off.'

Amira let her go. She was sure Francine was telling the truth about not seeing anything and she knew where to find her if need be.

'Come on.' Amira nudged Tia's knee. 'I know you're not afraid to tell it like it is.'

Tia held the fag between thumb and forefinger and blew on the burning end. 'I know he's a stupid wanker.'

'Because?'

'Because he'd got off the stones, hadn't he?'

Amira was shocked at the certainty in Tia's voice. Most people who went into rehab were back using within a week.

'You don't believe me, ask Daisy the Dog,' said Tia. 'Frankie got clean. Well, he was still using a bit of powder, but not crack, you get me? Then he rocks up this afternoon and he's sucking that pipe like it's cock. Him and some bald twat.' She sniffed and wiped her nose with her wrist. 'I mean, it's up to him, but it's fucking stupid when you've gone to all the trouble of doing your rattle.'

'Did you see him get shot?'

Tia finished her fag and ground it out in the grass. 'Nah.'

'Really?'

The girl got up, brushed the dust from her arse. 'Really. I was outside talking to some new kid.'

'You heard it, though?'

Tia nodded.

Amira stood and rubbed her knees. 'When did you realize Frankie had been shot?'

'When I saw him on the floor with a great big fucking hole here.' Tia placed her hands under her ribcage. 'Bit of a giveaway that one.'

Chapter 10

20 January 1990
At the crack of dawn, Connor drops me off around the corner from Orchard
Grove. I jump off the back of the bike and hand him the helmet. He pushes
my hair behind my ear, winks at me and roars away.

I sneak around to the back of the building, where my room looks out,
and pick up a stone. I throw it at the window but Vicky doesn't come. I
throw another and it glances off the glass with a loud ping. There's no
way she can't have heard that but she still doesn't come.

I swear under my breath. I cover for Vicky all the time but the one
day I ask her to help me out . . . All she had to do was stay in the bed-
room and, if anyone came to do a roll call, shout through the door that I
was asleep. Most of the staff never actually come in. In the first few weeks
when they're all keen, they might, which is probably why Hemma caught
us on New Year's Eve, but once she'd come across Imbo having a wank
and Vicky shredding the inside of her thigh with a pencil sharpener, she
stopped bothering.

I throw a stone at Imbo's window. He won't be best pleased to be
woken up at this time, but I need someone to let me in.

He opens his window, hot breath steaming in the cold.

'Let us in,' I hiss.

He gives a tight nod and slams his window shut. Christ, could he
make more noise if he tried? I steel myself for the abuse I'm about to get

for waking him up at this time, but when he unlocks the door, he's not pissed off with me and he's fully dressed.

'Thank God, you're here, Lib.'

'What's up?'

He drags me to the stairs. 'It's Vic. She's gone.'

'Gone where?'

He shrugs. 'She had a right barney with Hemma last night. Got gated again. I could hear her trashing the room.'

'She better not have touched my revision notes,' I say. She's normally pretty good and leaves my stuff alone, but there are times when she loses the plot and doesn't know what she's doing. That's how my radio ended up in bits on the pavement. She nicked me another, though.

'I sneaked in when it went quiet,' he says. I nod that he was wise to wait. Nothing good ever came of trying to talk to Vicky when she's in one. 'And I found this.' He flings open our bedroom door and I gulp. It's not trashed. Nothing on my side's been touched and nothing on her side is there any more. 'She's taken everything, Lib.'

I check her drawer. Empty. The wardrobe. Her half is empty. I bend and look under the bed. Just a couple of used-up cans of lighter fuel.

'That's all she's left,' says Imbo, pointing to my bed where her big hoodie that says, 'Feed Your Head' has been laid neatly. Imbo flaps his arms around. 'Do you know where she might have gone? She mentioned some bloke up the Crosshills.'

'Sean,' I say. 'I know where he lives.'

When we get up to the estate I use a short cut to Sean's. I used to live up here with Mam and Dad. A shabby flat that always smelt of damp and fags. A piece of plaster missing on the kitchen wall where Dad bounced Mam's head off it. Scratches on the floorboards in my bedroom from me pulling a dressing-table across the door to stop Dad getting in when he was off on one.

I don't say any of this to Imbo. His mum and dad are both alkies so I don't suppose his house was very nice either.

It's only as Imbo is knocking on Sean's door that I realize it's still early. Not even eight o'clock. I'm pretty sure that Sean's a junkie so maybe he won't have been to bed yet. He answers the door in jogging bottoms and a stained dressing-gown.

'What?'

'Is Vicky here?' I ask.

Sean rubs his chin. He's got needle marks on the front of his hands. 'Vicky who?'

'Vicky Tandy,' I say. 'From Orchard Grove.' When he still looks clueless I add, 'Long blonde hair and massive knockers, usually shouting her head off.'

'Oh, her,' says Sean. 'No, she's not here, why would she be?'

'Thought you were going out with her,' I say.

'Not really. She's not been round here in a couple of weeks.' He scratches his bare chest with dirty nails. 'But if you do see her, tell her she owes me a tenner.'

He shuts the door in our faces and Imbo starts shaking. It's freezing and he's only wearing a denim jacket, but I don't think it's that. I put my hand on his arm.

'Have you got any ciggies, Lib?' he asks.

'No.'

'Shit.'

We trudge away from the estate. 'We'll find her,' I say. 'I mean, how far can she have gone?'

'Maybe she went to London,' says Imbo.

'London?'

'To find her real dad,' he says.

'Is that where he lives?'

'Supposedly. Working as a bouncer, or so Vic's mam says. But that bitch will make her mouth say owt.'

I nod. Vicky's mam is a liar. She even gave Vicky's stepdad a false alibi when he was arrested for what he did to Vicky.

'Let's go back,' I say. 'Maybe she mentioned something to one of the other kids.'

Imbo shakes his head. 'If she hasn't told you or me where she's off, then she hasn't told anybody.'

Present day

Liberty's dreams came vivid and violent. Her mother's face as she fell from a balcony, eyes wide, arms and legs windmilling. The hard brick of a wall as Liberty's head smashed against it. The smell of her father's breath as he screamed at Crystal.

She started at a hand on her shoulder and found a nurse standing over her. 'Okay, love?'

Liberty wiped the dribble from her chin and rolled her shoulders. She'd fallen asleep in the chair next to Frankie's bed. 'Is there any change?' she asked.

'No.'

Liberty nodded. That was good, wasn't it? Her baby brother hadn't got any worse.

'Why don't you go and splash your face in the bathroom?' the nurse suggested.

Liberty shot a glance at Frankie.

'He's not going anywhere.'

Liberty smiled. She did need to stretch her legs and call Jay and Crystal, who had finally agreed to leave in the early hours. There was no point in them all staying and the doctors had said only one visitor at a time in Frankie's room.

The nurse checked the tubes that snaked from Frankie's nose, throat and arms and scribbled on his chart.

'Thank you,' said Liberty, and the nurse gave a little puff of air that said she was just doing her job.

Outside the hospital entrance, Liberty checked her mobile. The sun was up, weak but trying its best, and the surrounding streets were coming alive. A white van stopped and a lad jumped in, chugging on a bottle of Lucozade, shouting at the driver about a football match. Across the road a woman, still in her pyjamas and slippers, had a dog on a lead, urging him to do his business.

It seemed impossible that life was carrying on as normal while, three floors up, Liberty's brother was inches from death, skin, bone and internal organs in ruins.

Among her missed calls were three from Sol. Had he contacted her as a friend or as a copper? Was there a distinction when it came to him?

'Liberty?'

She looked up from her mobile and found a white Range Rover pulled over a few feet away, the engine idling. The passenger window was open and a face leered out at her. 'It's me.' The man tried a smile. 'Paul Hill.'

Liberty recognized him now. Cropped grey hair, green V-necked sweater over a white shirt. He might have been handsome once upon a time, but a life organizing deals in the dank back rooms of strip clubs had left him jowly and baggy-eyed.

The driver, a man mountain in a black leather jacket, opened the back passenger door.

'Step in out of the cold, Liberty,' said Hill.

Liberty frowned. She had no desire to get into a car with that man. 'I'm afraid I need to make some calls, Mr Hill.'

'Paul.' He moved his hand behind him to the open door. 'Please.'

Reluctantly, Liberty stepped up into the back seat of the car, the brown upholstery squeaking under her trousers. The man mountain closed the door.

'I know this is a difficult time, Liberty.' Hill leaned across the middle console and turned his body towards her. 'I hear he's had a reasonable night.' Liberty didn't comment. Hill clearly had ways to gather information and wanted her to know that. 'But we need to talk business.'

'Excuse me?'

The man mountain remained outside the car, but his silhouette filled the entire side window.

'I made a proposition to your brother and sister,' said Hill.

'I don't know anything about that,' said Liberty.

'It was a fair offer made in good faith,' Hill continued. 'If they had any questions they should have come to me in person.'

'If you want to speak to them about it you should go to them in person, Mr Hill.'

He cocked his head to one side and ran a finger over the walnut casement of the gears. 'Things need to be kept as calm as possible in the circumstances, wouldn't you say?'

Liberty shrugged. Whatever it was he wanted Jay and Crystal to know, he wanted her to pass it along.

'Remind Jay what I said at his party.' Hill smiled. 'Nature abhors a vacuum.' He reached out of his window and tapped the outside of his door, signalling for the man mountain to let Liberty out.

'I'll snap his head off his fucking shoulders.' Jay kicked a chair across the Black Cherry. 'And I'll make his slag of a wife watch me do it.'

Liberty had arranged to meet Crystal, Jay and Mel to tell them about her encounter with Hill. She'd decided that the club was a better place to fill them in than the hospital and she'd been right.

Mel scooped up the chair. 'Calm it down, Jay.'

'Calm down? Calm the fuck down?' Jay was raging now. 'He all but admitted he had Frankie shot.'

Liberty shook her head. 'No, he didn't say that. He just said that if you needed to ask any questions about the Delaney takeover you should have gone to him directly.'

'What fucking questions?'

Mel grabbed Jay's shoulders and pushed him down onto a stool at the bar. Then she stood behind him, hands still in place so he didn't spring back up.

'We need to find out what Frankie was doing up the Crosshills,' said Crystal.

'I think we can guess,' said Mel. 'He's on it again. We all know that.'

'So, it's just a coincidence that, of all the people sitting in that crack house, the only person who gets hurt is Frankie?' Jay asked.

Mel massaged his neck. 'Who knows what goes on in them places, Jay? It's like the frigging Wild West.'

Jay pushed her off. 'And I suppose it's also just a coincidence that the next morning Dog-breath Hill turns up talking all kinds of crap to Lib?'

Liberty raked her scalp. She needed a shower, a change of clothes and something hot to eat. She couldn't believe Paul Hill would be so stupid as to order a hit on their brother, but Jay was right about his strange dawn arrival at the hospital. Why the hell would he do that? 'We should listen to Crystal,' she said. 'We need to find out what Frankie was doing there.'

'We *know* what he was doing there,' said Mel.

Liberty put up her hand. 'You're probably spot-on, Mel, but we need to know for sure. If Frankie was just in the wrong place at the wrong time, then Hill is taking advantage but it doesn't make him involved in the shooting.'

'I'll still snap his head off,' said Jay.

Liberty pointed at him. 'You'll do no such thing. You'll go to the hospital and sit with your brother.' She glared at him until he nodded his agreement. 'I'll see what I can uncover about what went on up the Crosshills.'

'From your mate DI Connolly, I expect?' said Mel.

Crystal raised an eyebrow. 'Will he tell you anything?'

'Yeah,' said Liberty. 'He will.'

Amira moved from the printer to the clear board and tacked a picture of Jackson Delaney at the top, printing his name alongside. Underneath, she secured pictures of Chapman and Raj Singh. Bucky was pretty certain that the latter was straight, but Amira wasn't about to write him out of the story completely. Not yet, anyway.

Next up, she printed off the rest of the Greenwood clan. Crystal looked cool and harsh getting out of a car, unaware she was being photographed. On the other hand, Jay's eyes danced even though he was holding a number for his mug shot. Frankie, arrested a couple of years ago for beating one of the girls working in the Cherry, was sweating, obviously desperate for some drugs.

Underneath Frankie's picture, Amira scribbled the time and place he had been shot and the words 'arrived with bald friend'. Then she went to the list of names of the people who'd been at the crack house at the time of the shooting and ran the males on her laptop. Most had previous convictions and mug shots. Three were bald.

'What are you doing?'

Amira looked up to find Sol scowling at her across the office. Since it was obvious what she was doing, Amira didn't bother to answer but attached pictures of the bald men to the clear board.

'I thought you were trying to prove that Liberty's bent,' said Sol.

Amira noted that he had used her first name. Not Chapman. Not Greenwood. Liberty. She capped the pen and rapped the top of Frankie's head with it. 'This is connected.'

Sol's eyes moved from picture to picture and he rubbed his temple, as if he might have a headache. She took a step towards him and caught the smell of cigarettes. 'I thought you'd quit,' she said.

'Fuck off,' he said, but the fury had drained out of him.

Maybe they could get back to how things used to be. Was that a stupid thing even to think? Amira loved Sol. No doubt that was why she'd been so floored by his actions, but she could forgive him. Why not, if he did the right thing now?

His mobile bleeped but he ignored it.

'Is that her?' Amira asked. Sol let out a hard breath. 'If it is, you should call her back.'

The mobile bleeped a second time but Sol gave nothing away. It was as if his face had been injected with anaesthetic.

'All we're doing here is trying to find the truth,' said Amira.

Sol looked up at the sky. The recent sunshine had disappeared and troubled clouds scudded past. But even in the breeze he could feel the sweat trickling down his neck.

He felt like he had the worst hangover, but last night he hadn't touched a drop. After the hospital, he'd gone home and lain next to Natasha, listening to the rise and fall of her breath, tasting the smell of her face cream. Every night she slathered herself in lotions and oils. Rosehip for this, jojoba for that. And she did have the smoothest skin. But the smell, Christ, it was like going to bed with the perfume counter in Boots.

He dug in his pockets, retrieved a packet of paracetamol and threw two into his mouth, dry-swallowing them whole. He doubted they'd help.

Liberty's Porsche pulled into the hospital car park and she got out. The sight of her increased the tension in Sol's head.

'Thanks for seeing me,' she said.

'Why wouldn't I?'

A look of exasperation flitted across her face. 'Let's skip the bull-shit, eh?'

He had to smile at that, and the feeling that someone was cleaning the inside of his skull with sandpaper eased a touch. 'What can I do for you?' he asked.

'Can you tell me anything about what happened to Frankie?'

'Let's get in the car,' said Sol.

She slid back into her Porsche and he got in on the passenger side. The inside smelt of clean leather. There was no debris in the footwell, just her handbag.

'Are the OCU involved because you think Frankie was in-volved in organized crime or because you suspect the shooter was?' Liberty asked.

'No one seems to know who the shooter was,' said Sol, and wiped under his fringe, his fingers coming away wet.

'Are you okay?' she asked.

How to answer that one? No, he wasn't okay. He was a liar and a cheat. How could anyone be okay with that? And yet he'd lied and cheated so many times before without feeling like his body was giving up on him.

'The trouble with crack houses is that everyone's either off their tits or unconscious,' he said. 'They don't notice what's happening under their noses unless they can smoke it.'

'What about the dealers and the runners?'

'Not exactly forthcoming with information,' he said. 'You know how it goes.' He could leave it there. She didn't look like she'd press him, but he reached into his jacket pocket and pulled out three photographs. 'We think Frankie might have arrived with one of these men.'

He showed them to her in turn. She tapped the third one.

'Nathan Osborne,' said Sol. 'He works for a face called Paul Hill.'

'I know. I had a visit from the pair of them this morning.'

'What did they want?' Sol asked.

She leaned over and kissed him gently on the corner of his mouth.

Chapter 11

10 February 1990
Two weeks later and I've finished my exams.

It's a weird feeling. You still have this idea in your brain that you ought to be revising, but you don't need to. Mam used to say that having kids was the same. That you always felt like you should be doing something for them. To be honest, I don't remember her doing that much for us. She wasn't one for cleaning up or making our tea.

There's still no sign of Vicky, and I've been worrying about her. Maybe that's why Carl has sorted things out for me to see Crystal and Frankie. I don't care what his reason is. I'm beyond excited.

When I pass Imbo's door, I open it to tell him the good news, but he's already off his head. It doesn't matter, I know some people who will be chuffed for me.

At the Galaxy, Tiny is behind the counter cleaning up. She's got a black bin bag and is lobbing in apple cores and fag ends. Connor's leaning against the wall, reading the sleeve of a new EP by D-Mob.

'Guess what?' I say.

Connor puts down the record and takes my face in his hands. I love it when he does that. 'What?'

'I'm going to see Frankie and Crystal tomorrow.'

'About bloody time.' Tiny squeezes Jif over the counter top. 'It's criminal how they keep you lot apart.'

'Shall I take you?' asks Connor.

'You don't need to,' I say. 'They've given me a travel voucher and everything.'

Tiny scrubs with a cloth. There are so many rings, I don't think she'll get them off. 'Where have you got to get to?'

'A contact centre in Chapel Allerton,' I say.

'Christ.' Connor wraps an arm around my waist. 'You'll have to catch at least three buses. On Sunday service it'll take you all day. I'm giving you a lift.'

I kiss his cheek and then his neck.

'Hold up, Connor,' says Tiny. 'You might actually get a shag at this rate.'

The door opens and Fat Rob comes in, arms full of sandwiches, crisps and cans of pop. 'Hello, gorgeous.' He nods at me. 'If I'd known you were coming, I'd have bought double.' I eye the food. 'Don't even think about touching my Skips.'

Tiny unwraps a tuna roll, tears it in half and gives me the bigger piece.

'Fishy breath,' says Connor. 'That's something I like in a girl.' I stick out my tongue and shove the sandwich into my mouth. 'See the lengths she'll go to, to repel me?'

I laugh but he knows I don't want to repel him. I'd spend all day snogging his face off if I could.

'Have you heard from your mate?' asks Fat Rob, mouth full of egg mayonnaise.

'There's a rumour she might be in London,' I say.

'How would she survive down there on her own?' Tiny opens a bag of cheese and onion crisps. 'She can't sign on or get a job.'

'She'll manage,' I say.

'She'll need to nick a lorry load of batteries to get enough to live on,' says Connor.

'Oh, she won't just be thieving,' I say. They all look blank. Honestly, I'm the youngest, but you'd never know it. 'She'll charge men to do the two hundred and sixty-three bad things they like to do to girls.'

Fat Rob stops mid-bite. 'She's only fifteen.'

'I don't think the punters care,' I say.

The next day I meet Connor around the corner and he's got a carrier stuffed with something. He holds it out to me. 'Put this on.'

I open the bag and find a leather biker's jacket. Real leather.

'It's not safe riding about on a bike without one,' he says.

'I can't afford it.'

Connor sighs. 'I can.' He slides it over my back. 'And if you ever need anything else, just tell me. I can't bear the thought of you having to do what Vicky does. It's disgusting.'

'Don't judge her,' I say. 'There's not always much choice.'

He does my zip up for me. 'I'm not judging her. She's just a kid. But I will judge the social workers and her parents.'

The contact centre is like all the rest: cold, dark, full of stressed-out kids. Crystal and Frankie sit on plastic chairs, swinging their legs in time. When they see us, they fly over and throw themselves at me. I kiss their heads one after the other a million times.

Crystal points at Connor, cheek on my chest. 'Is this your social worker?'

'Bloody hell,' he says. 'Don't tell me I look like a social worker.'

'Don't swear,' I hiss.

'Sorry,' he whispers back. 'Not used to kids.'

'It's not them I'm worried about,' I tell him, and nod at the supervisors wandering around, making their endless notes. Sometimes I feel like I'm in a documentary.

We sit at a table of Lego, Crystal still glued to me. Connor makes a plane for Frankie.

'Are you Lib's boyfriend, then?' Crystal asks Connor.

He looks at me. 'Good question that one.'

'Yes.' I roll my eyes. 'Connor's my boyfriend.'

He holds up his palm and Frankie gives him a high-five.

'Can I sit on Lib's knee for a bit?' Frankie asks, but Crystal won't *budge. She's sucking her fingers, her head on my shoulder. I expect the social workers think she's too old for all this now she's ten and they'll be writing up their report as soon as they get back to the office.*

'I'll tell you what I've heard, Crystal,' says Connor. 'You're really good at painting.'

'I'm all right,' she says.

'All right? Lib says you're amazing. She says she'd love you to paint a picture for her, so she can put it on her wall for everybody to see.' Connor stands and holds out his hand. 'How about you do one for her now?'

Crystal thinks for a second, but then she slides off my knee and takes his hand.

'Make her roll up them sleeves, Connor,' I say. 'I'm not having them blaming me if her clothes get ruined.'

Connor frowns, but I know how it works.

Frankie straddles me, playing with my hair like he did when he was a baby. He shows me a wobbly tooth.

'Put it under your pillow and the Tooth Fairy will come,' I say.

'Is that even true?'

I cross my heart with my finger and watch Connor at the painting table, helping Crystal to choose the right colours and a brush. He crouches down and rolls up her sleeves as far as he can, so they're in bunches under her armpits. Then he stops and asks her something.

'Lib,' he calls over to me. 'Come here a minute.'

I put Frankie on my hip and walk over. Connor runs his thumb along the inside of Crystal's left arm. Her skin is smooth and white, but there are four round red marks, where someone has obviously grabbed her.

'I think we need to show somebody this,' Connor says.

Present day

Liberty met Jay outside Frankie's room, holding a basket of fruit, a pink ribbon wound around the wicker handle. 'Where did you buy that?' she asked.

'Not me.' Jay picked up an apple and rubbed the dark red skin against his shirt until it gleamed. 'The card says Raj Singh.'

'His wife will have sent it.'

'She knows our Frankie's been shot, right?' said Jay.

Liberty took the apple from him and bit into it, the juice running down her chin. 'She's just trying to be nice.'

'I doubt he'd eat any of this at the best of times.' Jay threw a grape into the air and caught it in his mouth. 'Not with his teeth.'

Liberty laughed. 'Is there any change?'

'Nope. Any news on the other thing?'

Liberty chewed the flesh of the apple. It had a bitter taste, which was welcome. When she was trying to get Dax to eat more healthily she sometimes cut up an apple for him, peeling it even. It was the only way to get a vitamin past his lips. He'd have spat this one out and opened a packet of crisps.

'Frankie was with someone yesterday.'

'Who?' asked Jay.

She swallowed, more for something to do than anything else. Jay was about to kick off. 'Nathan Osborne.' She swallowed again, even though her mouth was empty. 'He works for Paul Hill.'

Jay looked down at the basket as if he'd only just noticed it, then dropped it onto one of the seats in the corridor. A few grapes fell out and rolled away.

'That doesn't mean Hill's definitely responsible for this.' Liberty jerked her thumb in the direction of Frankie's room. 'He could just be a mate of this Osborne character.'

Jay tapped each stray grape with his foot as if they were cockroaches. Their skins split in turn. 'One way to find out,' he said.

Sol jerked his car into the nick's car park. He had all the windows open but his shirt still felt hot and scratchy. The pills he'd taken earlier were having no effect on his headache, which throbbed red and sickly in his temples.

He'd done undercover work many times in the past. This job should be no different. If Liberty had nothing to hide, there'd be no harm done, would there?

A fat drop of rain splatted the windscreen. Then another. The side of Sol's face was getting wet but he didn't put up the window.

If Hassani was right and Liberty was involved in anything criminal, he needn't feel anything but justified in what he was doing. Yes, she'd had a rough childhood, but which offenders hadn't? Sol would take a bet that the young Jackson Delaney had been half starved and beaten black and blue by a long line of stepfathers. It didn't mean people could do as they pleased, did it? It didn't excuse the harm that they in turn did.

Sol let out a hiccupy laugh. All this stuff was easy to say, a lot less easy to put into practice when he could still taste the woman involved.

He opened the car door, leaned out, put a finger down his throat and vomited into the puddles on the tarmac.

There was a second when Liberty could have made a different decision. She'd been sitting with Frankie, stroking his hand, running her finger over the scabs and scars as if she were reading braille, when Jay's text arrived: *Come to the Cherry. Ozzie's gonna answer a few questions.*

She could have just ignored the text. Instead, she calmly picked up her bag and asked Harry to take over waiting with Frankie.

When she pushed the drapes aside and walked through the strip club, blood was bubbling in her brain. She could have spun on her heel and walked out. After all, she'd got previous for doing just that.

A girl was on stage, peeling off an orange bikini top, throwing it behind her as she strutted away from the pole in a pair of white thigh-length boots. Over her left shoulder there was a tattoo of a tiger, its claws gripping the top of one breast.

Mel scuttled over to Liberty. She smelt of booze. 'I'm not convinced this is a good idea,' she said. 'Jay's all fired up.'

Sweat beaded across Mel's forehead, turning her thick foundation to paste. She never looked peachy but this afternoon she betrayed every one of her hard-lived years.

'The whole point was to avoid a war with the Hills,' Mel hissed.

'The whole point of what?'

Mel swore under her breath. 'Keeping things calm,' she said. 'Not overreacting. If we didn't care about the fallout we should have let Jay go steaming over to Paul Hill and start the ructions in person.'

Liberty's nerves jangled as she opened the door to the back office.

At first glance things looked normal. A stack of boxed vibrators teetered in the corner. Jay stood, back against the wall, sipping a bottle of beer. Crystal perched on the end of the desk, one leg swinging, jaw moving around her gum. Nathan Osborne was in a chair, his back to Liberty. It was still possible that the three of them were having a chat.

'I'm not happy about this, Jay,' said Mel.

'And I'm not happy that you're not happy,' Jay replied. 'But shit happens.'

'You should listen to the old bat,' said Osborne.

'Go check on the girls, Mel,' said Crystal.

Mel gave a cluck but stalked out of the room, closing the door behind her.

'Seriously, this is a bad idea,' said Osborne.

Jay nodded and placed his empty bottle on the desk. 'What do you think's going to happen, Ozzie? Are you expecting Paul Hill to charge in here and rescue you like you're a fucking princess?'

The bald man sat up straight. 'There'll be repercussions.'

Without warning, Crystal leaned back, grabbed the beer bottle and smacked it in Osborne's mouth. His lips gave a wet pop and blood sprayed in all directions. Liberty gave a gasp but the noise was drowned by Osborne's shriek.

Crystal grabbed his blood-covered chin and pushed back his head. 'And while you're waiting for the repercussions, dickhead, I'll be smashing your face to a pulp.'

Amira glanced up from her computer. 'You look awful.'

'Thanks,' Sol replied. He sank into the chair at his desk, looking like he'd aged ten years.

Back home, Amira had seen this regularly. Family, friends and neighbours, perfectly happy and healthy one minute, became old overnight. After another car bombing, one of her cousins had gone completely bald. He wasn't even involved, but that wasn't the point. What was the saying? The hair that broke the camel's back? 'Do you need something, Sol?' she asked. 'Glass of water?'

He squinted at her through his fringe and pulled out the photographs she'd printed off earlier. He thrust one in her direction.

'Nathan Osborne,' he said. 'Works for Paul Hill.' Amira took the picture. 'Looks like he went to the Crosshills with Frankie Greenwood.'

Amira scrolled through the notes to find out what Osborne had said after the shooting. Nothing much. According to him, he'd been passing and stopped to buy 'a bit of weed'. No mention of Frankie Greenwood.

'The Hills and the Greenwoods have joined forces now?' she said.

Sol shrugged. 'I don't think we can jump to conclusions. Osborne doesn't represent Paul Hill any more than Frankie represents the Greenwoods.'

That was true.

'If you've taught me anything, Sol,' she said, 'it's that coincidences are almost never that.' A shadow crossed Sol's face. 'We should get this character in, get him to explain a few things.'

'Something tells me he's already answering a couple of questions.'

A drop of blood from Nathan Osborne's exploding mouth bloomed on the sleeve of Liberty's shirt.

There was a pack of anti-bacterial wipes in her handbag and she was desperate to grab one and scrub at it, but knew that now was not the time.

Crystal was still holding the bottle, its base covered in viscous scarlet liquid. Jay stared at it. The look on his face unnerved Liberty. It was like everything that she recognized as her brother had disappeared.

Osborne leaned forward at the waist and spat out a mouthful of mucus, blood and tooth. Gingerly, he put a finger to the split in the lower lip and groaned.

'Now we've got that out of the way, let's get down to business,' said Jay.

Osborne looked up at him. There was hatred in his eyes, but also fear. He spat again.

'I think you've met my other sister.' Jay gestured at Liberty. 'The clever one.'

Liberty sighed inwardly. All her bloody life she'd been the clever one. Jay was the funny one, Crystal the pretty one and Frankie was the baby. Naturally, this gave them all a get-out-of-jail-free card when it came to any problems.

'My advice would be to answer Liberty's questions,' said Jay. 'That way Crystal will keep her feelings to herself. Okay?'

Osborne rolled each shoulder in turn. 'Fine.'

Jay nodded at Liberty. She understood why she was being set up as the one doing the asking. Good cop, bad cop. A tale as old as time. Plus, there was no way Jay or Crystal could be trusted to keep their cool. If Osborne gave an answer they didn't like, they might beat him to death.

She took the bottle out of Crystal's hand and placed it back on the desk. Osborne didn't take his eyes off it.

'Why were you with Frankie yesterday?' Her tone was shockingly even. 'At the flat on Crosshills?'

He didn't look at her. 'I wasn't.'

Again, Crystal snatched the bottle and this time slammed it across the bald man's left kneecap. There was a crunch, and Osborne leaned forward again, this time to throw up. Liberty side-stepped the gush neatly.

When Osborne finally sat up, his face had cracked, the features arranged truthfully. He was in pain and he was scared. His imagination must be boiling with all the ways in which Crystal could hurt him with the bottle.

Liberty let her voice drop low. 'What were you doing with my brother yesterday?'

'Taking drugs,' Osborne replied, breathing hard.

'Why?'

His eyes darted around the room, desperate for the right answer to avoid another smack from the bottle.

'I mean why with Frankie?' said Liberty.

Osborne nodded frantically, sending a fresh spurt of blood down his chin. Internally, Liberty winced. Externally, she didn't bat an eyelid. 'We bumped into each other in the pub, got chatting.'

'You weren't expecting to see him in there?'

Osborne shook his head with similar conviction, relieved that he knew the answer to another question. 'He never goes in there any more. Not since he went into rehab.'

Liberty looked down at the stain on her shirt. She lifted a finger to touch it, but pulled away at the last second. She'd throw the damn thing away when she got out of here. 'So, you got talking?'

'Yeah.'

'About what?'

The certainty left Osborne's eyes and they filled with panic. Liberty moved the bottle a few inches towards Crystal. It left a red smear on the desk.

'Just crap, you know how it is?'

'Enlighten me.'

Osborne stretched out his legs and groaned. The left kneecap was probably shattered. 'I don't know. Normal stuff.'

'Football?'

'Yeah.'

Liberty swallowed. Frankie wasn't interested in football. He was interested in doing drugs and girls. They were hobbies that required dedication, given the amounts of both he consumed.

When the blow came it was hard, the bottle wrecking Osborne's jaw. He toppled sideways from the chair, falling into his own blood and vomit. The noise he made was guttural.

'Fucking hell, Crystal,' said Jay. 'He's got to be able to speak to us.'

Crystal reached down and grabbed Osborne by the collar, dragging him back into the chair. He must have weighed twice what she did, but that didn't stop her. Instead, she smashed the bottle against the desk and held the jagged edge of it to Osborne's throat. 'Don't piss us around,' she said.

He closed his eyes and panted. Each breath released red droplets.

'We talked about business.' His words were thick and slurred. 'He said he was sick of working for Jay.' Crystal kept the sharp glass pressed to his jugular. 'He said he thought that taking over the Delaney patch was a good idea, even if Jay didn't.'

'Bullshit,' said Jay, and Crystal pushed the glass deeper so that it cut the skin.

'It's true. I swear.'

Liberty moved in close to his face. She could smell the acid bile and ferrous tang of blood. 'Did you see who shot him?'

Osborne's eyes popped open. 'No. If I did then I'd tell you. But I didn't.' He tried to lean away from the broken bottle. 'We'd done a few pipes and Frankie said he was out of money, so I went to find the runner and weigh in. Next thing there's a bang and all hell broke loose.'

Chapter 12

15 February 1990
Miss Chapman's office smells of oranges. There's a plate of peel on her desk so she must have been eating one before I arrived. I haven't got an appointment but she's squeezed me in.

'I've spoken to Crystal's social worker and she's looking into it,' says Miss Chapman, putting down two cups of tea on the desk. 'They're taking this seriously.'

'She's still with the same foster carers, though.'

'Yeah.' Miss Chapman takes a sip of her tea, wrinkles her nose and stirs it with her biro. 'The social worker didn't want to move her again in case it turns out to be nothing to do with the foster carers.'

'Who else could have done it?'

Miss Chapman sucks the end of the pen. 'Maybe a kid at school.'

'No way.' I shake my head violently. 'I got a good look at those marks and a kid couldn't have done it.'

'It's not exactly helping that Crystal won't say who did do it.'

'If they'd let me see her, I'd get her to tell me easy,' I point out.

Miss Chapman explains that the social worker thinks it's better for contact to be suspended during the investigation. Honestly, I want to scream. It's not Miss Chapman's fault but I'd like to throw my cup of tea at the wall.

Later, I go to Connor's house and tell him what's gone on. His mam tells me to try not to worry and makes us all a plate of egg and chips.

My helping's massive. She must think they don't feed me at Orchard Grove.

'Are you going to the bingo tonight, Mam?' Connor asks.

'Indeed I am. That one thousand pounds prize money isn't going to win itself, now, is it?'

Connor kicks my foot under the table and waggles his eyebrows suggestively. I cough and turn away. We're not having sex yet. Not proper sex anyway. I'm still a bit scared and Connor says there's no rush, but we still like to have time on our own. Lying on his bed, arms around each other, listening to Connor's latest records, there's not much better than that.

'Would you pop up to the Co-op for me, Connor?' she asks him. 'I've run out of Fairy Liquid.'

'Yes, Mam.'

When he's left the house, I help clear the table, stacking dirty dishes by the sink.

'Would you do me a favour, Lib?' his mam asks, snapping on a pair of Marigolds.

'Anything, Mrs O.'

'Could you not come round here again?'

I'm rooted to the spot, yolk-covered plate in one hand, salt pot in the other. Has something gone missing? Does she think I nicked it?

'I like you, Lib, really I do, and sure I know that all these terrible things that are happening in your life are not your fault.' *She squirts Fairy Liquid into the washing-up bowl. The bottle's almost full.* 'I just don't want Connor mixed up in any of it.'

'He's not.' *My words come out small and scratchy.* 'It's got nothing to do with him.'

'He's too nice to stay out of it, we both know that.'

She dunks the first plate in the water and rubs a brush over the grease. 'I just want what every mother wants for their son.' *She smiles at me.* 'To get a good job, meet a nice girl and settle down.'

'I'm a good girl,' I say.

She grabs the plate from my hand and plonks it into the bowl. There's a smear of sauce on it that won't come off. 'I just think that if you're as fond of him as you seem, you'd think about him in all this.'

'I do.'

'Well, then, you won't want to drag him down, will you?'

I excuse myself and go up to the toilet. It's spotlessly clean and smells of bleach. I put down the lid and sit, hands shaking. Connor's mam isn't being nasty: she just wants to look out for him, like I try to look out for my family.

I go along the corridor to his bedroom. It's a mess like always but there's a box of Maltesers on the top of his drawers that I know he's bought for me because he doesn't eat much chocolate, says it makes his teeth ache.

I run down the stairs and fish in my school bag for a paper and pen. The words come out in a rush and I press down too hard with the nib. When I'm finished I fold the paper in two and find Connor's mam in the kitchen, doing the drying-up.

'Give him this,' I say.

'You are a good girl.'

Present day

It was still raining and the steps outside the Cherry were greasy and covered in wet dog-ends.

'Come inside, Lib,' said Jay.

Liberty shook her head and rubbed the slickness with the toe of her shoe. Her brother sighed and moved outside into the rain to join her.

'Fine. Let's get pissed on.' He lifted his head to the heavens and held open his mouth, catching rainwater on his tongue. 'Ozzie had it coming.'

Liberty nudged away a half-smoked fag, watched it plop into a puddle and disintegrate. Whether Nathan Osborne had had a kicking coming or not wasn't why she was out here. She just couldn't take another second in the club with the girls circling like vultures in their knickers, the punters leering at them with undisguised hunger or hatred, touching their cocks when they thought no one was looking. And the music. Always the music banging away in the background.

'Do you think he was telling the truth?' Jay asked.

'Mostly.'

'About me?' Jay wiped the rain from his face with his sleeve. 'That our Frankie thinks I'm a twat.'

'I'm sure he thought it.'

'Why?'

'You and Crystal treat *him* like a twat,' she said.

Jay laughed. 'That'll be because our Frankie acts like a twat.'

A white van pulled into the car park and four lads in their twenties got out in their work clothes and boots – after a lunchtime pint and lap dance. They nodded at Jay as they skirted past. The last one, all pale Irish skin and black hair, at least had the decency to look sheepish as he caught Liberty's eye.

'You're bad for business, you are,' said Jay.

'Is that right?'

He was drenched now, hair wet, shirt beginning to stick to his broad shoulders. 'Can we please go back inside?'

She slipped through the door, immediately hit by the heat, the stench and the bass line. She lifted the drapes and watched the four lads at the bar, a girl already at their side, laughing at something one of them had just said even though she probably hadn't understood a word.

'Frankie might have thought certain things about you, but he would never have said them,' she told Jay. 'Not without a reason.'

'Have you met him?' Jay asked. 'He doesn't need a reason to do anything.'

'It's different when it comes to family.'

★　★　★

Amira pulled the band from her hair, raked her fingers through it to undo the plait and brushed. It was dry, the ends splitting. She was always so busy, these days – there was barely time to wash it, let alone take proper care of it.

As a child, it had been her grandmother's job to deal with the girls' hair. Which was just as well because their mother was more of a grab-you-by-the-chin-and-yank-out-the-knots type. Her grandmother, however, had had all the time in the world, pouring a few drops of scented oil into her palm and working it into Amira's hair from the roots to the tips, the smell intoxicatingly grown-up. Then, satisfied that the oil was distributed evenly, she would first use a wide-tooth comb made of shell, moving around the head, section by section, then finishing with a brush made of animal bristles.

Amira quickly redid her plait, pulled the clump of loose hair from the brush and threw it into the passenger footwell, where it landed on top of a half-eaten falafel wrap.

When she saw who she was looking for, she jumped out of the car. 'Tia.'

The girl had her hood up against the rain and was being half dragged by a Staffie on a lead.

'Tia.' Amira jogged after her. 'Wait up.'

The girl turned and frowned, her arm behind her as the dog continued to pull. 'Oi.' She yanked on the lead.

'Can I have a word?'

The girl gave a vicious tug and the dog jerked reluctantly towards her. As soon as it saw Amira it growled and Tia looped the black leather lead tighter around her hand.

'Shouldn't he have a muzzle?' Amira asked.

'That's pit bulls.'

The dog's teeth were bared and sharp, the folds of its chin splattered with frothy saliva.

'What's his name?'

Tia shrugged. 'I call him Star.'

Star lunged again and Tia pushed him back with her foot.

'You said a bald bloke was with Frankie when he got shot.' Amira pulled out the picture of Nathan Osborne. 'This him?'

Rain hit the paper, the sound of someone tutting, as Tia took a look. 'Think so, yeah.'

'You seen him before?'

'Not up at that flat.'

'But around?'

It was pouring down and the dog shook himself. Dirty water sprayed from his fur, covering the bottoms of Tia and Amira's jeans.

'For fuck's sake,' said Tia.

'Have you seen him around the estate, Tia?'

'Here and there,' she replied. 'Not regular, though.'

'Could he have been the shooter?' Amira asked. Tia kissed her teeth. 'Why not?'

'He's just some prick. No one.' Tia started laughing. 'He only had just enough cash for the food. You know?'

'Ozzie paid?'

Tia nodded. 'Listen, I'm off. I don't know anything else.'

When she turned, the dog wouldn't move, the lead digging into his neck. Instead he quivered and squatted as he did a massive shit. When he was done he trotted away with Tia.

'Aren't you going to clean up that mess?' Amira shouted after them.

Tia and Star didn't look back.

Every head in the Cherry turned to the stage as two girls began rubbing themselves against each other. The taller of the two reached round and pulled on the smaller girl's ponytail. She'd need to be more careful. Liberty could see from the bar that it was false, and might come off in her hands.

The four lads put their fingers in their mouths and whistled loudly. The girls responded by removing their bras.

While all eyes focused on four plastic breasts, Nathan Osborne was hustled out of the back room, limping, his arm around one of Jay's men for support. Someone had wrapped a scarf around his mouth. Not too gently, he was helped around the bar and through the back door. Len the pot man didn't even pass a side glance, just carried on emptying the dishwasher.

Mel waited until the injured man was gone, then clicked her tongue. 'That was a mistake.'

'Maybe,' Liberty replied.

'No maybe about it.' Mel poured herself a vodka and tonic. She'd clearly had a few already. 'Jay's a hothead, we all know that, but you're meant to be the sensible one.'

Liberty puffed out her cheeks. Clever *and* sensible? 'We needed to know a few things,' she said.

Mel made another clicking sound, this time somewhere in her throat. She spun the drink around in the glass and knocked it back. 'You won't find out anything important from Nathan Osborne,' she said.

'Actually, he did tell us something quite interesting,' Liberty replied. There was a breathless silence. 'Frankie was bad-mouthing Jay.'

Mel let out a half-laugh, half-cough. 'He'd never do that.'

Liberty eyed Mel coolly, watching as she fixed herself yet another drink. 'Not unless there was a point to it.'

'What point?' Mel asked.

Liberty leaned in close. 'You tell me.'

A cheer went up at the stage as the man with the fair skin held out a fiver to the tallest girl. Clearly he'd lost his earlier reticence. There was a logo on the back of his polo shirt 'Plumbing

Solution'. He spent his days with his hands down other people's toilets so he could shove the money he earned down the stocking tops of a stranger.

'Here's what I think, Mel,' said Liberty. 'Someone thought it was a good idea to try to find out what game Paul Hill is playing. And that someone thought it was a good idea for Frankie to do the digging.' She took Mel's glass from her and had a sip. It was strong, all vodka with only a splash of tonic. 'And now that person's shitting themselves that they put him in harm's way.'

'Rubbish,' said Mel. 'Frankie was in the wrong place at the wrong time.'

Liberty drained the drink and wrapped Mel's bony fingers around the empty tumbler. 'Let's hope so, eh?'

Sol was still technically on shift but he didn't care. He slid the key into his front door and went straight through to the kitchen. He plonked his mobile on the counter and searched the bread bin for something to make toast. Natasha didn't think he should eat too much wheat (wheatgrass juice, whatever that might be, was allowable) so there were often slim pickings in the bread department. Today he found a few slices of something brown and grainy that would have to do.

His mobile chirped. It was a text from Hassani: *Call me.*

Sol deleted it and waited for his toast to pop, then rummaged in the fridge for any substance that might look vaguely like butter. Chewing, he wondered if it would have been better if he'd just admitted to sleeping with Liberty, taken a disciplinary, maybe resigned. He knew plenty of ex-coppers who made decent money doing security stuff.

He could have kept it all from Natasha and convinced her that they should move away. She wasn't from England, let alone

Yorkshire. Sure, she had friends here but she wouldn't have made a fuss.

He glanced around the kitchen as if for the first time. There were three squat glass candle holders in a line, each with a recently burned scented tea light. A novel in Russian that hadn't been opened, by the look of it. Two unripe bananas hung from a special banana hook away from the other fruit. It was barely a life he recognized.

But he hadn't admitted to anything, had he? Caught out, he'd lied, then gone along with Hassani's suggestion of using his relationship with Liberty (could he call it that?). To be fair, he hadn't passed along anything very useful to Hassani. The stuff about the anonymous Delaney witnesses would have come out as soon as Singh made the application. In the same vein, he hadn't given Liberty any sensitive information about Frankie's shooting. The fact that Osborne had been at the scene wasn't confidential.

He was playing the game, like always, and he only had to last another couple of days. The DCI had given the say-so on surveillance until the end of the week. And then that would be it.

Hassani sent another text: *Where are you???????*

Sol pushed the phone away and it slid along the shiny worktop until it collided with the cappuccino machine.

Hassani would keep picking at him, as if he was a scab. As for Liberty, how long before she began to suspect that he was double-dealing? And what would she do then? Talk about being caught between a rock and a hard place.

The mobile went again and Sol was ready to throw it out of the kitchen window until he saw who it was from.

Rebecca was all wrong. The pink tunic clashed against the black of the drapes. A touch of nude lipstick accentuated the frown on her mouth.

Liberty marched over. 'Becca?'

Jay's wife blinked. Had she ever been inside the club? Her toes curled inside black patent Birkenstocks, each nail painted like a shiny little shell. 'Is Jay here?' she asked.

One of the girls passed by and gave Rebecca a puzzled look, fingers pulling the G-string out of the crack of her arse.

'He's in the office,' said Liberty.

Rebecca raised her chin towards the back of the club, but as she took a step there was a roar. To the left, the workmen had paid for a private dance and one was thrusting his hips in uncontrolled glee at the dancer while the other three cheered him on.

'I'll get Jay,' said Liberty. 'You wait here.'

As she moved alongside the lads' table she glared at them. 'Sit down.'

The one with the hips sneered at her. 'Who put you in charge?' Liberty flicked her finger at the girl, who grabbed her discarded knickers and scuttled away. 'Oi, I paid for her.'

Liberty put her hands on the table and leaned into their faces. 'Do you know who owns this club?'

'The Greenwoods,' said the one with the fair skin.

'Well, I'm Lib Greenwood,' she said. 'Nice to meet you.'

The one with the hips sat down. 'I did pay for her, though.'

'No, you paid for a dance and you got one.' She looked at them in turn, none of them above twenty-five. 'Why don't you go and find some real girls? Take them out for a drink or something. You never know you might even get to see a nice arse that you don't have to fork out for.'

Still shaking her head, she stomped to the office door and waltzed inside, immediately wishing she hadn't.

'Jesus, Lib.' Jay jumped away from a girl who was on her knees giving him a blow job. It was the small one from the lesbian act earlier and, true enough, her hairpiece came off in Jay's hand. He yelped and threw it across the room. 'What the fuck is that?'

The girl scrambled on all fours to retrieve it and Liberty pushed the door shut with her back.

'Come in, why don't you?' Jay hissed.

'Your wife is here,' Liberty hissed back.

'Becca?'

'You remember her name, then.' Liberty spoke through her teeth. 'May I suggest you do up your flies, wipe the dribble off your chin and find out what she wants?' Liberty pointed at the girl, still on the floor, clipping her hair back in place. 'You stay put until someone comes to get you.'

Liberty swallowed her anger and plastered on a smile as she walked with Jay towards his wife.

'Becca.' His voice was gruff. 'You shouldn't come to the club.'

Given what he'd just been doing, Liberty had to admire his cheek. Attack might be the best form of defence, but it took someone with *cojones* to switch as quickly as her brother.

'The boys have cricket practice,' she said. 'So, I went to the hospital with food and drink for you. I thought you might need it. Obviously, you weren't there.'

'We had a bit of business to attend to,' said Jay.

Rebecca glanced at the girl taking to the stage in a nurse's outfit, the skirt skimming pink buttocks. 'I can see that.'

'Jay needed me to check some paperwork.' Liberty put a hand on her sister-in-law's arm. 'With my lawyer's hat on.'

Rebecca seemed about to question that when the four workmen pushed aside the drapes to leave and the fair one pressed something into Liberty's hand. When she opened it, there was a phone number scribbled on a beer mat.

'I'm old enough to be your mother,' said Liberty.

The lad smiled. 'I like 'em more mature, then they can teach me something.'

'How about I start by teaching you some manners?'

'You can start anywhere you like, Mrs Greenwood.'

Liberty threw the beer mat at him. 'Get out of here while you've still got legs.'

When he'd gone, Jay's shoulders were shaking with laughter he couldn't contain and he dipped to kiss his wife's neck. 'It was nice of you to think of me, Becca, but you can see why I'm not keen on you coming here.'

Rebecca reddened but didn't push him away. 'Thing is, Jay, when I got to Frankie's room there was someone in there,' she said. 'He was really close to the machine, you know?'

A niggle of tension spiked Liberty's chest. 'Where was Harry?'

'No idea,' Rebecca replied. 'I only saw this man I'm telling you about.'

'Probably just a doctor,' said Jay.

Rebecca shook her head. 'No. Nothing about him said medic and, anyway, I asked who he was and he didn't answer me. Just went like this.' She put her finger to her lips. 'Then he left.'

Chapter 13

2 March 1990
It takes me nearly two and a half hours to get to the YOI. A bus, a train,
then another two buses. When I finally arrive, visiting's nearly over. Jay
doesn't go on at me, though, he just grins.

'What the hell have they done to your hair?' I ask.

He runs a hand over his fresh skin head. 'Makes it harder for anyone
to grab hold of you.'

All around us visitors are sharing bags of sweets and crisps with the
prisoners. I haven't got any spare money. I went to Boots to nick batteries
but that Sean from the Crosshills was already in there, hovering over
them.

'How are Frankie and Crystal?' *asks Jay.*

I don't have the heart to tell him so I say, 'Frankie's got a wobbly
tooth.'

'Them foster carers better leave him ten pence,' *he says.*

The Tooth Fairy never made many appearances at the Greenwoods'
but that never stopped our Jay trying his luck.

'What about your boyfriend?' *he asks.* 'He seemed all right.'

'We've finished.'

Jay frowns. 'He didn't hit you, did he?'

'What? Connor would never do anything like that,' *I say.*

'Why've you split up, then?'

I shrug. 'I'm busy with my exams and that.'

'You and your chuffing exams,' he says.

'You won't be saying that when I'm rich.'

'No.' He laughs. 'I'll be asking to borrow a fiver.'

Visiting time's over and it feels like I've only been there ten minutes. Jay leans into me and whispers in my ear 'Kiss me, Lib.' I'm surprised. I mean, he's fourteen now. 'Proper on the mouth.'

I pull away from him, laughing.

'I'm gonna make out like you're my bird to the other lads in here.' He gives me the cheekiest smile. 'Trust me, that sort of shit matters on the block.'

I shake my head and take his face in my hands, like Connor used to do to me, then I kiss him. When I move back he winks at me. 'Just so you know, I'm not going to shag you.'

When I finally get back to Orchard Grove, I'm knackered and I've missed teatime, but I find Tiny sitting on the wall outside, eating a bag of chips.

'Some lad called Imbo told me you'd gone to see your Jay,' she says. 'Cheeky beggar blagged three ciggies off me.' She pats the wall and I sit next to her. 'Is he all right, then?'

'He's just Jay,' I reply.

She offers me a chip. I take a fat one covered in salt. 'Seems like you've done a disappearing act on us lately.' She puts the chips on my lap and pulls a carton of Ribena out of her coat pocket. 'We miss you.'

'I miss you.'

She stabs the box with the little straw and sucks. 'What's up, then?'

'I just need to be on my own for a bit.' I eat another chip. 'I've got a lot on my plate.'

'What about Connor?' She puts the straw to my mouth so I can take a drink. 'He says he popped out to the shop and when he got back you'd left a letter telling him he was dumped.' The carton makes a burpy gurgle. 'Want to riddle me that one?'

I wouldn't even know where to start so I just take another chip.

Tiny stands and wipes her greasy hands down the front of her jeans.

'He's driving me doo-lally tap, to be honest. Will you just talk to him? Then he might stop breaking my brain in two.'

When we get to Connor's street, I start to drag my feet. Apparently, his mum's at another christening, but I'm still nervous.

Tiny knocks on the door and a figure appears at the other side of the frosted glass. It seems to be naked.

The door opens and Fat Rob peers out in just his pants. He sees me and gives me a bear hug.

'Oh, my chuffing eyes are falling out,' says Tiny, and pushes him back inside.

The lounge is in chaos, covered in plates of food, cans of beer and over-flowing ashtrays. Danny is fast asleep on the settee and Connor's building a spliff on the coffee table. He looks like he could do with a bath.

'Visitor,' Tiny trills.

Connor seems shocked to see me.

'It smells like a skinner's yard in here.' Tiny points at Connor. 'I know you're heart-broken but open some windows, will you?' She bends over Danny. 'And has anyone seen him awake at all today? Or shall I call the undertakers?'

In the kitchen, Connor makes us both a cup of tea. 'How's Crystal?' I shrug that I don't know. 'I was talking to this bloke who knows a bit about that sort of thing,' he says. 'Well, he's had all his kids taken into care so he's a fucking expert. Anyway . . .'

'You didn't do anything wrong, Connor. I just had to end things between us.'

'Can I ask why?'

I don't look at him. 'A lot of crap things are going on at the minute.'

'I know that,' he says. 'And if someone gave me three wishes I'd use the first one to sort them all out for you.'

'What about the other two?'

'I'd wish for a million pounds, no, a billion, and world peace. Or maybe for Leeds to win the double. It's a toss-up, that one.' I smile at him then. 'That's more like it,' he says.

159

Even with dirty hair and stubble he's handsome.

'I just don't want to drag you down with me,' I say.

He puts a hand on either side of my face, fingers still warm from his mug. 'You don't ever drag me down, beautiful. You just make me happy.'

I want to kiss him, but I know his mum's right: Connor doesn't need to be involved in all my problems. It's like I'm a black hole sucking everyone in that comes too close. Vicky's disappeared, Jay's in the nick, Crystal's being beaten and our Frankie's still wetting the bed.

'I can't,' I say, as much to myself as Connor.

'Right,' he says.

Present day

The rain had finally stopped but it felt like a temporary reprieve. The air was still hot and laden with moisture. What Mam would have called muggy. Liberty pushed her hair from her face as she hurried into the hospital with Jay.

Rebecca wasn't a drama queen. She was solid and stable, just the sort of woman Jay needed in his life. She certainly wasn't one to worry unnecessarily.

'Where the hell is Harry?' asked Liberty.

'You tell me,' Jay replied. 'When I catch up with him, he's going to wish I hadn't.'

They'd agreed to take shifts sitting with Frankie. Not because they'd thought anyone might try to harm him again, but in case he woke up. Or that had been what Liberty had assumed.

Jay stabbed the button for the lift five, six, seven times.

'It won't come more quickly that way,' said Liberty.

Jay glared at her and stabbed it two more times. They rode to the third floor in silence. When they arrived at Frankie's room, a nurse was in there adjusting some of the tubes.

'What are you doing?' Jay barked.

It was the nurse who had been kind to Liberty. 'I beg your pardon?'

'Jay.' Liberty grabbed for his hand. 'Stop it. She obviously works here.'

Jay avoided her grasp and strode to the bed. He ran a finger from Frankie's ear down to his jaw. The tenderness stung Liberty.

'Sorry,' Liberty said to the nurse. 'We're all really on edge.' The nurse nodded and carried on with her work, changing a bag of saline, squeezing the new pouch. 'I don't suppose you saw anyone else in here? Someone who wasn't supposed to be?'

The nurse shook her head. 'We don't really let anyone in ICU except immediate family.' The saline began to drip steadily. 'Police maybe. Given what happened.'

Jay glanced at Liberty. If a copper had been here why would he be touching Frankie's machine? Unless he was the sort of copper who worked for Paul Hill.

Crystal stuck her head in the door. She'd changed her clothes since what had happened with Osborne. Liberty checked herself. Something hadn't 'happened' to Osborne. Her family had grabbed and beaten him. And she'd been part of it.

'Where's Harry?' Jay snapped.

'I thought he was here,' Crystal replied.

'Well, he's not.'

The nurse frowned. 'You can't all be in here at once and certainly not while you're arguing.'

Jay locked on a space in mid-air above the nurse's head, a tactic he'd used as a kid when he refused to engage. Liberty sighed and left the room, dragging Crystal with her.

'What the hell's up with Jay now?' Crystal muttered.

Liberty filled her in about what Rebecca had told them, watching the colour drain from Crystal's already alabaster face. Her sister grabbed her phone and tried her husband. No answer.

'Could he be at home?' Liberty asked. 'Getting a shower or something?'

Crystal looked down the corridor, desperate to find Harry there. 'I've just come from home. I think I'd have noticed him.'

'You could have missed each other by seconds.'

'But why would he go home when he knows he's meant to be here?'

Liberty threw up her arms. How was she supposed to have the answer to everything? Crystal tried Harry's number again but there was still no reply.

'Go home and check,' said Liberty. 'If he turns up here in the meantime, I'll call you. And hopefully manage to stop Jay knocking his head off.'

Amira sent Sol another text. She was certain he'd ignored the others.

They couldn't keep Chapman under twenty-four-hour observation, though Amira would have loved to, but if she and Sol tag-teamed, they could have at least an idea of her whereabouts most of the time.

Back at the station, they'd agreed that she would do some digging on the Crosshills estate and Sol would contact Chapman. He'd looked terrible and was clearly unhappy with the whole thing but he'd agreed.

Now he was on the missing list.

She slammed the steering wheel with the heel of her hand.

Sol's involvement with Chapman was the perfect in. Amira had clearance to watch the lawyer, but Sol could access ears and nose. The shooting of Frankie Greenwood was the icing on the cake. Another reason for Sol to be in regular contact with Chapman and another thing to tip that woman into doing something dodgy.

The apple never fell far from the tree. And the Greenwood tree was laden with rotting fruit.

She punched Sol's number and got his voicemail.

'I don't know what you think you're playing at, Sol, but just so you know, you can't run away from this.' Amira tried to keep her voice steady. 'I won't let you do that. I've spoken to someone who was at the scene of the shooting and I want to know what Chapman thinks of what they have to say.'

She hung up and tossed her mobile onto the passenger seat.

A moment later her phone sprang to life.

'What's with the three-act drama?' Sol spat. 'Liberty's at the hospital visiting her brother.'

'Then that's where you should be, Sol.'

He hung up.

Liberty sat outside Frankie's room, elbows on knees, head in her hands. So often in her life, this was how things had gone. Everything around her spiralling out of control, everyone she loved getting hurt. She had fought and fought to stop the wheels of chaos turning. But it had never worked.

The only time when that chaos didn't reign was when she stopped fighting and stepped away. When she kept things at a distance, she couldn't infect them. She shifted awkwardly in her seat, moved one hand to the back of her neck, trying to knead out a knot. Maybe she should step away now. Maybe that was the answer she'd been struggling to find. She could pack up her stuff in less than an hour. To be honest, she could leave most of it and not miss it. She'd never got around to renting out her flat in London, unsure how long she was staying in Yorkshire. In less than three hours, she could be lying on her sofa in Hampstead, a glass of good red wine in her hand.

Her old boss, Ronald, would probably take her back. Not at the same level, but still on the sort of money most people dreamed of.

The idea held Liberty for a few more seconds. But she couldn't just leave Frankie half dead, could she? How would that help? And what about Jay? He could barely keep control of himself. God knew what he'd do, left to his own devices. Even Crystal acknowledged that Liberty was needed right now. Then there was Dax. She'd made a promise to herself to keep him out of trouble. If she went back to London, he'd surely follow and would be back out on the road in seconds.

It wasn't a choice between fight or flight. She needed to be rational. She needed to box clever. After all, wasn't she meant to be the clever one?

It was so hot and she felt groggy when she needed to be sharp. She forced herself upright and slapped her cheek.

'Lib?'

Jay was standing in the doorway. He looked worse than Liberty felt. Her brother was a good-looking bloke. Six two, thick hair, the sort of smile that often stared out of magazines. When he laughed, which he did all the time, it carried people along.

'You look like shit,' she told him. He laughed and slid into the seat next to her. 'And you smell worse. Go home and get a shower.'

'Any sign of Harry?'

Liberty shook her head. 'I'm staying anyway.'

Jay lifted his shirt, bent and breathed in. Given he'd spent the last few hours beating up a gangster then shagging a stripper, what did he expect to smell like?

'Fine,' he said. 'But if anyone turns up that you think seems even vaguely off key . . .'

'I'll batter him with an empty beer bottle,' said Liberty.

'If you're going to take the piss I'm off nowhere,' said Jay.

Liberty elbowed him in the side. 'I'll get the nurse. Obviously. And there's a bloody alarm button in there for an emergency.'

Satisfied, Jay got up. 'I'll be back in a couple of hours.'

Onions sizzled on the iron hotplate of the burger van.

'Do you want some of these, love?' asked a woman with more blue hairnet than hair.

'Please,' Sol answered.

He watched her scrape a good scattering on top of the burger, then hand it to him wrapped in a paper napkin.

'That looks almost edible,' said Bucky.

'Can I buy you one?' Sol asked.

She cupped a breast in each hand and jiggled. 'My body is a temple.'

Sol reached for the ketchup and squeezed a generous amount in a crisscross pattern over his tray of chips. His lunchtime toast hadn't touched the sides.

'What's up, then, Bucky?' he asked. 'Why the cloak and dagger?'

She reached over, took a sauce-smeared chip and blew on it. 'Raj hasn't made an application yet.'

'Give him a chance.' He took a bite of his burger. 'I expect everything's a bit up in the air with Frankie getting shot.'

'Either that or Hassani's information is wrong.'

Sol took another bite of burger. The onions had been a mistake. 'It's not wrong.'

'What the hell's going on, Sol?' Bucky was still holding her chip. 'Surveillance on Raj Singh? I know Delaney's a big fish, and I want to catch him as much as the next man, but this does not seem right.'

Sol moved away from the van and sat on a nearby bench. He put the chips between them and gestured for Bucky to help herself.

'Amira's got a problem with Chapman,' Sol said. 'It goes back to last year.' Bucky chewed her chip thoughtfully. 'She convinced the DCI that we should put eyes on her. But only for a week.' Sol put down his burger on top of the chips. The almost raw yet greasy onions were making his stomach roll. 'That's where the intel on the application comes from.'

'If this buggers up the Delaney trial in any way shape or form . . .'

'It won't,' said Sol. 'In a week's time when there's nothing on Chapman, the surveillance will end and no one will be any the wiser. We'll just get on with prosecuting Jacko.'

Bucky picked up the half-eaten burger, sniffed it, took a bite. 'Fuck me, them onions! I've got a date later and I haven't even got a toothbrush with me.'

'Fazeel?' Sol asked.

Bucky scrabbled in her handbag for a heavy bottle of perfume and sprayed it on her tongue, choked and sprayed again. 'Fazeel? He's about ten,' she said. 'Plus, he's the wrong sort.'

'What do you mean wrong sort?' Sol asked. 'Muslim?'

Bucky looked at Sol like he was an idiot. 'A man, you dick-head. Did you not know that we bat for the same side?'

'We should go out for a beer some time, Bucks,' said Sol, with a roar of laughter that felt good.

She still had the perfume in her hand and squirted some on each of her wrists, the side of her neck and then, as an after-thought, down her top. 'When we send Delaney down, we'll go on a bender, DI Connolly.'

'Amen.'

Bucky stood to leave. 'In the meantime, on the off-chance that Hassani is right about this application, I've been through the anonymous statements.' She smoothed down her skirt over her arse. 'There are three possible problems.'

'That doesn't sound good.'

Bucky held up her hand. Each nail was short and glossy red. 'I'm probably being overcautious, but I've emailed them to your private addy. Let me know what you think.' She waved. 'Maybe don't tell Hassani until we've had the chance to talk again.'

Sol nodded and watched her walk away.

'You need to wake up now.' Liberty kissed Frankie's cheek. 'You've made your point.'

She sat in the chair beside the bed, pressed her forearms into the mattress and rested her chin on top. The machine was bleeping steadily at the other side of the bed. Sometimes she couldn't even hear it any more, like in a submarine: apparently, the crew were deaf to the endless sound echoing through the ship, out into the ocean, talking over it, sleeping through it. But the second it stopped, they knew the shit had hit the fan and jumped to attention.

'Of all the ways we thought you might die, this wasn't one of them,' she said. 'To be honest, my money was on Jay strangling you. If you deny him that, I think we'll all be disappointed.'

Liberty watched the gentle rise and fall of Frankie's chest pump and breathed in time with it. She reached out and stroked her brother's hand. He felt cold. Or was she just too hot? 'Another reason you can't die is that there's stuff I need to talk to you about,' she said. 'For one thing, I've met someone. It's not exactly ideal circumstances but still.' She laughed. 'Jay will have a fit when he finds out who it is, so you'll want to be around for that at least.'

She watched and waited, as if her brother might open his eyes and ask for more details. When he didn't, Liberty pushed herself to her feet and went to the window. Outside, dusk seemed to be arriving quicker than usual. Darkness was already edging its way out of the corners.

Behind her the door opened and Liberty stiffened, but it was only the nurse. 'My last round of this shift,' she told Liberty. 'If you want to nip out, now's your chance. My replacement's coming from Bank.' She tutted. 'Always late, often useless.'

'Give me two minutes?' Liberty asked.

The nurse smiled her agreement.

Liberty peed as fast as she could and washed her hands, reading a warning about norovirus that was stuck to the mirror. She washed them again.

Back in ICU, the overhead lights had been dimmed. The patients in the ward were all so ill that they slept most of the day. Many, like Frankie, weren't even conscious, but the rhythms of the real world were still respected.

As Liberty passed the room nearest to Frankie's, she peered inside. A broken body on a bed. Tubes. A machine.

Who would want to work here? Surely medical staff wanted to make people better. What were the chances of any of these patients making it out?

As she approached Frankie's door, Liberty decided she would buy the nurse a gift. Not flowers or a bottle of wine. No, she'd find out what the woman actually liked and get it for her.

'So, what do you do when you're not mopping fevered brows . . .'

Liberty stopped short. The person in Frankie's room wasn't the nurse. It was a man. Cropped hair, dark skin, good-looking.

In the split second while Liberty considered what to do, the man was across the room. He grabbed her by the back of the neck, pulled her inside and slammed the door behind her.

'Say a word and I'll break it.'

There was no doubt in Liberty's mind that he meant it and could do it. His hand was huge, easily spanning her neck, the grip vice-like. She bit her lip, desperate not to scream as he frog-marched her to the side of Frankie's bed. Then he pushed down, forcing her face into the blanket that covered her brother's lower body. The smell of washing powder filled Liberty's nose and mouth. She couldn't breathe. The more she inhaled, the more blanket she sucked in. She clawed at it and tried to jerk her head away, but the man was far too strong.

'Calm down,' he said.

The voice was a scratchy rasp in the quiet of the ward. He released his hold slightly, allowing Liberty to thrust her face to the left. When he reapplied the pressure, her right cheek disappeared into the blanket, but at least the corner of her mouth and one nostril were unobstructed.

Liberty concentrated all her effort into getting her breathing under control. In and out. There were only two noises in the room, her breath and the machine. The man was behind her, silent, unmoving.

'I'm not here for you,' he whispered.

Relief flooded through Liberty's body. He wasn't here to kill her. Then the words came looping back to her, like that game Swing Ball. He wasn't here for *her*. From the position the man had her in, Liberty couldn't see Frankie, but she could feel him. The baby of the family. This man was here to kill him.

Liberty swallowed twice, trying to lubricate her throat. 'Someone will be here any second.' The man pressed his fingers deeper and Liberty choked. She had to fight to get words out. 'Jay will kill . . .'

A strange gurgle came out of her mouth and her vision blurred. She reached behind her to claw at the giant hand that squeezed the air out of her, digging her nails into the skin. The man grunted, but didn't release her.

The room began to swim and Liberty felt as though she were falling. Black dots appeared in her eyes. Her mouth was still open but nothing was going in or coming out. She had seconds before she passed out.

Something flitted through her mind. A picture of Jay smiling. Sunglasses on his head, chin tilted up, like he was laughing at something Liberty had said. His words came out trance-like and Liberty had to listen very carefully.

'If you're going to take the piss . . .' she had been taking the piss because that was what you did with your brother '. . . I'm going nowhere.'

Don't worry, Jay. Nothing's going to happen. Nothing at all. And if it did there's the . . .

Up on the wall, next to the machine, was the red button. The alarm. She stretched out her arm, but there was at least a foot between it and her fingers. Then she couldn't see her fingers or the button. Everything was turning inky black.

No point in reaching up to the man's hand. Better to reach down. With the last atom of strength she had left, Liberty scrabbled behind her and grabbed the man by the balls. Then she twisted with all her might.

Instinct kicked in and the man jumped back, releasing her. Liberty hoped air would rush into her lungs but her throat still felt closed. Her chest was on fire. She did the only thing she could and threw herself at the alarm, collapsing onto the floor as it went off.

Chapter 14

3 March 1990
It's a dirty afternoon. Wet, foggy and cold. But I don't want to go back to Orchard Grove.

They've moved Silent Leanne into my room. Carl says they haven't given up on finding Vicky, but in the meantime it will be nice for me to have the company.

'She doesn't speak,' I pointed out, but Carl waved that little detail aside.

Turns out, though, that silence is the least of my worries: Imbo spends half his life in our room. I wouldn't mind so much if he were quick and quiet, but he gives a chuffing running commentary on every hand job.

'Why can't you take her into your room?' I ask Imbo.

'It smells better in here, Lib.'

I keep walking through town until I'm near Carter Street. A car stops at the kerb and a man asks if I'm working. I give him my middle finger so he calls me a cunt and drives on. When another car pulls up, I'm ready to call the driver every name going, but the passenger door opens and Vicky gets out. She wobbles across the road in a pair of turquoise high heels, oblivious to the traffic.

'Vic.' I chase after her. 'Wait up.' She doesn't seem to notice me until I'm virtually next to her. 'Vic, it's me.'

Her face looks a bit blank. The scabs around her mouth are worse than when she left and there's a cut under her eye.

'Vic?'

She laughs and throws her arms around my neck. 'Fucking hell, Lib, I thought I was tripping.'

She takes me into the café on the corner and buys me a hot chocolate with whippy cream and sprinkles. Her legs are bare even though it's freezing out. One of her shoes has rubbed the back of her heel raw.

'Why did you take off?' I ask.

She spoons up some froth. 'I'd had enough.'

'Me and Imbo have been worried.'

'Sorry,' she says, but she doesn't sound it.

'Where are you living?' I ask.

'In a squat.' She shrugs. 'Only temporary, though. As soon as me and my boyfriend have got enough money we're going to rent a flat.'

I put down my mug. 'Not that Sean.'

'No.' Vicky laughs. 'His name's Billy and he looks after me really well.'

I don't know what to say. She's living in a squat, covered in cuts and bruises, and turning tricks for a living. How much actual looking-after is this Billy doing?

'What about you?' Vicky asks. 'Finally shagging Connor?'

'I finished with him,' I say.

She abandons her drink, pulls a cig she's nipped earlier from her pocket and lights up. 'Why? It's obvious that he's mad about you.' A woman comes in, all permed hair and gold chains. She looks around the tables. Vicky eyes her through the smoke. 'And he's got plenty of this.' She rubs her finger and thumb together.

'He hasn't even got a job,' I say.

She bursts out laughing and smoke comes out of her nose. 'Of course he has.' She taps the sleeve of my leather jacket. 'Bought that for you, didn't he?'

The woman with the perm comes over and stands at our table. 'Billy says to get a wiggle on.'

Vicky sighs, takes a last drag, grinds out her fag and gets up. 'Don't tell anyone where I am, Lib.' I shake my head. 'And stop worrying about other people. You can't watch out for everybody. Do what makes you happy for a change.'

It takes me ages to walk to Connor's street, and by the time I get there, it's teeming down.

I stand in the rain, my hair plastered to my face. Is Vicky right? Thing is, if she's supposedly doing what makes her happy, it looks a complete nightmare.

Fuck it. I ring the bell.

The door opens and the central heating floods out. It's Connor's mam, a suitcase at her feet. She must be not long back from Ireland.

'Oh, it's you,' she says.

'Is Connor in?' I ask.

'No,' she says, and goes to shut the door in my face.

'Mam?' Connor appears in the hall behind her. 'What are you doing?'

Her face changes. I think she's a bit scared. I could land her in it and tell Connor she told me to stay away. She could say I was lying, of course, but it would be her word against mine. Thing is, I don't want to cause any problems between Connor and his mam. She was only doing what she thought was right.

'Why are you shutting the door on Lib?' Connor asks.

'I think she thought you wouldn't want to see me,' I say. 'Which is understandable, seeing as how we're finished.'

'We're still friends,' he says.

'Sure, I didn't know that,' his mam replies. 'I've not been home, have I?'

She bustles away, without looking me in the eye.

'Do you want to tell me what's going on?' he says.

I shake my head and, like a wet dog, I manage to spray the walls in the hall. 'Shit.' I rub some of the dirty drops but make things worse.

Connor cracks up. 'Come in. Let's get you a towel and a cuppa.'

He turns and walks ahead of me. I don't go in yet but blurt out after him. 'I think I love you, Connor.' He stops but keeps his back to me.

'Actually, I don't think that. I know that.' Now he turns to face me. *'Is that okay?'*

'I suppose I can live with it.'

Present day

The alarm assaulted Sol as soon as he opened the door to ICU. It filled the corridor, along with medics racing towards Frankie Greenwood's room.

His stomach lurched. He wasn't a fan of Frankie, but he didn't want him to die. For one thing, Liberty would be crucified if her little brother didn't make it. The guilt of leaving all those years ago was already an almost physical presence. If he died before she had a chance to make amends, she'd never get over it.

He hurried along the corridor. When he reached the door to Frankie's room the alarm stopped and, for a moment, the doctor who was speaking didn't modulate his voice.

'Has he arrested?'

There was a male nurse checking the machine by the bed. 'Nope. Vitals are all fine.'

Then Sol noticed the female nurse helping Liberty to her feet and dived towards them. 'What's happened?'

'Can you leave the room, please?' the nurse said.

Sol scrabbled for his warrant card. 'I'm police.'

'I don't care if you're the pope,' said the nurse. 'Clear the room.' When he didn't move she glared at him. 'Now.'

Sol backed away, a chicken bone of anxiety lodged in his throat. What the hell was going on?

At last, Liberty staggered out, helped by the nurse, who slotted her into a chair. The nurse then took a pencil torch from her pocket and shone it in each of Liberty's eyes.

'Did she bang her head?' Sol asked.

Liberty tried to speak but the words were crushed and she collapsed into a coughing fit. When it eased, she lifted her hair and Sol's eyes widened. The skin of her neck was punctuated with furious red finger marks. 'She's been attacked,' he said.

The nurse checked the marks. 'Jesus.' She lifted Liberty's chin. 'Who did this?' Liberty shook her head again.

Sol took Liberty's hand in his and she looked at him. 'Okay?' he mouthed.

She blinked a bloodshot yes.

Someone arrived with a paper cup of water and encouraged Liberty to take a drink, but even a tiny sip resulted in another barrage of coughs.

'Easy does it,' said the nurse. 'Just wet your lips first.'

Almost child-like, Liberty did as she was told, licking the film of water from her mouth, then trying again.

'Good girl,' said the nurse. Liberty opened her mouth to speak but the nurse stopped her. 'Not yet. Let's get you checked over first.' She shouted down the corridor, 'Can I get a wheelchair here, please? I need this woman to be taken to A and E right now.'

Sol was still holding Liberty's hand and she squeezed it tight, pointing to Frankie with her other hand.

'He's fine, love,' said the nurse.

Liberty held Sol's gaze and pointed again. Stay here, she was telling him. Don't leave Frankie. He squeezed back that he understood.

The doctor left Liberty in the cubicle, curtain drawn across the entrance.

She scooted to the very end of the bed and pressed her toes into the floor. Tears welled in her eyes but she pushed them back down. Her mind kept floating off to a dark place, but she dragged it back.

The doctor returned with a smile and a bottle of medicine. He let some of the pink liquid glug onto a plastic spoon. 'Because of the angle of the attack, your windpipe isn't damaged.' He held out the spoon to Liberty. 'But, obviously, you're going to be in pain.' Liberty slurped the medicine. It felt warm and soothing as it went down. 'I want to keep you in for observation, though.'

'No.' Liberty's voice came out as a gasp. She tried to clear her throat. 'I need to be with my family.'

'Someone has assaulted you, Miss . . .' he checked the notes where Liberty had scribbled her name '. . . Miss Greenwood. I can't in all conscience let you just walk out of here.'

'I'm not going anywhere,' Liberty replied. 'I'll be in ICU with my brother.'

The doctor didn't look happy but Liberty didn't care. She needed to be with Frankie. The man who had strangled her was out there somewhere, possibly still in the hospital. What if he came back to finish what he'd started?

'I'll sign a waiver,' she said.

The doctor sighed and shook his head to indicate that he'd accepted there was no point in arguing.

Sol was on hyper-alert. Every noise and movement made his muscles twitch. Whoever had hurt Liberty had legged it from ICU when the alarm had gone off, but that didn't mean he'd left the hospital. He glanced at the red button and imagined Liberty smacking it even as her assailant was squeezing the life from her. He held in check a small smile of pride.

'What have you done this time, Frankie?' he asked the man lying unconscious on the bed.

The shooting had clearly not been a warning. Someone wanted Frankie Greenwood dead.

When the door opened, Sol was ready, hand on his Taser. When he saw Jay Greenwood he relaxed slightly, but Greenwood crossed the room, arm pulled, ready to strike.

'Back off,' Sol warned.

Greenwood launched his body at Sol, knocking him backwards, pinning him to the floor.

'How much did you get paid?' He grabbed Sol's hair and smashed the back of his head into the tiled floor. 'How fucking much?'

The blow rang through Sol's skull and black stars crowded his vision. When Greenwood cracked his head for a second time, Sol bit his tongue and tasted blood. As he prepared himself for the third wave, he clasped his fingers around his weapon, dragged it out and pushed it against Greenwood's chest.

'Taser,' he shouted. Greenwood still had his fingers in Sol's hair. 'Fifty thousand volts to your heart.'

Greenwood looked down at the black and yellow gun Sol aimed at him. He was raging but he wasn't stupid.

'Move away.' Sol's voice was calm. 'Now.'

Greenwood lifted himself from Sol and sat back on his heels. His eyes were on the Taser but he wasn't scared, not really. Jay Greenwood didn't do scared.

'Liberty asked me to stay with Frankie,' Sol said.

Greenwood's eyes snapped from the Taser to Sol's face. 'Why?' He looked around the room as if he might find her there. 'Where is she?'

Sol sat up, rubbing the back of his head with his free hand. There was a lump the size of an egg but no cut. Nothing wet.

'A and E,' he said. Greenwood's face fell. 'Someone was here. Presumably for Frankie. Liberty fought him off.'

Greenwood was on his feet, stumbling for the door. At the last second, he turned to Frankie.

'I told her I would stay here and watch him,' Sol told Greenwood. 'And that's what I'm going to do.'

As Liberty limped from her cubicle, the next patient passed her, holding an arm at an unnatural angle, his T-shirt riding up to reveal a pink football of a belly. He spoke to the doctor in what sounded like Polish and the doctor in turn mimed for him to sit on the bed.

Liberty pressed her palm to the side of her neck. Her throat felt as if she'd swallowed a stone and it was stuck sideways.

'Thank you,' Liberty mumbled at the doctor, but he was already snapping on a fresh pair of latex gloves.

When she reached the waiting area, the full glory of Accident and Emergency greeted her. A woman in a wheelchair gagged into a Tesco carrier bag. A huge extended family clamoured around a man with a bloody tea-towel covering his hand, taking it in turns to look underneath and grimace at the damage. The only thing missing was a kid with a plant pot stuck on his head.

By the time she'd reached the exit, the walls were closing in on her and suddenly she was in a box. She leaned heavily against the glass, taking deep breaths.

'Get out of the way,' a woman shouted as she ran in, a child on her hip.

Liberty staggered to the left, her hand still outstretched. She needed to sit, but also to leave. Gently, she brought her fingertips to the bruises on her neck. The man's hands had been strong, like a pair of pliers. She shuddered.

Outside, night had fallen and car lights scudded past, forcing Liberty to shield her eyes. She needed to get back to ICU, to Frankie and Sol, but her feet didn't want to move. She couldn't bear another second on her own, yet her own body rebelled against her.

At last, when she thought she might have to sink to her knees, she saw a figure charge towards her. Black shirt, black trousers, black hair.

'Jay,' she cried, voice little more than a whisper.

He threw his arms around her, lifting her from the floor and she buried her nose in his neck, like a cat. 'What happened, Lib?'

She knew she'd have to give him the details. Just not yet. 'Is Sol still with Frankie?'

'That copper is up there. Connolly.'

'That is Sol, you muppet.'

'We should get back.' Jay slid a hand into hers. 'Whatever his name is, I don't trust him as far as I can throw him.'

In ICU, Liberty gave the best description of the attacker that she could manage. Jay had wanted her to tell him privately, but several medics and Sol had pointed out that it wasn't just the Greenwoods who had skin the game.

'This ward is full of vulnerable people,' Sol pointed out.

Jay wasn't happy. He wanted to keep the whole business in the family, but Liberty understood that if it had been a nurse and not she who had interrupted the man they, too, might have been attacked.

'We'll get an officer stationed outside Frankie's room,' said Sol.

Jay growled. He had plenty of people who could make a better job of securing the ward, but there was no way they'd be allowed access. He curled his lip as Sol went to make the necessary calls.

'It's for the best, Jay,' said Liberty. 'We can't be here twenty-four seven.' She leaned in. 'Especially if we want to spend any time finding out what's going on.'

That seemed to hit the spot. Jay was not one for standing around and waiting.

'I still say this is down to Paul Hill,' he muttered. 'We should hit back now. Teach him that you do not mess with the Greenwoods.'

His fury was easy to grasp. As the fear gradually seeped away from Liberty, it was fast being replaced by cold anger. Whoever thought they could do this to her family was going to regret their actions. 'Not yet,' she said. 'We need to identify who did this.'

'I'll start asking around,' he said. 'See if your description rings any bells.'

'And I'll ask the police.'

'What?'

'Think about it, Jay,' she said. 'What are the chances of the Organized Crime Unit not having files on all Hill's people? If I can go through them and I see our man,' she snapped her fingers, 'job done.'

'They'll never give you access.'

Liberty glanced at Sol, who was still on the phone. 'You don't have a dog and bark yourself.'

Natasha answered the door in black yoga pants and a cropped top. The skin of her stomach was smooth and firm and tanned.

Amira sucked in her own stomach, covered in stretch marks, and smiled.

'Oh, my God.' Natasha's hand covered her mouth. 'What's happened?'

At first, Amira didn't know what Natasha was talking about, but then she realized what the woman must be thinking. 'It's okay, Natasha.' She stepped forward and placed a hand on Natasha's bare arm. That, too, was smooth. 'Nothing has happened to Sol. Can I come in?'

In the kitchen, Natasha gave one of her tinkly little laughs as she made some herbal tea. 'You scared me right there,' she said, in her strong Russian accent.

'Sorry.'

A lot of the blokes at the nick took the piss out of Sol's choice of wife. They said he'd bought her online. Amira had always refused to laugh at the gags, telling the comedians they were jealous. Sol took it all in his stride.

Natasha handed her a glass mug full of water, containing a teabag on a string that was gradually leaking yellow fluid. It smelt a bit like lemon toilet cleaner.

'It's very good for the digestion,' said Natasha.

Amira nodded and had another sniff. 'Can I talk to you about Sol?' she asked. 'In confidence?'

Natasha nodded. '*Da.*'

There was a photograph in a frame on the wall. Natasha and Sol, sun-kissed and smiling, an expanse of twinkling blue ocean behind them. Natasha caught Amira looking at it.

'What is it you come to say?'

When was the picture taken? On holiday? Maybe their honeymoon? They looked happy. Amira took a sip of the tea. It tasted like hot water with a squirt of lemon toilet cleaner. All day she'd only eaten half a KitKat so her digestion didn't actually need any help.

'Amira?' Natasha gave a pretty frown. 'Please.'

She'd come to destroy Sol's life. Well, that wasn't the aim as such, but that was what would happen if she told his wife he was having an affair.

On the way over to his house, she'd felt so bitter she could taste it on her tongue as she went through the situation repeatedly. Sol had done something bad, but he'd been given an opportunity to make amends. Didn't everyone want that? A chance to right wrongs? The fact that Sol wasn't taking the chance offered to him was even worse than his original transgression. He had to be made to see that there was no other choice. Amira owed him that.

'Sol's a good man,' said Amira.

She'd tried everything else. She'd reasoned with him. She'd argued with him. She'd laid it all out for him. The only thing left was to accelerate the process of revealing his lies in the hope that he might come to his senses.

'Drop the bullshit.' Natasha's frown was no longer pretty. 'Just tell me what's going on.'

Chapter 15

9 March 1990

Tiny's having a flat-warming party. She moved in a couple of days ago and we helped to ferry her stuff from a car she borrowed from her dad's girlfriend's next-door neighbour. There was so much stuff, clothes, records, books, an entire box of plates and cups and that.

When I'm a solicitor, I'm going to get a place of my own and fill it with things like that. I'll buy each of the kids their own bed and let them choose a quilt cover.

Fat Rob has set up a sound system in the lounge and he's blasting out 'All For Lee-Sah'. Tiny's invited all the neighbours so hopefully no one will get the monk on. She skips around the flat, taking pictures of her guests with a Polaroid camera.

The front door opens and a group of girls fall inside, laughing, already pissed by the look of them. One of them is Mrs I-Need-To-Put-Some-Clothes-On and she makes a bee line for Connor, who is rummaging through the records Fat Rob's brought with him. She's had her hair done in loads of little plaits, each end secured with a plastic bead. When she leans in to say something to Connor, the plaits cover both their mouths, like a curtain.

I chew my lip and go to the bathroom. As I'm going inside, Tiny shouts, 'Wait up. I'm not queuing in my own bleeding house.' She pushes me inside. 'Hurry up, I'm bursting.'

'I just want to wash my hands anyway,' I say.

I run them under the tap as Tiny has a wee. There's no soap and no towel so I wipe my hands down the back of my jeans.

'You don't need to worry about that lass, Lib,' Tiny says, pulling a used tissue from her pocket and using it to wipe herself. 'You don't need to worry about any lass to be honest.'

'No?'

She yanks up her trousers, grabs me and makes me stand in front of the mirror. 'You're not blind, Lib.'

I'm not. I see Dad's eyes looking back at me so I turn away.

Tiny dips the tips of her fingers in the stream of cold water and flicks them at my face. 'Connor's been besotted ever since you first set foot in the Galaxy.'

'Shut up.'

Tiny laughs. 'I'm not bloody joking. He drives us all crackers going on and on about you.'

Back in the lounge, Danny's already dancing so I join in. Soon Connor is behind me, hands around my waist, kissing the back of my head.

'How's your mate?' I ask him.

'Not as attractive fully dressed, to be honest.'

I elbow him in the stomach and he pretends to double over. Then he picks me up and carries me to the door. 'Breath of fresh air, Mrs I-Always-Keep-My-Clothes-On?'

We step outside into the cold night and Connor lights a spliff. He takes a few drags and hands it to me.

'You do know I'm joking, Lib?' He's suddenly serious. 'I don't expect you to . . . you know. I'm happy to wait until you're ready.'

I nod and take a drag. The weed crashes through me, immediately making me light-headed. I giggle and he kisses me. I love this boy.

'I am ready,' I say.

He's still got his lips on mine, but he's not kissing me any more. He's just sort of stuck, like he doesn't know what to do next.

I step back. 'I said I'm ready to have sex, Connor. Tonight, if that's okay with you.'

BANG TO RIGHTS

The look on his face is an absolute picture and I'm laughing hard when Tiny comes out of the flat, waving her camera. 'Say cheese.'

The photograph slides from the slot and Tiny blows on it. There I am, the biggest smile on my face. And there's Connor looking bewildered.

Present day

As Sol drove Liberty home, she regained control of herself. She damped down the fear and the anger until they were a compact ball in her gut. She could manage the discomfort like she always had.

He took out a packet of Marlboro Lights. 'Do you mind?'

When she shook her head, he opened his window and lit up, cheeks sinking in as he took a deep drag. 'It's been a really long couple of days,' he said.

When they got to Empire Rise, he pulled up outside her house. She didn't bother to ask him how he knew where she lived. 'Do you want to come in?' she asked. Her voice had improved. Now she just sounded as if she were on the tail end of a bout of flu. 'There's a bottle of Jack Daniel's with our names on it.'

The house was in darkness, and when Liberty turned on the lights, there was no sign of Dax. She showed Sol into the sitting room, then checked the kitchen and Dax's bedroom. No discarded bowls of cereal. No T-shirts draped over any chairs. No towels left in a wet heap on the floor.

She poured out two generous measures of bourbon and slid ice cubes into both. 'What time is it?' she asked.

'Just gone three.'

Where the hell was Dax? A few weeks ago she'd have started to worry, maybe gone out to look for him, but there wasn't enough head space for that right now. He was sixteen and ten times more street smart than most. With any luck he was holed up with some girl, telling her how she reminded him of Rihanna.

She handed a glass to Sol, clinked hers against it and took a long drink before she'd even sat down. It burned her already sore throat but she didn't care. When she'd taken a second gulp, she noticed that Sol had already drained his glass.

'I'll get the bottle,' she said. She retrieved it from the kitchen, sloshed more into both glasses and plonked it on the coffee table. 'Can I ask a favour?'

'Name it.'

'I want to check your files on Paul Hill's people.'

He picked up his glass, voice husky from the alcohol. 'You're assuming we have them.'

'I am, yeah.'

'And if you find the man you're looking for,' he pushed her hair to one side to reveal the still livid fingermarks, 'will you tell me so I can arrest him?'

The bourbon zipped through her and she smiled. She had no idea what she'd do if she found the man she was looking for. She might let Sol deal with him. Or she might tell Jay. Alternatively, she might hunt him down herself.

'You can't drive now, Officer Connolly.' She topped up his glass. 'You'll have to stay over.'

A wood pigeon outside the window woke Sol with its repetitious song. Ooh-ooh-oh. Ooh-ooh-oh. He'd cheerfully take his Taser to the little bastard.

The lack of any throbbing in his head told Sol he was still half cut. No hangover yet, but it was in the post. He needed to pee but didn't want to wake Liberty, who was still asleep next to him, hair spread across the pillow, the weals on her neck angry.

He reached to the floor where he'd tossed his phone. So many missed calls. Hassani. Natasha. Bucky. He was the most popular man alive.

186

BANG TO RIGHTS

When his bladder pointed out that he wasn't seventeen any more, Sol slipped from the bed as quietly as possible and padded out to the bathroom. As he took a leak, he prodded the lump on the back of his head. The fact that he wasn't in agony was more confirmation that he was still drunk.

When he'd finished, he opened the window above the sink and leaned out to gulp some fresh air. The garden below was covered with white droplets of dew. A man appeared from next door, stopping on the path as he checked his pockets. From above, Sol could see his hair was thinning on top. He wore a white shirt and a green fleece bearing the name of a local garden centre that Sol had once visited to buy some tubs that Natasha wanted to put on their patio. It had been packed with people mooching around, as if choosing a lavender plant was the highlight of their weekend. There was even a café offering home-made cakes, freshly filled sandwiches and jacket potatoes (who would spend actual money on a cup of tea and a tuna baguette in a garden centre when they were only ten minutes from home?) and every table was full.

Sol shook his head. Other people were a mystery to him. Not the criminals he put away. He got them. Their thought processes were understandable and predictable, which was why he was good at catching them. But supposedly normal folk? Sol had no idea what made them tick.

He washed his hands and reached for the towel hanging from a silver ring on the wall. A couple of spares were folded neatly on top of a wooden stack of drawers. And on top of the spares a can of Lynx lay casually on its side, as if someone had used it and tossed it there, too lazy to put it away.

Sol picked it up and found that it was almost full.

He opened the first drawer of the stack and found cleansers, cotton pads, and tubes of serum by someone called Eve Lom. Below that was a drawer of make-up: pencils, mascaras, a bag of tiny pieces of sponge cut into triangles. The bottom drawer, however, contained what he was looking for: hair wax, clippers, a bottle of aftershave by David Beckham.

Sol shut the drawer, left the bathroom and moved along the landing to the bedroom next to Liberty's. He pushed open the door and found the spare room. It was neat, the bed made but unused, an empty suitcase placed on top.

He went to the last bedroom on the landing and entered. It was as if it didn't belong in that house. The floor was littered with jeans and trainers and free weights, the duvet half on, half off the bed. Sol counted three mugs and four bowls crammed on a shelf. The curtains were shut and the room smelt of testosterone.

'What are you doing?'

Sol turned and found Liberty watching him. She'd put on a blue silk kimono, tied with a belt, that skimmed her thighs.

'You're snooping.' She answered her own question.

'Habit,' Sol replied.

'And what have you uncovered, Officer Connolly?'

'That you don't live alone.'

Liberty tightened the belt around her waist. 'I never said I did.' She hadn't told him anything much about her living arrangements. Why would she? The elephant in the room had always been Sol's wife. 'Anything else?' she asked.

'That I'm a little old for your tastes.'

The taxi driver had the radio on full blast, laughing as a DJ tried to convince a girl band to reveal the colour of their knickers.

'Love it,' he repeated on a loop. 'Love it.'

Sol closed his eyes and tried not to groan. When they reached the nick, the driver leaned over the back of his seat. 'Signing in, mate?'

'What?'

'Bail conditions to sign in every morning.' The driver grinned. 'I get a lot of you in here. A tag would be easier, eh?'

Sol slapped a fiver into the driver's hand and got out.

'Do you want me to wait?' asked the driver.

'Nah,' Sol replied. 'Something tells me I'm gonna be here a while.'

Hassani was already in the incident room, fiddling with the air-conditioning. According to Sol's phone she'd called five times. Only one time fewer than Natasha. She lifted up her plait and clipped it to the back of her head. Something was getting Amira Hassani hot under the collar.

'Morning,' he said.

'This is knackered and it's boiling in here.' Hassani smacked the top of the unit. Sol's mother used to do the same when their telly was on the blink. 'I can't work like this.' Her cheeks were pink as she looked Sol up and down. 'You didn't go home last night, I take it.'

'You wanted me to get inside enemy lines.' He logged onto the system and began to scroll through the files for Paul Hill and the people who were known to be or suspected of working for him.

'Have you spoken to Natasha?' Hassani asked.

'Nope.'

Hassani gave up on the air-conditioning and marched over to the water dispenser. She grabbed a paper cup, filled it and took a drink. 'It's not even cold.' She flicked the tap and an air bubble rushed through the barrel with a loud gurgle. 'Did you show Chapman the witness statement?'

'Not yet.'

'You had all night, Sol.'

He drafted a quick email and attached some files. 'I was busy.'

Up on the clear board, Hassani had tacked a picture of a girl. She was pretty but her eyes were harsh, on constant lookout for trouble. Sol had seen those eyes a thousand times on kids who knew better than to expect good things. He'd seen those eyes staring out at him from all the Greenwoods, including Liberty.

'Look, I get it. The woman was attacked and you feel bad about that.' Hassani wrote the words 'Tia Rainsford' next to the girl's face. 'I feel bad about it. I'm not made of stone.' She threw the pen onto her desk where it bounced and fell onto the floor. 'But I'm not going to get distracted and neither are you.'

Sol sent the email to his personal address.

'And if you need something to help you concentrate,' said Hassani, 'call Natasha.'

'Are you threatening me, Amira?'

'It's got way past that point, Sol. I'm just pointing out that if you want to salvage your life right now, you need to stop pissing about.'

Up the road from the strip club, Sun Studio – 'Yorkshire's Premier Tanning Salon' – was being boarded up. Clearly there wasn't enough money in skin cancer.

It was mid-morning and clammy, another storm brewing, and Liberty felt flushed. She'd tried to camouflage her injuries with make-up, but had decided that a beige neck looked even worse. Given the concealer would now be dissolving, she'd made the right choice.

Inside the Cherry, Crystal stood at the bar and barked orders at Len.

'Where's Mel?' Liberty asked.

'Good question,' Crystal replied. She lifted Liberty's hair, as if it were a dirty sock, checked the damage and dropped it.

'You heard what happened?' Liberty asked.

'Jay called me. He's absolutely screwing. Worse than I've ever known him.'

A group of girls arrived, including the small one with the hair-piece. She scanned the club.

'He's not here,' Liberty shouted over. 'With his wife, I expect.' Liberty held out her hand and tapped her ring finger. 'You get yourself ready or look for another job.'

The girl pouted and stomped away.

'Maybe it's Mel who should look for another job.' Crystal snorted. 'You could take over.'

'I work for Raj.'

Crystal's mobile rang and she pressed it to her cheek. 'Harry?' While her husband spoke, Crystal tapped her foot in irritation. 'Where the fuck have you been?' She pressed her finger in her free ear and moved to the door at the back of the bar, kicking it open. 'You picked a really bad time, Harry.'

She slipped outside, leaving Liberty with Len.

'I've no idea where Mel is before you ask,' he said.

Harry, Dax and now Mel. What was the story? Wasn't there enough going on without the Lord Lucan routines?

Crystal returned, face like a werewolf's at full moon. 'I've got to go, Lib. Can you hold the fort?'

'Not bloody likely.'

'It's important,' Crystal retorted.

Something about Crystal's tone told Liberty this wasn't just a pissing contest as to who had more pressing things to do. If she was worried about Harry, then something was up.

'I can do a couple of hours,' said Liberty. 'Then I've got to find the bloke who was at the hospital before Jay loses it completely.'

Crystal slid her phone into her back pocket and grabbed her car keys from the bar. 'That copper going to help, is he?' Liberty nodded. 'Be careful there. No one ever does anything for nothing.'

★ ★ ★

Amira had never drunk alcohol in her life and had never really been tempted. Watching her colleagues getting pissed in the Feathers had only ever made her convinced her decision was the right one. Their sweaty-cheese faces and thick, slurred voices were hardly an advertisement.

As she watched Bucky describe a drunken brawl to the magistrate in Court One, she wondered why anyone bothered.

'The defendant, having been evicted from the nightclub by security, then broke into a neighbouring building site where he stole a spade.' Bucky read directly from her file. Somehow the mechanical tone made more impact. 'He then returned to the Vox and proceeded to attempt to smash down the door with the spade.'

The man in the dock played with the end of his tie, which Amira thought she recognized from the local comprehensive. It was difficult to tell if he was even listening.

'When one of the security staff came out to stop the disturbance, the defendant attempted to hit him with the spade but fortunately missed his footing and banged his head against the kerb, knocking himself unconscious and losing several teeth.'

The magistrate asked a question and Bucky riffled through her papers. Amira had been hoping for a word, but this wasn't going to be a quick hearing.

The door to the back of the court opened and Fazeel slid in. Quietly, he approached the advocate's bench and placed a bright pink Post-it note on top of a file, before slipping away. Amira followed him.

'Fazeel?'

He smiled at her. '*Assalaam alaikum*, sister.'

'*Wa alaikum assalaam*,' she replied. 'Can I have a word?'

'I'm in a bit of a rush, to be honest,' he said. 'I need to call the lab about a missing swab. If Bucky has to ask for another adjournment she'll string me up.' He rolled his eyes. 'I sometimes wonder why I didn't pick a nice easy job like bomb disposal. If you can talk and walk?'

Amira forced a smile and tried not to notice the trickle of sweat squirming down her back.

'Can I ask about the Delaney case?' she said, as they strode towards the CPS room.

'Sure.'

'Have the defence made any recent applications?'

Fazeel unlocked and held open the door for Amira and she skirted past him, hoping he couldn't smell her. 'I don't think so but I couldn't be certain. Why not just ask Sol?'

'He's not contactable today,' Amira replied.

'Right.' Fazeel didn't seem suspicious. 'Give me a second.' He flipped the lid on a laptop and tapped. Amira kept her back to the window in case a dark patch had appeared on her blouse. The glass amplified the sunlight and made her skin prickle. 'Nope. Raj hasn't done anything as far as I can see.'

Amira nodded. It was possible that Singh & Co were behind schedule because of the shooting of Frankie Greenwood. Or it was possible that Sol had lied.

'I have a sore pussy.'

Liberty crossed her arms and sighed.

A dancer who went by the name of Cherish but was actually called Agnetta cupped her crotch. 'Terrible pains.'

In the changing room, the other girls clucked in sympathy.

'Do you want to go home then?' Liberty asked.

A dark-haired girl, sitting in front of the mirror, applying indus-trial quantities of foundation to a love bite, took a sharp breath.

'I cannot afford,' said Cherish.

Liberty counted to ten in her head. 'So, what do you want me to do? I'm all out of magical pussy-healing powers.'

Cherish moaned, one hand still between her legs.

'Have one of these.' Liberty pulled a packet of Nurofen from her bag. 'And put a smile on it.'

She didn't wait for the next round of complaints but stalked out of the room.

Downstairs at the bar, Sol was waiting for her.

'How did you know I was here?' she asked.

'I took a guess,' he said.

Liberty went behind the bar and poured them both an orange juice. Then she lifted up a bottle of vodka. 'Hair of the dog?'

'You don't know how close I am to saying yes,' Sol replied. 'Can we talk?'

Liberty told Len to keep an eye on things and led Sol into the back office. It smelt of disinfectant. Someone had given it a thorough clean after Nathan Osborne. She lifted a box of fur-lined handcuffs from the chair and realized she didn't feel embarrassed.

'Sit.' She plonked the box in the corner and perched on the end of the desk, Crystal-style. 'Tell me what's on your mind.'

Sol lowered himself into the chair, the glass of orange juice still in one hand. The other brushed the back of his head and he winced. 'What's going on with us, Lib?'

She hadn't seen that one coming. Not that she hadn't been asking herself the same question, but because she had assumed it was a subject from which he would want to steer well clear.

Sol stood and placed his untouched glass of juice on the table next to Liberty. Then he pressed a hand onto each of her knees and leaned close. 'Do you even like me?'

'Are you serious?'

He started slightly when music began in the main part of the club. 'I am.'

'I don't often have sex with men I don't like.'

'So that's what this is? Just sex?' he asked.

She slid a hand around his neck. 'We're sitting on different sides of the fence, Sol.'

'I thought the Greenwoods' business had nothing to do with you?' he said.

She rubbed a finger against his hairline. 'I *am* a Greenwood.'

This was his chance to walk away and she wouldn't blame him if he did. It was no longer about the company she kept, but about who she was. He stared at her and she could feel his breath on her mouth. 'I can't help what I am, Sol.'

'You don't have any choice in the matter?'

'I thought I did,' she answered. 'I thought I could be a part of this family but stand on the sidelines.' She laughed. 'Crystal told me that was bullshit.'

'What happened to the kid who wanted to get away from all this and make a new life for herself?' he asked.

'She's been there, done that, worn the T-shirt,' she said, 'and it doesn't fit.' Silently, she challenged him to tell her that she was wrong and didn't belong here. That he'd been attracted to a good person with a moral compass and this woman in the back room of a strip club, only recently wiped clean of blood, wasn't someone he wanted to be with.

He took one hand off her knee. There was the door right behind him and all he had to do was walk through it. He must know that she wouldn't stop him. Instead he reached into his jacket for his mobile. 'I've got the files you asked for.'

'What?'

He tapped the screen and accessed his emails. 'Paul Hill's men.' He sat on the table next to her and held out his phone. 'If you ID the man who attacked you, will you let me arrest him?'

'I can hardly stop you.'

He raised an eyebrow. They both knew what he meant.

'But I need to speak to him first,' she said. 'I've got to find out if he shot Frankie and if Paul Hill gave the order. If I don't do that, matters might get out of hand. I'm doing my best to avoid that. Do you understand?'

The phone was still in Sol's hand, his thumb hovering over the icon to open his emails.

'I know I'm taking advantage of our situation asking for this,' she said.

He laughed. 'Our *situation*?'

'Well, what would you call it, smartarse?'

'God only knows.'

She laughed back. 'All I'm saying is that I know it's not right to ask you for this.'

'But you're asking all the same.'

'Yeah.'

He sighed and opened an email sent from his police account. 'Just promise me that you won't let Jay kill him.'

Chapter 16

24 March 1990
It's been over six weeks since I've seen our Crystal and Frankie and it's doing my nut in.

I keep ringing the social worker and Miss Chapman, but they just say the same thing. There's an ongoing investigation and I have to wait for the outcome of that before I can get a contact visit.

Carl says I need to stop bothering folk about it.

'Bothering folk?' Tiny grabs the fag from between Fat Rob's lips and takes an angry puff. 'This is your little sister they're talking about.'

The Galaxy's busy for once, with people queuing up to buy tickets for DreamSkool. The organizers have only let a few places sell them, so Tiny's helping behind the till. They'll be sold out soon but we're all on the guest list so it doesn't matter to us.

'Can't you just turn up?' Fat Rob asks.

'They'd never let me in,' I say.

A customer holds out a fiver and Fat Rob takes it in fingers stained burgundy from putting henna in his hair. It doesn't really suit him, but I'm not going to say anything.

'I bet the foster carers wouldn't have the bottle to send you packing,' he says. 'Them sort of people never do.'

'I bet they would.'

He takes the fag back from Tiny. 'Then you'd be in no worse position than you are now, would you?'

He's right. What punishment can anyone give me? They've already suspended contact. I can't even ring the kids. I keep worrying that Crystal thinks I'm not even trying. If I could just see her for a few seconds, so that she knows I haven't abandoned her, it would be better than this.

Connor arrives and puts on a new EP.

'I'm off to see Crystal and Frankie,' I tell him. 'I'm sick of waiting for all this to get sorted out so I'm just going round there.'

'Good idea,' he says. 'I'll come with you.'

Fat Rob sells the last ticket and shouts his apologies to the folk still waiting. People groan but most hang around anyway, listening to the music, looking at the records. Fat Rob's going to do well today.

'What time do the kids go to bed?' Connor asks.

I don't have much of an idea, but foster carers usually like to get the kids out of the way as early as possible. 'Probably before eight o'clock,' I say.

'Right then, we'll turn up tonight around seven when they're bound to be in,' he says. 'Your Crystal might even open the door.'

I don't know why I haven't thought of this before. I always stick to the rules and look where it's got me. Precisely nowhere. From now on I'm going to bend them and break them, if that's what it takes. What can Social Services do? Arrest me? It's not actually against the law to knock on a door, is it?

'Come back to mine now,' says Connor. 'I'll make you some tea before we set off.'

From the grin on his face, I know he's got more than sausage and chips on his mind.

'Where's your mam?'

'Visiting some woman from church who's had a hip replacement,' he says. 'Won't be back until tomorrow.'

I kiss him. I like having sex with Connor and I'm not embarrassed about it. He makes it all feel perfectly normal, like it's just what you do if you love someone. Not like the lads at Orchard Grove who bug all the girls to let them do it, then talk about it non-stop with everybody else. Which is chuffing boring over your Rice Krispies.

Later in his bed, he twists a piece of my hair round and round his finger.

'You're bloody lovely, you are,' he says.

'You're not so bad yourself,' I reply.

'I wish you could stay here all the time.'

I laugh. 'I don't think your mam would be too happy about that.'

'Not here, then.' He kisses my nose. 'But somewhere we could, you know, be together.'

I look at the ceiling. I'd love nothing better than to get a flat with Connor when I leave care, but I won't have any money, will I? Carl's talked to me about going to a place called a 'halfway house'. Halfway to where, I've no idea.

'Is there enough time to get a bath?' I ask him.

Connor checks his watch. 'If I get the water on right this second.'

I squeeze his arm. He knows I love to have a bath here and sit in the bubbles with no one banging on the door to tell me to hurry up. He sighs, but he's not really pissed off and gets out of bed to turn on the immersion heater.

While he's out of the room, I reach onto the floor for my knickers. When I can't find them, I bend down to look under the bed. It's dusty under there and big balls of fluff wink at me. Connor's mam keeps their house spotless but he bans her from his room as best he can. She's not been under here with a Hoover in years by the look of it.

At the back, near the wall, there's a sandwich box. It's blue with a clear lid. I dread to think how long it's been there and what sort of minging remains it's sheltering. Mrs O would have a breakdown if she knew it was nestled there, breeding germs and attracting mice.

I slide off the bed and reach for the box, my fingertips only just managing to grip the lip of the lid so I can pull it towards me. As I peel it off, I'm expecting to retch, but instead I just sit there, stark naked on my knees, staring at what's inside.

Drugs. Weed, pills and powder to be exact. All ready in their little plastic baggies. There's also a huge roll of notes, held together with an elastic band.

When Connor bounces back into the bedroom, there isn't time to push the box back where it belongs. Anyway, I'm not sure I want to do that.

'Hot running water in approximately twenty minutes, my lady.' He stops when he sees me. 'What are you doing with that, Lib?'

'What are you doing with it more like?'

'Just put it back,' he says.

'I will,' I say. 'When you tell me what it's doing here.'

'Come on, Lib, you of all people know the score.'

Me of all people? Why me? I don't take drugs and he knows that. I smoke a bit of weed here and there but that's it. I don't even really get pissed that much.

'Look,' he says, 'it's a few odds and sods for people who want to enjoy themselves when they're out. People who know exactly what they're doing.' He shrugs. 'I'm not pushing heroin.'

I look down at the contents of the box. People we know take this stuff all the time. Tiny does. Fat Rob does. Danny's never off it. And looking back now it's bloody obvious they're all getting it off Connor. Even Vicky tried to tell me, for God's sake. I mean, where did I think Connor got all his money from?

He sits next to me on the floor in his pants and takes the box from me. He puts the lid back on and slides it under the bed.

'It's illegal,' I say.

He laughs and touches my cheek. 'Lucky for me my girlfriend's gonna be a solicitor.'

'Don't even think of coming to me when you get yourself nicked.'

He laughs even harder. 'Like that, is it?' He stands up and pulls me to my feet. 'I'd better stop then and get myself a real job.'

'Yes, you bloody well had,' I agree.

'And you'd better get yourself a bath,' he says. 'We don't want to get to your Crystal's too late and give them foster carers any excuse to stop you seeing her.'

Present day
Kane Lester, a.k.a. K–Dog, had grown up on the Crosshills. His father had jumped bail after he'd been arrested for GBH and had never been seen again. Funny that, seeing as how his first wife and six kids still lived in his hometown of Kingston, Jamaica.

K–Dog had first been nicked at twelve, done his first lump at fifteen. However, since his last stretch he'd stayed out of trouble for three years. Working for Paul Hill was either keeping him on the straight and narrow or the coppers Hill kept in his back pocket were earning their keep.

Liberty had tried not to react when K–Dog's photo loaded on the screen, but Sol had felt the tightness in her shoulders. Thirty-two, handsome, with high cheekbones the colour of hot chocolate, Kane Lester was about to find himself on the wrong side of the Greenwood clan.

Sol should put a stop to whatever was about to happen. All those years ago in police training it had been drilled into them that their job was to protect and serve, not to make moral judgements. He'd believed it too. And not just as a green–arsed cadet, naïve and hopeful, but throughout his career, mostly because it just seemed logical. He laughed as he put his key in his front door. Where was his logic now?

He hadn't been home since yesterday lunchtime, but immediately sensed something was wrong. For a start, there was a cold breeze coming from the kitchen, as if the window had been left open (and that was something Natasha, raised in one of the most violent cities in the world, would never do).

His first thought was that they'd been burgled and instinct kicked in.

'Police,' he called, and removed his Taser. 'Police.'

He marched down the hallway and opened the kitchen door fully. There was nobody there but not long ago someone had completely trashed the place. Sol sucked in a breath. The windows were smashed, the cupboard doors flung open, a couple were off their hinges and the floor was a carpet of broken plates and glasses.

He pushed aside Natasha's favourite casserole dish with his boot. The crack across the bottom opened up and the dish fell apart. No more baked beetroot. Every cloud.

Suddenly he heard a noise upstairs. The bastard was still in the house. Anger ran through Sol, like an electric shock, and he raced from the kitchen and up the stairs.

'You have so picked the wrong house, pal,' he roared, and kicked open the bedroom door.

The room was in a similar state to the kitchen, with the mirror shattered, clothes ripped and thrown in a heap on the bed, shower gel poured over them, then the bottle thrown against the wall, leaving a lurid green smear.

He raised his Taser to the sound of someone in the en-suite bathroom. He needed to get himself under control or he was going to do some serious damage.

'Get out here now,' he shouted.

The door opened and his mouth gaped at the sight of Natasha, mascara running down her cheeks, hair wild and a pair of scissors in one hand, his polka-dot tie in the other.

'Tash?' He hadn't called her that in a long time. 'What the hell?'

She pointed the scissors at him. 'Stay away from me, Sol Connolly.'

He raised both hands, realized he was still holding the Taser and lowered that hand slowly, placing the stun gun back in its holster.

'Natasha?'

'You promised me, Sol,' she shouted. 'You swore.'

'What? What did I swear?'

Spit flew from Natasha's mouth. 'That things were different with me and you. That you were done with all the shit you pulled on Angie.'

Sol knew he should feel panic coursing through him, but he didn't. He looked around the room at the chaos he'd brought on himself and felt numb. 'Did Amira tell you?' he asked.

'She didn't need to,' said Natasha. 'She came here all worried for you. "Oh, Sol is acting so strange, can you have a small word with him?" I knew exactly what she was not saying to me. Don't try to deny anything.'

He didn't intend to.

As if she had just remembered she was holding the tie, she snipped it in two with the scissors. The lower half fell and Natasha threw the piece she was holding at Sol. 'I hope she is worth all this.' Natasha waved her arms wildly around the room, then let the scissors drop to the floor. 'Otherwise, you've made the biggest mistake of your life.'

Liberty found the flat easily enough above Tip Top Pizza just off Carter Street. The bins outside released a smell that would ward off death itself. As she lifted her knuckle to knock the door, she felt the weight of the gun shift in her waistband. She'd taken it from the safe at the Cherry after Sol had left, wondering if she had lost her mind. Now she was glad she had it. Insurance, she told herself. Nothing more than insurance.

The door opened and Mel stared out. 'What do you want?' She'd clearly been at the bottle.

'I need a favour,' said Liberty.

Mel nodded for her to come through. Following her inside, Liberty almost laughed at the fluffy slippers the older woman was wearing. At the club, Mel only ever tottered around in heels of at least four inches.

'Can I get you something?' Mel asked.

'Why don't we both have a coffee?' Liberty replied.

The inside of the flat was surprisingly homely, and a wooden heart swung from a cupboard handle in the kitchen. 'All you need is love,' it declared. Not true, but a nice sentiment all the same.

Mel brought out two cheery yellow mugs and spooned in some Nescafé. 'You know I didn't mean anything bad to happen to Frankie,' she said. 'I mean, he gets right on my tits but I wouldn't want him to get hurt.' She pulled a carton of milk from the fridge and sniffed it. Satisfied, she poured it into the mugs. 'I suppose you've told Jay what I did?'

'Why would I do that?'

Mel shrugged and heaped sugar into the coffee without asking. 'Families shouldn't keep secrets, don't you think?'

'I'm no expert on families.'

Mel cackled and clinked her mug against Liberty's. 'Me neither.'

'Never been married?'

Mel shook her head. 'Nah. Blokes are just a liability mostly.'

'Kids?'

Mel looked at her feet. 'I had a girl. She was a pretty one like you.' She smiled to herself. 'But her personality was more like your Crystal's.'

'What happened?'

'We weren't exactly the Waltons, you know what I mean?'

Liberty laughed. 'Oh, yeah.'

'Jay helped me try to find her once, but we didn't have any joy,' she said. 'She probably doesn't want to be found. You of all people know how that goes.'

Liberty put down her coffee. There might be a million reasons why Mel's daughter had taken off and all of them or none of them might be Mel's fault. More likely, some of them were and some of them weren't.

Without warning Mel kicked off her slippers and slid her feet into a pair of skyscraper black ankle boots covered with gold zips. 'Right then,' she said. 'Are you going to tell me why you've got a gun in your pocket? Or are you just pleased to see me?'

The DCI's room was airless and a cloud of his aftershave hung low and thick.

He waved Amira in, but didn't offer her coffee.

'Anything to report on Chapman?' he asked.

'It's been tricky, sir,' Amira replied. 'Her brother was shot.'

'Are the family cooperating?'

Amira felt dog-tired. After seeing Natasha last night, she hadn't been able to sleep, and when she finally nodded off around three, Rahim had woken up screaming. It had taken an hour to settle him back down in her own bed, where he'd spent the rest of the night squirming and farting.

'The family say they don't know anything, sir, and Frankie Greenwood is still unconscious.'

'Usual wall of silence from all the witnesses?'

Amira nodded.

'And nothing to prove Liberty Chapman is involved in any criminal activity?' the DCI asked.

'We need more time, sir. I'm sure if we keep watching her she'll slip up.'

The DCI smiled. 'I said eyes to the end of the week, Amira, and that's what I meant.' He put up a hand to prevent further discussion. 'After tomorrow, if you don't have anything concrete, you leave the lawyer alone.' His smile faded. 'You understand what I'm saying here?'

The phone on his desk rang and he answered, turning his chair from Amira. She was dismissed.

'Are you sure about this?'

Mel ignored Liberty and indicated that she should pull the car over outside a primary school. They were using Mel's little Citroën, so as not to draw attention, but Mel was still far too pissed to drive. The kids in the school were on their lunch break, racing around and screaming, each wearing a little white hat with a flap covering the neck like mini Foreign Legionnaires. One boy took his off and threw it high in the air with a whoop. Liberty smiled. Frankie would have been the first kid to do that.

'Tyson Fitzgerald,' a playground assistant, her own head bare, bellowed. 'Put that back on before you get sunstroke.'

Liberty killed the engine and scanned the street. She spotted a teenage lad in a bus stop, checking his phone.

'Him,' Mel said.

'He might be waiting for the thirty-two,' said Liberty.

Mel sighed. 'How about you just shut up?'

Liberty watched the boy. He looked like Dax, all baseball cap and lip ring. Once again, she wondered where Dax was. Please, God, he hadn't headed back down to London without telling her.

After a few minutes, another lad cycled around the corner and skidded to a halt at the bus stop. Mel had been right all along. The two boys exchanged a few words, laughed about something and shook hands. Then the second lad cycled away. They could be mates shooting the breeze, but Liberty knew full well that things had been passed between them. The first younger had handed over the drugs and the second had slid across the cash.

Soon another younger arrived, a girl this time, and the same routine took place.

'How long will we have to wait?' Liberty asked.

'I'd say another swap at most.' Mel flicked the air freshener hanging from her rear-view mirror. 'Hill won't let young-fella-me-lad have a lot of food on him.'

'Then if he gets caught he can say it's a bit of personal?'

Mel snorted. 'You think Paul Hill gives a shiny shit if any of these kids do time? They don't carry much so that if they caught Hill won't find himself too badly out of pocket.'

Five minutes later, the girl returned. The lad said something that made her give him the finger. Then they took care of business and she cycled away, shouting, 'In your dreams.'

Exactly as Mel had predicted, the lad didn't wait for another deal, but got on his phone. When he'd finished speaking, he sauntered up the street towards the bookie's. An old man was outside having a fag, his trousers slightly too short, displaying his towelling socks. He gave the younger a stare, ground out his fag and went back inside. The younger spat on the pavement and waited.

At last a man came out and Liberty's chest constricted.

'That him?' Mel asked.

Not yet trusting herself to speak, Liberty just gave a tight nod. She could feel his hands around her neck as she gasped for air.

'Jay was bang on, then,' said Mel. 'This is all down to Paul Hill.' She shook her head. 'Lord knows what he'll do.'

'Which is why my brother's not invited to this particular party,' said Liberty. Outside the bookie's, K-Dog and the boy spoke briefly before shaking hands. 'I'm surprised he's risking his arse, carrying drugs.'

Mel tutted. 'He's not. K-Dog takes the money. The younger's got to go to one of the flats for more gear. Watch.'

As the bookie's door shut behind K-Dog, the younger didn't go back to the bus stop, but cut across the road and headed down an alleyway that led to the estate beyond.

'All your man's got to do is sit in there, watching Sky Sports, and collect his pretty green,' said Mel. 'Nice work if you can get it.' She turned to Liberty and grinned. 'Shall we ruin his day?'

'Let me do all the talking,' said Liberty. Mel mimed zipping up her mouth, then held out her open palm. Liberty reached into her waistband and brought out the gun. 'You've handled one before, I take it?'

Mel rolled her eyes. Of course she could use a gun. She checked it was loaded, removed the safety and slipped it into the inside pocket of her jacket.

'Just so we're clear, Mel,' said Liberty, 'we're not here to shoot him.'

'I'm not a complete idiot.'

'We get the answers we need, then I call Sol,' said Liberty. 'K-Dog, or whatever he calls himself, can rot in jail.'

Sol was on his second pint when Hassani arrived. He knocked back a double Jack Daniel's and took a long drink of lager.

'Is that a good idea?' she asked.

'I can't think of a better one.'

It was a busy lunchtime in the Feathers. Someone's birthday, by the look of it. A big group of uniform was laughing and ordering food at the bar. Sol should probably get himself something to eat.

'I didn't tell Natasha anything.'

'You just gave her a great big hint,' Sol answered. 'And she worked the rest out herself.'

Hassani rubbed her hand across her face. She looked knackered and grubby. There were crusty bits at the corner of each eye and her lips were dry, skin flaking off.

'Can you talk her round?' she asked.

Sol laughed. His house was wrecked, his clothes cut to shreds. 'I think that's highly unlikely.' He lifted his pint to Hassani. 'Still, you got what you wanted. My life in ruins.'

Hassani shook her head. Her hair was greasy and needed a brush. Sol could almost feel sorry for her. 'That is not what I wanted, Sol, and you know it.'

'Do I?'

'You know full well that I just wanted you to do your job like you've always done. Like you taught me to do.' She tapped the table with her finger. 'If the shoe were on the other foot and I was shagging Jay Greenwood, what would you have said? "No harm done, Amira, enjoy yourself." No, you bloody well would not.'

Sol finished the pint and burped. The alcohol sat on top of last night's, separated only by the picture of Natasha's face as he'd left the bedroom. 'None of it matters now anyway.'

Hassani jumped to her feet, her chair clattering away behind her. She grabbed Sol's empty glass and hurled it at the wall. The coppers celebrating at the bar, threw down their sandwiches and charged over.

Sol put up a hand. 'We're job.' He called over to the landlord, 'Bad day here, mate, but we'll sort it.'

The landlord nodded slowly. Over the years he'd seen it all: tears, blood, puke. They always worked it out among themselves and always paid for any damage.

The uniform dissolved away and left Sol and Hassani to it. She was still on her feet.

'What we do counts, Sol.' Her teeth were gritted. 'It counts. Why else would we put up with all the shit?' A tear ran

209

down her sweaty cheek. 'The Greenwoods hurt people, you can't deny that.'

Pieces of glass glittered on the dingy carpet and Sol had to resist an urge to pick up a shard and squeeze until it cut through his palm. Anything to feel something.

'You can still do the right thing, Sol.' Hassani was crying openly, her nose running. 'And you can salvage your life.'

'It's fucked.'

Hassani wiped away the snot with her sleeve. 'You still have a job you love – at least, you used to love it.'

So that was it. If Sol didn't help her, Hassani would go to the DCI. There was now more than enough evidence and he wouldn't be able to talk his way out of it. Suspension, dismissal, the end. Did he even care?

'You need to make a choice right now,' said Hassani. 'Are you with us or are you with them?'

Sol thought about all the people he'd tried to help, all the people who didn't have a choice. The working girls, the junkies, the gamblers. And all the innocent bystanders who got caught up in the chaos that organized crime brought. Mothers by gravesides, old folk too terrified to go back to their homes after a burglary, kids in care when their parents were sent inside.

'Kane Lester attacked Liberty,' he told her.

Hassani sat back down. 'K-Dog? Doesn't he work for Paul Hill?' Sol nodded. 'So, what's happening? A turf war?'

Sol shrugged. 'Looks that way.'

'Will Chapman make a statement against him?'

'She says so,' he said.

'You don't believe her?'

'I don't know what to believe.'

Liberty had said she would help Sol send K-Dog down, but she'd said a lot of things since he'd met her. Not all of them true.

'You think the Greenwoods would rather deal with him?' Hassani asked.

'I suspect that's a possibility.'

Hassani held out her hand to Sol, her fingers smeared black from her eyeliner. 'Then let's go and catch them.'

Chapter 17

24 March 1990

'All right for some,' says Connor.

I know what he means. The house where our Crystal and Frankie are living is dead posh. There are two cars parked on a drive covered in them crunchy pebbles and a plant in a silver pot on the steps. A tall hedge makes sure the neighbours can't see in.

'When you're a solicitor are you going to buy somewhere this big?' Connor asks, with a laugh.

'Twice as big.'

'I suppose we'll need the space if we have six kids,' he says.

'Six!'

'I'm Irish, remember.'

I smack his arm and get off the bike. He takes my helmet and pushes my hair off my face.

'Just act completely normal,' he tells me. 'It's no different to when you knock for one of your mates, or me.'

I don't ever knock for mates, though. People at school steer clear, and I don't need to go anywhere to see the kids at Orchard Grove, do I? And since that thing with Connor's mam, I don't knock for him either. I only go to his house now when I'm already with him because I can't risk being on my own with her. Connor doesn't seem to have noticed.

'Smile.' He kisses my head. 'It'll be fine.'

BANG TO RIGHTS

I feel sick as I walk up to the door. I lift my hand to ring the bell, but quickly look back. Connor is lighting a cig and ushers me on with the lighter in his hand. The bell makes three musical notes when I press it and a woman answers. She's got thin stringy hair cut into a bob, the top of her ears peeping through at each side.

'Yes?' she says.

'Can I see Crystal and Frankie?' I ask.

She looks me up and down. 'Are you from Social Services?'

'No, I'm . . .'

Frankie charges down the hall in a little pair of blue pyjamas with buttons. He launches himself at me. 'Lib,' he shrieks.

I can't help but laugh and pick him up. He smells of shampoo.

'Elizabeth?' says the woman.

'Yes.'

'Oh dear,' she says. 'I don't think you're meant to be here.'

'I know, and I'm sorry for just turning up, but I really needed to see them,' I say, and she doesn't seem angry at all. It's more like she's worried. 'I didn't know what else to do.'

'Crystal,' Frankie shouts into the house. 'Crystal, come here. It's our Lib.'

The woman's hands flutter to her face. 'That's not a good idea, Frankie.'

Good idea or not, he shouts out again and footsteps come banging down the stairs until I can see Crystal, all ready for bed in a long nightie. With Frankie on my hip, I throw out my free arm towards my sister, but when she gets close, I gasp. Her left eye is purple and almost closed.

'Oh dear,' says the woman.

I grab Crystal's arm and pull her to me, then I start backing away, but Crystal can't walk on the pebbles and stumbles. I lean down and pull her up by her arm. A man appears in the doorway now, presumably the foster dad. He's much older than the woman and has a grey moustache.

'What the hell do you think you're doing?' he shouts at me.

He takes a step towards me and grabs Crystal's other arm. She screams as we both try to pull her. Suddenly, Connor's there and bats the man's hand away.

'Call the police, Jennifer,' says the man.

'Yes, Jennifer,' I shout. 'Call the police right now and explain why my sister's got a black eye.'

'Sister?' the man says.

Crystal hides behind me and I scoop my arm around to protect her. The man moves towards me.

'Put one hand on her and I will deck you, mate,' says Connor.

The muscles in the man's neck strain. Perhaps in his younger days he'd have taken Connor on, but not now. He turns to his wife and glares at her. 'Why the hell did you bring the children out to her?'

'I didn't.' The woman looks scared now. 'They just ran out.'

She tries to put a hand on his arm but he jerks it away. Mam used to try things like that whenever Dad got into one of his moods.

'I thought you were going to ring the police,' I say to her.

She gives a hysterical little laugh. 'Come on, now, that's not necessary, Elizabeth. Just let the children come back inside and we'll say no more about this.'

Is she completely mental? Does she really think I'm going to let Frankie and Crystal go back in there? I can see exactly what sort of man her husband is.

'Ring the police,' I tell her.

She gives her husband a terrified look but he's staring at me.

'You're going to regret this, Elizabeth Greenwood,' he says.

Present day

Inside the bookie's the old man was checking the odds in the *Racing Post* and filling out a betting slip.

There were roulette crack machines on the far wall. A middle-aged man in overalls smacked the screen of one with his palm and walked away. Those things let people play every twenty seconds. Bang, bang, bang. Again, and again, and again. When he got to the door, he walked back to his machine and sat down, hand already in his pocket.

K-Dog was at a table in the far corner, watching the television where an old football match was playing. He nursed a can of chocolate Nurishment, mobile in his other hand.

'Ready?' Mel asked.

Liberty nodded. Actually, she wasn't ready, she was bricking it, but she knew this had to be done. Together they walked over to the table. Before K-Dog had had a chance to notice them, Liberty slid into the seat next to him and Mel stood close behind.

K-Dog went for his pocket.

'Don't,' said Liberty, and he froze, clearly now aware of the gun Mel was pressing into the small of his back. 'Let's go for a little walk.'

This had always been the part that concerned Liberty. If K-Dog simply refused to move, what could they do? Mel had laughed and said there was no chance he would stay put with a bullet inches from his spine. Again, she was right and he got up without a word.

As the three of them moved through the bookie's to the door, the old man looked over from the *Racing Post*. He didn't know what was happening or didn't care. The man at the crack machine didn't even notice.

Outside, Mel guided K-Dog to the car, pushed him into the front passenger seat and slipped in behind him, the gun now pressed against the side of his neck. Liberty got into the driver's side and placed her hands on the steering wheel.

'Did you shoot Frankie?' Liberty asked.

K-Dog ran his tongue along the pink inside of his bottom lip, then smiled. If he was scared about the possibility of having his throat explode, he didn't show it.

Liberty kept her voice very calm. 'If you don't want to talk to me, that's fine.'

'You'll let her pop me in here?' he asked, with a sneer.

'I might.' Liberty reached for her mobile. 'Or I might just ring my brother and sister. To be honest, you'll be begging Mel to finish you off once Jay and Crystal get their hands on you.'

K–Dog's face remained unmoved, but Liberty could see the throb at his temple. The Greenwood reputation was evidently well known.

'Just answer my questions,' said Liberty.

Mel tapped the base of his skull with the gun. 'Come on, sunshine, you know it makes sense.'

'Fuck's sake.' K–Dog sighed. 'I didn't shoot Frankie.'

'But you were at the hospital to finish him off?' said Liberty.

'Something along those lines.'

'Who sent you?' Liberty asked. 'Your boss?'

K–Dog kissed his teeth. 'This whole thing is messed up.'

'Did Paul Hill order you to kill Frankie?' Liberty asked. 'Yes or no.'

'You're being played. You and the rest of your family.'

Liberty frowned. 'What do you mean?'

K–Dog's laugh turned to a groan as Mel cracked the back of his head with the gun. He lurched forward and smacked his face on the dashboard. Liberty grabbed his hair and pulled back his head. His nose had burst and blood was splattered across the car's upholstery.

'What do you mean, we've been played?' Liberty asked.

Grunting, K–Dog brought his hand to his face. 'She broke my fucking nose.'

'I'll break your fucking skull as well if you don't answer the question,' said Mel.

'Think about it.' K–Dog puffed air at Liberty. 'I thought you were supposed to be the clever one.'

Liberty still had her fingers in his hair when she heard the siren. Then an unmarked police car screeched to a halt in front, another to the side. Hassani jumped out of one and raced to Liberty's car door, throwing it open and dragging her out. The tarmac was hard and hot as Liberty's face hit it.

'Liberty Chapman, I am arresting you on suspicion . . .'

She didn't hear anything else said to her as she caught sight of Sol's boots moving across the pavement.

Amira sucked in her cheeks as she wrote up the details of her prisoners on the board in the custody suite.

It didn't do to crow. Sol had taught her that. For once thing it pissed off other officers who were bringing in suspects on lesser offences. For another, it made you look naïve. 'Arresting someone is the easy bit,' he always said. 'Getting it to stick is another thing altogether.'

She printed the names. Liberty Chapman, a.k.a. Greenwood, and Melanie Tandy. Then the time of detention and the rest. In the offences column, she stuck to serious arrestable offences. SAOs. She would have loved to list all the crimes she suspected both women of committing but SAOs looked so much more understated and classy.

Sol hadn't come down yet. Even though he was the senior officer, he'd let Amira arrest Chapman and he was letting her write it up. Just the sort of thing that made Amira love him.

She was sorry about what had happened with Natasha. It hadn't been her intention for them to split up. She thought that if she dropped a hint to Sol's wife, there might be a scene, some awkward questions to answer just to prove to the stupid man what he was risking. Maybe it was for the best. Natasha had never been a good fit for Sol, with her kale smoothies and balanced chakras. He'd go home from work having just told some poor woman that her son had been stabbed over a six-quid bag of draw and Natasha would attempt to make it all better with a scented candle.

In the end, he'd made the right choice about Chapman and her family and that was the main thing. The choices a person made at difficult times showed what they were like deep down. Amira, of all people, knew that. When she'd arrived here, terrified and traumatized, a splash of her mother's blood still visible on her *abaya*, she could have chosen a different path, but she hadn't. Perhaps that was why she despised Chapman so much. The woman had made all the wrong choices.

Amira looked over to the bench in front of the custody desk where Chapman sat in silence. Her cheek was swollen and scarlet from where she'd hit the kerb. Mel was by her side, seething. It was incredible how such a small person could radiate so much fury.

'I want to speak to my brief,' said Mel.

'Got the details for me?' the custody sergeant asked.

Mel pulled out a card and slid it across the desk with a long pink nail.

The sergeant read it and spoke to Chapman. 'Do you want to see him too?'

Chapman nodded.

'And you'd better get a doctor while you're at it,' Mel hissed. 'Have you seen the state of her face? Police brutality right there.'

The sergeant made the call and Amira led them to the cells. Chapman didn't look at her or even acknowledge her existence.

'I hope *you've* got a good lawyer,' Mel said to Amira. 'Cos you're going to need one.'

When she'd locked them both in different cells, Amira gave her cheeks another suck. Chapman's injury was a pain in the arse but there had been fears for the victim's safety. Sol would back her up on that.

At the desk, the sergeant finished a call and stuck a piece of Nicorette in his mouth. 'Doc will be here in ten, solicitor in twenty.'

'I'll interview them in number two,' said Amira.

She wanted the room with video equipment. In all likelihood, Chapman would go no comment but Amira would want the jury to see how cold she was. Kidnapping a man, breaking his nose and threatening to kill him meant nothing to her. Her family were vicious criminals and she was cut from the same block of ice.

'Word to the wise,' said the sergeant. 'If you're going to film it, get yourself cleaned up first. I've seen homeless glue-sniffers look better.'

The cell was eight feet by eight, and the only things in it were a bed and a toilet. The bed was a metal block bolted to the floor covered with a mattress that Mahatma Gandhi would have considered too thin. The toilet was metal and had no seat or lid. It did, however, house a turd the size of an engineering brick.

Liberty leaned against the wall, her heart an overtied knot in her chest. Mel was being her usual cocky self, but it was bravado. Had to be. They'd been caught red-handed holding a man at gunpoint. A man with a gash on the back of his head and a smashed tomato where his nose had once been.

The cell door opened and Hassani stood in the gap, holding something white in her outstretched hands.

'I need your clothes,' she said. 'For evidence.'

She placed the paper suit on the bed and waited.

'You're going to watch me undress?' Liberty asked.

Hassani crossed her arms and Liberty shrugged. She'd never been ashamed of her body. It had never let her down yet. She took off her shirt and jeans, dropping them in a pile on the floor. The matching red underwear followed.

Liberty stood in her cell, naked and defiant.

'Put the suit on,' said Hassani, and bent for the clothes.

Liberty could have kicked her then; a knee under the chin would have knocked the smaller woman out, broken her jaw at the very least. Hassani left as Liberty zipped up the rustling suit, something on her face not too far from a sneer.

The worst thing about all this was Sol's involvement. He'd led Hassani right to Mel's car. Liberty bent double at the thought of it. The man she'd been in bed with only eight hours ago had betrayed her. She hadn't been stupid enough to think he was in love with her, but she'd assumed their connection meant something to him. That had been her mistake right there.

She straightened herself and pressed her hands against the wall behind her. Under her fingers were deep gouges in the concrete and she rubbed the pad of her thumb against them until the skin broke.

Fuck the police

Someone before her had carved out that message. Fuck the police. Liberty sucked the blood from her thumb. Fuck the police. Fuck DC Amira Hassani. And most of all fuck DI Sol Connolly.

'I don't suppose you can give me a clue as to what's going on?' Raj perched at the end of the bed in the cell, scooting up to avoid a rip in the plastic mattress, exposing yellow-stained stuffing. Against every instinct Liberty sat next to him.

'It's Hassani,' she said. 'Remember when she nicked me last year and nearly tore my shoulders out of their sockets? Well, this time she went for my face.'

Raj tilted Liberty's chin and peered at her cheek. 'I'll get the doctor to look at that. I did stick my head into his room but some bloke was already in there, drowning in his own vomit.'

'What are they actually saying I've done?'

Raj opened the notebook on his lap. 'They say you and Mel kidnapped this bloke.' He ran a finger across his scribbled notes. 'Kane Lester. At gunpoint no less. Then you assaulted him in Mel's car. Apparently, it's covered in claret.'

'His nose was bleeding,' Liberty replied carefully. 'Then the police arrived and Hassani attacked me.'

Raj snapped shut the notebook. 'Are you okay in here while I go and ask some tricky questions?'

'Like what?'

'Like what this Lester bloke has actually said.' Raj stood and picked at some bits of fluff on his trousers. 'As far as I can see, he hasn't made a statement yet. Then there's the small matter of what Hassani was doing at the scene. If I find out that she's been following you, there'll be holy hell to pay.'

'Get you, hot shot.'

Raj patted his belly. 'What's the point in being big if I can't throw my weight around the shop when I want to?'

Singh was a hard one to fathom. Growing up in the sludge-coloured seventies couldn't have been easy for the fat kid with the foreign name that Amira imagined he'd been. How that had translated into a life spent helping ne'er-do-wells was harder to imagine. By the look of his frayed cuffs, it didn't even pay that well.

She sat him down at the far end of the canteen and offered to get him a cup of tea, which he declined. Sol arrived a few seconds later and took a seat, holding a water bottle from which he repeatedly drank.

'I've a few things I need help with.' Singh opened a notebook, each page covered with what looked like hieroglyphics. 'First is Kane Lester's statement. I want to see it.'

Not a question, a demand.

'When it's been taken, you'll get it,' she replied.

'Do I understand you don't have a statement from him then?'

She gave a laugh. 'He's in hospital, Mr Singh. Sixteen stitches in the back of his head and a broken nose. When the doctors tell us he's okay, we'll take a full statement from him.'

'You know what line of work he's in?' Singh asked.

'Are you suggesting we shouldn't take action if the victim has previous criminal convictions?'

Sol took another glug of water. Amira appreciated that he was leaving all the talking to her, but she wished he'd put down the bloody bottle.

'I wouldn't dream of telling you how to do your job,' said Singh. 'I'm just wondering what the chances are that someone in his line of work will actively cooperate with someone in your line of work.'

He was trying to rile her. She'd seen defence briefs do the same a hundred times. Drawing lines in the sand with their sticky fingers, inviting the police to cross them.

'I think having your head bashed in tends to make people want to cooperate,' she said.

Amira knew that wasn't necessarily true. How many times had she had to let some lowlife go because his wife was adamant she'd walked into a door? She'd learned the hard way that you couldn't win them all. Or even close to half.

'But has he said anything at all that makes you believe he'll even talk to you?' Singh smiled. 'What about when you made your arrests? Maybe you could check your notebooks.'

Amira knew there was no point checking her own. She'd been at the other side of the car to K-Dog, tackling Chapman. 'Sol?'

He made a show of finding his notebook and flipped through the pages. 'Mr Kane only said one thing to me during the arrest and that was "No comment."'

'"No comment"?' Singh pretended to be puzzled. 'Did he think *he* was being arrested?' K-Dog probably hadn't given it too much thought. His instinctive reaction on seeing any police officer would be to shout, 'No comment'. 'You'd think someone who'd supposedly been kidnapped at gunpoint would realize that you'd come to help him and be grateful for it, wouldn't you?'

'I expect he was in shock,' said Amira.

Singh carried on looking at Sol. 'What about Miss Chapman and Miss Tandy? Did they have anything to say on arrest?'

'Chapman didn't say a word,' said Amira. 'You'd think someone accused of kidnap at gunpoint would realize they had an opportunity to set the record straight and be grateful for it, wouldn't you?'

'I expect she was in shock,' Singh replied. 'What with you bashing her head into the kerb.' He still had Sol fixed in his sights. 'How about Mel? Anything?'

Sol coughed and read his notes mechanically. 'She said, "Are you completely out of your mind, you ugly cunt?"'

Singh nodded, as if this were a perfectly normal response. To be fair, it wouldn't have been the first time Sol had been called that in the course of his duties. 'Okay, then,' he said. 'It's fairly clear that no one at the scene said anything to confirm that any crime had even taken place.'

Amira wished Singh had accepted the offer of tea. Right now, she'd have chucked it in his face and enjoyed watching it drip off his turban. Of course, Chapman and Tandy had admitted nothing at the scene. And they wouldn't admit to anything later either. They might be evil but they weren't stupid.

'How about we just crack on with the interviews?' she said, forcing a cheery note into her voice.

'Fair dos,' said Singh. 'I'll just make sure Liberty's finished with the doctor before we kick off. That cheek is looking nasty.' He took several steps from the table, then turned back. 'By the way, what were you doing at the scene?'

'Excuse me?' said Amira.

'The two of you.' Singh waggled a finger at them. 'On the same road, in separate cars, where my clients just happened to be.'

'I'm afraid that's not information we can give out at this time, Mr Singh.'

He dipped his head as if expecting that answer and made his way from the canteen. Amira waited for every nylon-covered inch of him to be out of the door before rounding on Sol.

'You could have backed me up about how Chapman got injured.'

Sol shook his head. 'Don't be daft, Amira. Raj Singh knows full well that I was dealing with K-Dog and Mel, who was hardly coming quietly, was she? If I say I saw the whole thing with Liberty, he'll rip me apart. Let's just stick to the truth.'

Liberty's fingers worried the message on her cell wall once more. She thought about adding her own. Something derogatory about the size of Sol's dick, but he'd know she'd done it and she wasn't going to give him the satisfaction of showing any emotion.

She remembered the Latin inscription Offred had found in her closet in *The Handmaid's Tale*. Maybe she could do that. Say what she wanted to say in Latin? But then no one would ever know what it meant, would they?

Her cheek felt ridiculously tight. Like someone had turned a screw at her ear and pulled everything back. She touched it with a cautious fingertip.

The door hatch slid open and Liberty scowled. Fuck the police.

'Miss Chapman?' The voice was well spoken and soft, the face polite. 'I'm the FME. May I come in?'

Liberty almost smiled. She was banged up, yet he was asking permission to enter, like a gentleman come a-courting. 'Sure,' she said. '*Mi casa, su casa.*'

He laughed and the door opened. 'I'd take you to the medical room, but it's being cleaned. My last patient had drunk his body-weight in supermarket vodka. He's gone off to get his stomach pumped but not before he turned my room into a Jackson Pollock.'

Liberty returned his laugh. 'Ow.'

'Let's take a look at that.' The doctor held out his hand. 'Jonathon Bloom.' She shook his hand, then he snapped on a pair of latex gloves. 'How did this happen?'

'I was in my friend's car when a police officer opened the door and pulled me out.'

He pressed along the cheekbone more firmly than she'd expected and she tried not to wince.

'Did you fall?'

'Nope. I was pushed to the ground.'

He didn't react to that statement. Liberty guessed he wasn't meant to engage in the who-did-what-to-whom. Instead, he made a note and smiled. 'You'll be pleased to know that it's not shattered.' Liberty wiggled her mouth from side to side. 'I can give you a painkiller.' He held his pen next to her injury and noted down the length. 'Though nothing sexier than a paracetamol. When you get out of here, I'd hit the chemist for something stronger, if I were you.'

'I'm not sure I'm getting out of here anytime soon,' said Liberty.

Bloom raised an eyebrow but didn't pursue further details. However, when she pushed her hair from her face, he sucked in a breath. 'Good grief. Did you sustain those during your arrest?

'What?'

'Your neck.'

The pain in her cheek had made her forget about the injuries to her neck. 'As much as I'd like to pin these on Officer Hassani, I got them last night.'

'How?'

'I was at the hospital visiting my little brother and I disturbed someone trying to kill him,' she said. 'I was attacked.' Bloom's eyes were saucers as he cleaned her cheek and slipped antiseptic cream along it. 'I think it's fair to say that these last couple of days have been a bit crap.'

Raj appeared in the cell doorway. 'You've patched her up then, Doc?'

'Indeed,' said Bloom.

'And recorded everything?'

'Notes written and measurements taken.' Bloom pulled out his iPhone. 'A quick couple of photographs and we're done.' He turned to Liberty. 'Could you look that way?' He pointed at the wall and she read the message once again. Fuck the police.

'We're going to need a statement from you, Doc,' said Raj. Bloom pursed his lips. 'I know it's a ballsache for you, but I can't let this one slide.'

Bloom took off the gloves. 'You know they'll say she fell.'

'Course they will.' Raj mimed tripping in the cell, his arms out in front to protect himself. He then grabbed Liberty's wrists and rolled up both her sleeves displaying the unmarked skin. The only blemish was the slice on the pad of her thumb.

Bloom took photographs of Liberty's arms and hands, turning them to get shots of both sides. When he was finished, he smiled. 'Good luck, Miss Chapman.'

When the doctor had left the cell, Raj sat on the bed. 'You'll be glad to know that Sol's not backing up Hassani about what happened when she arrested you.'

'What did he say?'

'Absolutely sweet Fanny Adams,' Raj replied. 'Which is interesting.'

Liberty narrowed her eyes. Sol was a snake. If he was saying nothing about Hassani using Liberty's head like a basketball, then he had a reason. And that reason had nothing to do with helping Liberty. Fuck DI Sol Connolly.

Chapter 18

23 March 1990

There are two coppers sat opposite me. One thin, one fat. One black, one white. One woman, one man. All bases covered.

The fat white man is doing all the talking.

He reminds me of Mr Scott, one of my PE teachers. All chunky thighs and burst blood vessels. Some of the kids say he's having it away with the new French teacher, Miss Spencer, but I don't believe she'd touch him with a bargepole.

'You know you're not meant to come over here, Elizabeth,' says Fat White Copper.

'It's a good job she did,' says Connor. 'Have you had a good look at Crystal's eye?'

Fat White Copper looks at Connor like he's shit on his shoe. 'And you are?'

'Connor, Lib's boyfriend.'

I like the way he doesn't crumple. Like the police really don't scare him one bit. Not all mental like Vicky gets at the first sign of a copper, just calm.

'Boyfriend, is it?' Then Fat White Copper looks at me. 'And how old are you, Elizabeth?'

'Sixteen,' I say.

'Just about legal.' He's marking Connor's card. 'But old enough to know better, young lady.'

228

'Better than what?'

'Better than to turn up unannounced.'

'They won't let me see the kids whether I announce myself or not,' I tell him. 'And now we know why.'

'Let's not jump to any conclusions.'

Connor shakes his head. 'Conclusions? The little 'un looks like she's gone ten rounds with Mike Tyson.'

The thin black copper hasn't said a word and her lips are getting thinner with every second.

'If Jennifer and Colin had anything to hide, I doubt they'd have asked you into their home,' says Fat White Copper.

We are sitting in their kitchen, I suppose, but they hardly invited us in. They argued the toss for the best part of half an hour, me and Connor shivering in the cold where we'd wrapped our jackets around the kids. It was only when Frankie peed himself and thin black copper said he either had to go inside for a change of clothes or be taken to the nearest police station that Jennifer begged her husband to let us all in.

I know what Fat White Copper's thinking. He's looking at the clean cupboard doors, the alphabet magnets on the fridge spelling out the words 'cat' and 'dog'. He clocks the stone jars on the side marked 'tea', 'sugar' and 'biscuits'. All these words tell him a story about a couple who wouldn't dream of hurting the lucky foster children they take in. Kids with rotten teeth. Kids who have bad dreams and wet the bed.

'You know there's already an investigation?' I say. 'About some bruises on Crystal's arm.'

That puts the cat (and the chuffing dog) among the pigeons.

'Kids hurt themselves all the time,' says Fat White Copper, but he sounds much less sure of himself. 'Jennifer and Colin say that Crystal's a bit clumsy.'

Jennifer and Colin. It's like they're his mates. Oh, Colin's a good sort, life and soul of the party. His wife's a bit quiet but she makes a mean Sunday roast.

At last the thin black one speaks up. 'Maybe we should call Social Services.'

We have to wait well over an hour for the duty social worker to turn up, and during that time they keep Crystal and Frankie away from me like I'm some sort of danger to them. I can't work it out. The coppers know full well that our Crystal's got a black eye and that it can't have been me or Connor who did it, so why are we being treated like the criminals here?

When I need the toilet, the thin black one insists on coming with me. At the top of the stairs a bedroom door is open and I catch sight of a little bed in the shape of a train. Frankie's not in it, though.

The duty social worker finally turns up in a bit of a fluster. Her name's Valerie and she's new in the area and doesn't know anything about the Greenwood file. She's got a runny nose and a sore throat. When she's spoken to Crystal she accepts a cup of coffee from Jennifer. Nobody offers anything to me or Connor. I glance at the biscuit jar and wonder what sort are in there.

'I've spoken to Crystal and she confirms that she walked into a door,' says Valerie.

'There we go then,' says Fat White Copper, with a grin.

Are this lot really going to swallow that? Mam used to give that excuse all the time. No one was ever daft enough to believe it. Just like they didn't believe her when Dad broke her thumb and she told the doctor that she'd got it stuck in the lift. For a start that lift was barely ever working, and the odd time it was, there was a sensor to stop it shutting if something was in the way.

'How many times have you heard that one?' I ask.

The thin black one at least has the decency to look down at her hands.

'Come on now, Elizabeth,' says the fat white one. 'You've had your pound of flesh.'

Connor thumps the table and Valerie jumps at least two feet in the air. 'You think this is about Lib wanting to punish somebody? You're off your rocker, mate.'

'I've got your number, lad.'

Connor stands. 'Yeah, and I've got yours.' He points at the thin black one. 'And yours.' He pulls me to my feet. 'There's a little girl in this house that's been badly hurt and it's not the first time. And when something worse happens, and it will, then you lot will have some explaining to do.' He drags me out of the kitchen to the front door. Then he shouts over his shoulder. 'Frankie? Crystal? Your sister loves you more than anything in the world. Don't ever forget that.'

Present day

Interview Room Two had been painted since Liberty had last been inside it. A year ago, when Hassani had arrested her, Liberty had been put in there instead of a cell by the custody sergeant. A cup of tea had even been part of the deal. Raj had managed to get her released before a fuming Hassani had had a chance to ask a single question. It wouldn't go that way this time.

Liberty sat at the table next to Raj. It was empty except for the audio recorder. A video camera was attached to the wall.

Raj nudged her and showed her two words he had printed in his notebook.

NO COMMENT!

She smiled at him and nodded. It was just like Dax had explained. Not her job to help the police build their case.

Hassani entered and began to fiddle with the camera. Liberty had refused to look at her until now and she was shocked. The woman was a mess. Her shirt was sweat-stained and creased, her eyes were red-rimmed and her hair, usually thick and glossy, was greasy and limp.

Satisfied with the camera angle, Hassani took her seat. 'We're just waiting for DI Connolly.'

The sound of Sol's name stung, but Liberty buried her reaction deep inside. What would she do when he walked in? Ignore his very existence? Or throw him a you-are-nothing-to-me look? Maybe she should lick her lips, giggle and call him Sol.

At last he arrived, a plastic cup of water in each hand, which he set in front of Raj and Liberty. She'd seen him do something similar on the Delaney tape and thought it was a sign of his inner decency. It turned out it was just part of his routine. Boy, had he reeled her in.

She picked up the cup, held it high and said, 'Cheers, DI Connolly.'

Shock fluttered across his face. This was his first glimpse of her injured cheekbone.

'Not a pretty sight, is it?' Liberty asked him.

Raj scribbled frantically and shoved his book on her lap.

SHUT THE FUCK UP!!!!!

'If we're all ready?' Hassani asked.

'We are,' Raj replied.

'Just to remind everyone that this interview is being recorded both visually and in audio.' Hassani pressed the recorder on the table. 'Liberty Chapman, you do not have to say anything but it may harm your defence if you do not mention when questioned something which you later rely on in court. Anything you do say may be given in evidence. Do you understand?'

'Yes,' Liberty replied.

'Are you sure?' Hassani asked. 'I can explain it in simpler terms if need be.'

Liberty covered her mouth to catch the expletive about to escape. She had a first in law from Oxford University. She'd won a prize at law school for the best average scores in the country.

'My client understands the caution,' said Raj.

Hassani smiled. 'For the sake of the tape, I'm going to ask everyone to introduce themselves. I am Amira Hassani of the Organized Crime Unit.'

'DI Connolly,' said Sol.

'I'm Raj Singh, here to provide legal representation for Miss Chapman.' Raj picked up his water and drank. 'Who on my advice won't be answering any of your questions today.'

'She understands that, if she chooses to do that, inferences may be drawn by a jury in court?'

Raj tilted his head. 'She knows that's technically possible, yes, but my advice remains the same. Now is quite simply not the right time.'

'Your client won't get another opportunity to explain herself, Mr Singh. I think a jury might question why any innocent person wouldn't want to clear their name.'

Raj glanced up at the camera, reminding Liberty to ensure her injuries were on display. 'I think any sensible jury will understand when they hear that only last night Miss Chapman was almost killed by an assailant while visiting her brother who is in a coma. Had she not managed to hit the panic button, I doubt we'd be having this conversation at all.'

Liberty pulled a hairband from her pocket and pinned back her hair. She didn't look directly at the camera. When the band was secured, she realized Sol was still watching her. Had he been staring the whole time? His intensity had been what had drawn her to him in the first place. A barely covered rawness that sat just under his skin. He hadn't presented himself as a good man and hadn't seemed to care that Liberty was not a good woman. But that had been bullshit. He'd been biding his time, waiting for his moment. She remembered the second when K-Dog's face had hit the dashboard, the sound of the crunch as the bone broke, the smell of the blood in the heat of midday. She pictured Sol instead, his head jerking forward, her own hand on the gun.

'And that's before we even mention the injury sustained by my client on arrest,' said Raj.

'The FME has checked her out and stated she's fit to be interviewed,' Hassani retorted.

Raj leaned forward. 'Oh, physically she can speak, I grant you. But up here?' He tapped his head. 'What state would you be in if you'd been assaulted twice in the last twenty-four hours?'

'Are you saying we need to bring in a psych to declare her fit for interview?' Hassani asked. 'Or are you qualified yourself, Mr Singh?'

'Nope. I'm just explaining why she's not going to answer your questions.'

'Whatever.' Hassani waved a grubby hand. 'Just don't go saying your client didn't have the chance to tell us the truth.'

Amira's cheeks were starting to burn, she'd been sucking them for so long. But the sight of Chapman in the interview room had been like *iftar* during Ramadan.

Back home, after sunset, her mother would place a jug of water on the table and carefully pour everyone a glass. Even though she and Zaid were dying of thirst, they would follow the adults' lead and drink slowly. Samyaa had been too young to fast but had copied her brother and sister anyway. Then their mother and the aunties would carry a procession of platters from the kitchen. Snacks piled high for everyone to pick at, the noise of chatter building up. Amira's favourite, *dolma*, were made by her grand-mother, who would spend patient hours filling vine leaves with spiced lamb and rolling them with arthritic fingers. If they had special guests breaking fast with them, there might be *masgouf*, which her mother would serve with wedges of lime and chutney.

It was hard to get carp in England. And the neighbours cer-tainly wouldn't appreciate the smell if she roasted it for hours in the garden, as they had back home. But one day, when Rahim was old enough to understand, Amira would create the sort of *iftar* she'd enjoyed.

The interview had gone as expected. Singh was no shop egg and Chapman had displayed her cuts and bruises, like a kid after a fight. With everything that had gone on, she didn't imagine that the no-comment responses would hurt the defence in the long run, but there was plenty of other evidence.

Sol had rushed away as soon as they'd finished, saying he had to have a word with Bucky. No matter, he was back in the saddle, and by the look on Chapman's face she was raging. Hell hath no fury like a woman scorned. Lucky for Sol, this particular woman was being led back to her cell by the custody sergeant.

'Charge or release?' he asked Amira, when he was settled behind his desk.

'Neither just yet.' She laughed at the look on the sergeant's face. 'I'm not playing silly beggars, Sarge. But I might want to interview her again when I've spoken to the victim.'

'And when are you planning to do that?'

She pulled out her phone and waved it at him. In answer, he tapped his watch.

K-Dog answered after the first ring. 'Yeah?'

'It's Amira Hassani,' she said.

'Who?'

The door to the custody suite opened and two coppers pushed in a screaming woman, her hands cuffed behind her back. Her face was covered with a tangled mass of hair containing twigs and leaves. There was a brown stain on the seat of her tracksuit bottoms that Amira hoped was mud.

'It's not my day to be here,' the woman wailed. 'You know it's not my day.'

Hassani skirted round them and slipped from the custody suite while the door was still open. 'Hassani,' she repeated to K-Dog. 'The copper who saved your arse today.'

He laughed but it turned into a wet squeak.

'Are you okay?' she asked.

'No,' he replied.

She didn't care how he was feeling, to be honest. He was a means to an end. 'Are you still at the hospital?'

'Yeah. Waiting for test results or some other shit.'

'Can you come to the station when you're done?' He made another noise that sounded like someone drowning. 'You need to make a statement, K-Dog.'

'I'll come tomorrow,' he said. 'If I'm done by then. Or I could still be here. Makes you wonder why we pay tax.'

The chance that Kane Lester had ever paid tax was slim to remote. Funnily enough, he tended not to declare his earnings from dealing drugs and beating the crap out of people for Paul Hill.

'I'll come to you,' she said. 'I need this statement tonight so I can keep the women who did this to you inside.'

'You want to do that. Because if I get my hands on either of them bitches, I will tear them new ones.'

Liberty's legs were aching but she really did not want to sit on the bed. Instead she slid to the floor with her back to the wall. The contents of the toilet now stank. At some point, she would need to go herself. The thought made her want to throw up.

The interview had gone as well as expected but she was still going to be charged. How could she not be, with K-Dog's nose all over the car and Mel caught red-handed with a gun? Hassani would oppose bail, no doubt about that. Raj would argue the toss, but with a firearm involved she'd be sleeping in the cell tonight. Or not sleeping. Tomorrow Raj would try to convince a magistrate to give her bail, but her chances were non-existent. Then she'd be shipped off on remand. Once upon a time a wicked witch had told Liberty that girls like her always ended up in jail, on the game or worse. She'd refused to believe it. It turned out these things were just a matter of time.

Bucky had two pints in front of her. She was halfway through her own and pushed the full one at Sol when he arrived.

'I thought you were a Pinot Grigio kind of girl,' he said.

'Have you tasted the piss they call wine in here?' she asked. 'It's not even in the fridge half the time.'

The Feathers wasn't the sort of place where anyone drank much wine. Sol didn't think he'd ever had a glass of it in there, and he'd pretty much got down everything else from Cointreau to Pale Ale. One famous night, when he was still married to Angie, he'd necked seven Malibu and Cokes for a bet.

'You never called me back about the statements on the Delaney case,' she said.

'Sorry.' He took a gulp of lager. After the day's events, it was like sunrise. 'Been manic.'

'This is top priority, sunshine. Trust me.'

'I'll take a look as soon as I get home.'

He stopped short. He wouldn't be going home tonight. Where the hell would he go? He didn't even have a toothbrush. When Angie had finally kicked him out he'd escaped with a fat lip and no shoes. But he'd sloped off to Natasha who had given him (herbal) tea, sympathy and a blow job.

'What's up, Sol?' Bucky asked. He didn't want to tell her. 'Sol?'

'Amira arrested Chapman.'

Bucky froze, pint in hand, top lip covered with froth. 'Tell me you've taken a new job in cabaret.'

'It's serious,' he said. 'Kidnap. Assault. Threats to kill.'

'Fuck. Me. Sideways.' Bucky downed what was left of her pint in one motion, her throat pumping. When she was done, she placed her empty glass down carefully. 'Evidence?'

'Amira texted me to say she's gone to take the victim's statement right now. He's at the hospital.'

Bucky reached into her handbag and retrieved the same bottle of perfume she'd used the other night and sprayed a generous cloud down her cleavage.

'Another date?' Sol asked and Bucky nodded. 'Same woman?'

'God, no. I like it as hard as the next woman, but I'm not sixteen any more.' She stood. 'I hope to God that you know what you're doing with Chapman, Sol.' Her mobile buzzed like a wasp and she read a text. 'Raj Singh. He says he'll see me in court tomorrow and I'd best be wearing riot gear.' Someone from the bar wolf-whistled and Bucky gave him the finger. 'If this goes tits up, Sol, I'm holding you responsible. Hassani's a dumb kid, but you know the score.'

Two hours later and someone in a neighbouring cell was still howling. A proper howl, like a frightened animal. At first, Liberty had felt sorry for whoever was doing it, but now she'd cheerfully put them down herself.

Other prisoners banged their doors and swore but that just seemed to make the howler worse. Every barrage of abuse ramped the screeching up a notch.

Liberty put her head into her hands. When she'd been in care, there'd been a girl who'd thrown herself under a train. What was her name? How horrible that Liberty couldn't remember her name. That girl had cried out like that at night, her sorrow filling the children's home. Then one day she'd got up at the crack of dawn, and walked barefoot to the bridge. Apparently, she'd sat there for a bit, in the cold. Liberty imagined her feet, mucky from the rain, swinging in the air, heels tapping the stonework. They'd found her body a fair way up the track because trains can't stop quickly. Obviously.

BANG TO RIGHTS

The cell door opened and the custody sergeant held out a tray. Liberty pushed herself to her feet and took it from him. 'Try to get something down you,' he said. The screaming reached an ear-shattering crescendo. 'She'll stop in a bit. She always does.'

When he'd locked the cell behind him, Liberty laid the tray on the bed as far from the rip as possible. There was a cheese roll, the slice of cheese thick and square, fighting against the clingfilm. She picked up the carton of orange juice. It was warm and the straw was missing. She tried to tear off the corner but in the end she had to bite it off and managed to spill half of the juice down the front of her paper suit. Wouldn't that look the business when she appeared in court tomorrow? She grabbed the paper napkin to wipe herself down and her mouth dropped open. Underneath was a mobile phone. She looked around the cell as if someone might be watching, then grabbed it. It was a cheap pay-as-you-go job with only one number programmed into the contacts. Liberty pressed call.

'Lib?'

'Crystal.'

Chapter 19

31 March 1990
Since Silent Leanne topped herself, Imbo spends virtually all his time in
my room. I don't mind. He mostly just lies in Vicky's bed. All that wank-
ing is a thing of the past. I think the cider and the glue are messing with
his dick as well as his head.

He nods at the letter I'm reading. 'Is that from your Jay?'

'Yeah.'

'Isn't he out yet?'

I shake my head. 'He battered some kid for calling me sexy so he's
having to do his full sentence.'

'Daft cunt.'

Of all the cunts, our Jay is certainly one of the daftest. The whole point
of making me out to be his bird was to get respect on the wing. But
obviously I'm not his bird, so when somebody said they fancied me he
didn't actually have to protect my honour.

'What about your Crystal?' Imbo asks.

'They've moved her,' I say.

'Good.'

'Yeah.'

I mean it's good that she's away from that Colin, who I'm convinced
was the one who gave her the black eye. But she's had to go to a family
in York and our Frankie has gone to Skipton and I'm still not allowed
to see either of them. Carl says I haven't helped my case.

240

BANG TO RIGHTS

Miss Chapman told me she's making a proper application to court so I can get an order stating I have to be allowed contact. A piece of paper that no one can argue against. It might take a long time, though.

I push Jay's letter under my mattress with all the others. He writes a lot. Who else would he write to? He can't spell for toffee but they still make me laugh out loud. Our Jay can turn anything into a joke.

The Feed Your Head hoodie that Vicky left me isn't exactly clean but I give it a sniff and decide it will do. I'll be sweating cobbs by midnight so it doesn't matter.

'You off to DreamSkool?' Imbo asks.

'Yeah,' I say. 'Wanna come?'

It would do him good to come out. I mean, he's a complete liability, but all the same.

'Think I'll just chill out here, Lib.'

He pulls out a canister of gas. I don't like leaving him to do it on his own. He's got no off button and one of these days I'm going to find him cold and white and in a bath of spew.

'It'll be good,' I say, but he's already huffing.

On my way, I kiss him on his head. He stinks of chemicals and worse.

'Lib.' His voice is already scratchy. 'When you leave here, will you come back and visit me?'

'No,' I say. 'You'll come and visit me and I'll make you egg, chips and beans.'

The music pours out of the Cube. The DJ is on fire and the crowd are screaming for more. The lad on the door asks for my ticket.

'I'm on Fat Rob's guest list,' I tell him. 'Pretty Lib.'

He looks me up and down. 'He's not wrong there, is he?' He stamps my hand and rubs my wrist with his thumb.

Tiny comes out. 'Bloody hell, it's like a siren goes up from the bat cave.'

'What?' I ask.

'*You.*' *She's laughing and wraps an arm around my waist.* '*You haven't got a clue, have you?*'

She drags me inside. The crowd is like a wall. Everyone with their hands in the air, glow sticks waving, whistles in their mouths. I laugh, and it's as if the bass jumps into my open mouth. Danny is on a podium, a cricket hat on his head. He holds out a hand and hauls me up.

'*I love you, Lib.*'

'*I love you, Danny.*'

We dance until the sweat is stinging our eyes.

'*Oi.*'

I look down and see Connor. He opens his arms and I let myself fall into them.

'*Where've you been?*' *he asks.*

'*Dancing with Danny.*'

He hugs me. '*Oh, I see how it is.*'

A girl taps him on the shoulder. She whispers something to him and he nods. Then she pushes something into his hand. He leans in, kisses her cheek and presses the packet into her back pocket. When she's on her way, he picks me up and spins me around.

A couple of hours later, we stagger outside. I take off Vicky's hoodie. It's so wet I could wring it out.

'*Can I ask you something, Lib?*' *Connor asks.*

The rain hits my skin in lazy splats. '*Of course.*'

'*You'll leave Orchard Grove when you turn seventeen, won't you?*' *I nod and suck some rain off my arm. I'd rather not think about it.* '*And then you can live where you want?*' *Not exactly. I won't have any money so I'll have to go wherever Social Services put me and hope for the best.* '*I was wondering if you'd come and live with me.*'

I groan. '*Your mam will never have it, Connor. You know that.*'

'*Fat Rob's brother is moving out of his flat and we thought we'd take it on.*' *Fat Rob's brother is gay. His boyfriend is a bloke called Omar from Chapel Town. The pair of them have been talking about going to work on the cruise ships for months now. 'We both think you should live with us,' he says.*

The lack of cash sits on my back, like a rucksack full of the heaviest books in the world. 'I can't.'

'I'll pay your rent,' he says. I stand very still. 'I don't mind.' He wipes the rain from my face. 'You can finish school and I'll take care of things until then.'

I'm stunned. No one has ever offered to look after me. I think I could be happy living with Connor and Fat Rob. Tiny and Danny would visit. And I could make Imbo those eggs, chips and beans.

'I'll pay you both back,' I say. 'When I get qualified as a solicitor, I'll buy us all a house.' He laughs as if that's a load of rubbish. 'No. I mean it.'

He cups my face in his hands. 'You don't need to do all that now.'

'Do what?'

He doesn't answer because a police van screams down the street and judders to a halt in front of us.

Present day

'Are you a complete moron?' asked Crystal. 'Taking Mel to deal with K-Dog?'

Liberty held the mobile away from her ear. The howler was losing her sting. 'How the hell did you get this phone to me?'

Crystal sighed. 'It's my job, Lib. Just like yours is drafting contracts or whatever.'

It was impossible to comprehend how her sister could compare writing up a goods and services agreement with smuggling a phone into a police cell.

'Why didn't you wait for me or Jay?' Crystal demanded.

'Because you were sorting things out with your missing husband and Jay was about to start World War Three.' Liberty couldn't quite believe she was fighting with Crystal, given the current circumstances. 'How is Harry, by the way?'

'Don't ask.'

Christ. Weren't they past all this? Hadn't she proved time and time again that she could be trusted?

'I am asking.'

'Now's not the time.'

'I don't know about you, Crystal, but I'm not exactly busy.'

There was a silence on the line, and for a second Liberty worried that her sister had hung up. Then she heard breathing.

'Harry has kids. From another woman.' Crystal's voice was toneless. 'One of them needed him.'

Liberty looked around the cell. How many people who had spent the night in here had no one in their lives? No one who wondered where they were or when they might get out?

'When did Harry have these kids?' Liberty asked.

'A few years ago. When we'd split up for a bit.' Crystal sighed. 'Do we have to talk about this?'

'Why did you split up?'

'Because I'm not exactly ideal wife material.'

'I love you, Crystal.'

Crystal laughed. 'Piss off.'

'When I go down will you do something for me?' Liberty asked.

'You're not going down.'

'Of course I am.'

'You know the trouble with you, Lib?' asked Crystal.

'I've a feeling you're about to tell me.'

'You give up too easily.'

Liberty's head felt as though it was filled with stones and she couldn't hold it upright. There was no fight left in her. Presumably this was how the girl who had jumped off the bridge had felt. Not angry or miserable. Just bone-achingly tired.

'K-Dog won't give evidence against you,' Crystal said.

'Gangster's code?'

'Don't take the mick.'

'I need you to look after Dax for me,' Liberty told Crystal.

'Dax?'

'He's only sixteen and he thinks he knows all the answers,' said Liberty.

'Sounds familiar.'

Liberty smiled sadly. She didn't have the answers, never had done. Crystal's voice changed, suddenly energized. 'Listen, Lib, I've got to go.'

'Is Jay with Frankie?'

'Yeah. We'll swap over later,' Crystal replied. 'See you.'

The line went dead but Liberty kept the phone to her ear.

The custody sergeant had been bang on the money. At some point during the night, the howling had stopped. Liberty refused to lie on the bed but closed her eyes where she sat. The beds in prison would likely be much worse and she'd have to get over herself, but not tonight.

The hatch of the cell door opened, waking Liberty with a start. How long had she been asleep? She wiped a string of dribble away with her hand. Hassani peered in, a rigid smile in place that looked like she'd borrowed it.

'Come with me, please.'

The door opened and Liberty followed her to the custody desk. Raj was there, reading a document, face stony.

'That's Kane Lester's statement,' said Hassani. 'I'm sure Mr Singh will confirm that it's in order.'

So much for the gangster's code.

The custody sergeant read out the charges but Liberty wasn't listening. They were all offences that attracted long custodial sentences. When asked if she had anything to say, Raj stepped up. 'My client is innocent and will produce evidence in due course.'

The trouble was, Liberty wasn't innocent and wouldn't be able to produce any evidence to prove it.

Seven in the morning, and Liberty received the police station breakfast tray. Scrambled eggs and beans on a paper plate, the orange sauce spilling over the side. The carton of juice was apple and had its straw.

Back in London, Liberty almost never ate breakfast in her flat. She used to call at the same stand on the way to work. The owner knew her and would have a coffee and a muffin ready. At the sight of the Porsche he would scuttle over with a grin and pass them through the window. Liberty never waited for the change.

Out of the cell, Liberty found herself corralled with the other prisoners waiting to be transported to the magistrates' court. Mel arrived last, ridiculous in her own paper suit and no make-up.

She winked at Liberty. 'Looking good, Greenwood.'

The motley crew of missing teeth and home-made tattoos gave one woman a wide berth. She whimpered in the corner, clumps of dirt and leaves still stuck in her hair as if she'd literally been dragged through a hedge backwards. Even from the other side of the holding area, Liberty could smell that the woman had shat herself.

A few prisoners nodded at Liberty and Mel as if they knew one another. Maybe Mel did know them.

A door at the back opened and a security guard stepped in, bomber jacket bearing their company logo. 'Hands,' she shouted.

The prisoners held out their hands, wrists together.

'It's not my day to be here,' the woman in the corner shouted. Everyone, including the guard, groaned. 'Not today.'

246

Mel stalked over and put a finger to her lips. 'Know who I am?' The woman nodded. 'Know who that is?' Mel nodded at Liberty and the woman nodded. 'Then stop creating.'

The woman began to cry but did so as quietly as she could.

Order restored, the guard snapped metal cuffs on the prisoners, each set attached to a cord that ran between them.

'Okay, folks,' the guard called. 'Let's get out of here. Your carriage awaits.'

Beyond the door was a courtyard where a prison van was parked, the windows high and tinted. Another guard helped the prisoners inside one at a time. As they waited for their turn, Mel gestured behind her and Liberty saw Sol walking towards them. He looked almost as bad as hedge woman.

When he came close, he grabbed Liberty's upper arm. She could feel the heat of his fingers through the paper suit. 'Tell Raj to check the chain of evidence.'

Liberty shook him off. 'Don't touch me.'

A cream-cheese sandwich from Boots helped calm Amira's stomach. If possible, she liked to start the day with a cup of her father's coffee and to feed Rahim. These days, he wanted to feed himself and a lot of his food ended up on the floor or in her hair. She couldn't risk that this morning, and talked Zaid into doing his duty.

She'd left as a dollop of porridge landed on the lens of her brother's glasses.

As she skipped through security at the court, she told herself that there was nothing to be nervous about. K–Dog's statement had been emailed to the CPS last night and it covered all the bases. Sure, he might have overegged the pudding here and there, but essentially it was a fair account of what had happened to him. More importantly, it tallied with his injuries.

Sol caught up with her outside the CPS room. His hair was still wet from a last-minute shower, presumably at the nick. He was wearing yesterday's clothes. From what she'd gathered, Natasha had shredded everything he owned and there wouldn't have been any time to buy new.

'Ready?' she asked him, and he nodded.

Inside the CPS room, Bucky was already on the warpath, bellowing at Fazeel about a missing set of photographs. 'You can't mistake them, pretty boy,' she shouted. 'They're of a leg. On its own.'

'I know what they are, boss,' Fazeel screamed back. 'It's not like I mixed them up with my holiday snaps.'

The sandwich repeated on Amira and she pushed a fist against her chest as they waited for the prosecutor and her assistant to sift through the stack of files on the table. At last the photographs were located, inside a fraud case.

Bucky held up a photograph of a severed leg, the toes black and rotting. 'This is all I've got left of my victim so I can't afford to lose it.' Amira gave the sort of laugh she thought was expected. 'Right then. Officers Connolly and Hassani, talk to me about Liberty Chapman.'

'You've seen the statement?' Amira asked.

'I have,' Bucky replied. 'And I'm impressed you got a scrote like Kane Lester to talk. Forensics?'

'The car's being swept but it was dripping with Lester's blood. Plus, we have both defendants' clothes. The results will be back in a day or two,' said Amira.

'Both women gave a no-comment interview?'

Amira nodded. 'As expected.'

'Then all I need to see is the paperwork on the gun,' said Bucky. 'Chain of evidence and all that crappola.'

★　★　★

The cells in the courthouse were packed. Liberty and Mel were shoved in with a woman already lying on the one bed, forearm covering her eyes, and two young prostitutes, who shivered against the wall in their PVC miniskirts, arms covered with bruises and needle marks.

The woman on the bed didn't object when Mel moved her feet and sat on the end.

When the hatch slid open, five sets of eyes jumped to attention. 'Is it a private party or can anyone join in?' asked Raj.

Liberty gave a hollow laugh and put her face into the small rectangular space. 'Morning, Raj.'

'You okay?'

'Not too bad,' she said.

'Spoken like a true northerner.' He held up a folder. Liberty and Mel's names had been written on the front and Raj had drawn a smiley face. 'I'm going for bail obviously.'

'I'm not expecting to get it.'

'The problem is, these are serious offences and they've already got Lester's statement.'

'I know, Raj,' said Liberty. 'You can only do your best.'

'See you up there,' he replied, and turned to leave.

As she watched him walk away, she called after him, 'What's the chain of evidence?'

'It's the statements that show the movement of a piece of evidence,' said Raj. 'From a copper to Forensics and what-have-you. It proves something can't have been tampered with. Why?'

'Doesn't matter. I think someone was trying to wind me up.'

Amira's pulse was hammering in her temples as she stared at Sol. She was trying to keep her cool, to register what he was saying, but it was impossible. Bucky, too, looked like she was about to lose the plot.

'Why would I have bagged the gun?' Sol asked. 'I didn't even see it.'

Amira lifted a hand but forced it down before she slapped him. Her voice when it came was too loud. 'Mel had the gun. You took it when you arrested her.'

'I think I'd have noticed if Mel had a gun,' he replied.

Amira blinked wildly. Mel had been holding the gun when she'd wrenched open the driver's door. She'd needed to get Chapman out of there to make the arrest and had left it to Sol to sort out Mel. He had to have seen it.

'I didn't know anything about a gun until you mentioned it in the interview,' Sol said. 'So, I assumed you'd bagged it.'

This wasn't right and she squared her shoulders at him. 'Have you done this deliberately?'

'Why would I?'

'Because of Natasha.'

Sol's eyes remained expressionless. The shutters were down. 'I didn't see a gun, Amira.'

Bucky slammed both palms against the table. 'Shut up, both of you, or, so help me God, I will chuck this case out of court right now and report you both to Police Standards.'

Amira swallowed hard. This was the last chance she would ever get to send Chapman down. The room was silent, all eyes on her. Fazeel and a couple of other prosecutors froze, waiting to see what would happen next.

Bucky reached behind her for the file, removed K-Dog's statement and read. No one moved. No one breathed. When Bucky was finished she looked up at them.

'Mr Lester didn't see a gun either.'

'Of course he did,' Amira replied.

'Nope. He felt it pressed against his back and thought it was a gun.'

Amira laughed harshly. 'Mel cracked his head open with it.'

'She cracked his head open with something Mr Lester assumed was a gun.' Bucky smacked the statement with her fist. 'Not once does he say he actually saw it.'

Suddenly the door to the CPS room flew open and Singh breezed in, plastic slip-on shoes slurping against the carpet tiles. 'Right then, you lot. About this gun.'

Chapter 20

12 April 1990

I was lucky to get a visiting order for today because tomorrow's Good Friday and all the buses are on a reduced service until next Tuesday.

It'll still take me hours to get to the prison but school's broken up so I've plenty of time on my hands.

I tighten my ponytail as I walk past the corner shop. I would have liked to wash my hair this morning but the water was off. Imbo head-butted the boiler when Hemma told him he couldn't go to Silent Leanne's funeral. Apparently her family want it to be private.

When I get to the bus stop, Connor's mam is waiting there. Just what I need. I can't turn back, though, because she's already seen me.

'Lib,' she says. 'Can I have a word?'

'I'm on my way to see him.'

'Sure, I know that,' she says. 'I won't keep you.'

We sit side by side under the shelter. Connor's mam is wearing some new perfume. It smells of lavender and old ladies.

'This is a terrible business,' she says. 'Absolutely terrible.'

I nod. I've been crying on and off since Connor got arrested. I hung around outside the police station for hours, hoping they'd let him out. In the end, the copper on the duty desk told me they'd charged him with possession with intent to supply and he wouldn't be getting bail.

'He'll get five years his solicitor told me,' she says. 'Even with good behaviour he'll do three if not four.'

I know all this. I've had two letters from Connor. They're not like Jay's, all jokes and drawings of knobs. Connor's are line after line of how he doesn't think he can do this.

'You could help him, of course,' she says.

'I'm trying,' I tell her. 'I've told him I'll stand by him.'

'I mean something that will really help.'

Of course I'll do anything to help him. If I had three wishes . . .

'You could tell the police the drugs were yours,' she says.

I laugh. She must be joking. Her face, though, tells me that she's not. Not at all.

'They were in his pocket, Mrs O.'

'You could admit you put them there when the police arrived and Connor didn't say anything to protect you.'

'They wouldn't believe that.'

'Don't be stupid,' she says. 'A girl with your background? It's what people are saying anyway.'

A girl with my background. A girl with no parents. A girl in care. Naturally I'm the one dealing class A drugs. It's what people are saying anyway. I get to my feet and start to walk away.

She jumps up. 'Come back here.' I don't but she's caught up in an instant. 'If you loved him you'd do this.'

'If I loved him I'd go to prison for him?'

'Why not? Girls like you always end up in jail, on the game or worse.'

I'm in tears on the bus and an old lady hands me a packet of tissues. I blow my nose. When I finally get to see Connor, I'm done in. I tell him what his mam said, the words catching in my throat. He goes quiet.

'Connor?'

'Thing is, Lib, if you did say it was you, they probably wouldn't even send you down.'

'I'm pretty sure they would.'

He shakes his head and grabs my hands in his. 'You'd get Miss Chapman to tell the court about everything you've been through with your mam and your dad and now your Crystal. It's called mitigation.'

I pull away. 'I know what it's called.'

Next to us, a woman in a purple tartan jacket puts her hand under the table and passes something to her husband. Quickly, he pushes it into his mouth and swallows.

'Seriously, Lib, I don't think I can do this,' says Connor. 'You don't know what it's like in here.'

I look around the visitor's centre. The men are all angry and desperate. Connor doesn't belong here, with his cheeky good looks and a smile that makes knickers drop.

'With a drugs conviction on my record they'll never let me become a solicitor,' I say.

He frowns at me like he's irritated.

'What?' I ask.

'Whatever you decide, that's never going to happen, Lib.'

'Yes, it is.'

'Oh, grow up, Lib,' he says. 'Girls like you don't end up as solicitors.'

Present day

Amira's blood was pounding so hard in her ears she could barely hear the voicemail recording on K-Dog's phone.

'Yo, this is K-Dog. Leave a message.'

Yo? Half these idiots thought they were in an episode of *The Wire*, rather than sending kids out to sell crack in the arse end of Yorkshire. They wouldn't last two minutes where Amira was from.

'It's Amira Hassani,' she snapped. 'Call me back immediately.'

Bucky had managed to get rid of Singh, explaining that she was 'looking into' the chain of evidence for the gun, and that Hassani was going to contact the victim for 'further clarification' on a few points. It was a temporary reprieve. A brief like Singh could smell bullshit and he'd be back.

When K-Dog hadn't returned her call in ten minutes and her

second attempt also went straight to voicemail, she contacted the station for his address.

The house was at the end of a terrace, the upstairs window covered with the flag of Jamaica. Amira knocked on the door but there was no answer. She opened the letterbox and called but only silence greeted her.

She rang K-Dog's number and from somewhere inside the house she heard the ringtone: some rap song about a bitch that wanted it all night long.

'I know you're in there, K-Dog,' she shouted.

When he didn't answer she took a step back, broke the glass in the door with her elbow, reached in and unlocked the door.

'K-Dog,' she shouted. 'It's Hassani and I'm coming in.'

He was probably busy hiding a stash of rocks and cash. She listened but the house was still.

'Kane?'

The door opened into the sitting room. A sofa and chair stood empty, facing a flat-screen television, PlayStation plugged in, a pile of games waiting; Grand Theft Auto, Football Manager, Call of Duty. A coffee table in the middle of the room was littered with money, tens and twenties wrapped into dealer folds. A mobile phone lay face down on the glass. Amira rang K-Dog's mobile once more and the tune erupted.

Could the Greenwoods have grabbed him again? Chapman and Frankie were otherwise disposed, but Jay and Crystal were still at large. Plus the family had an army of foot soldiers they could use.

Amira's anger rose. If they had snatched her witness, the Greenwoods were going to feel the full force of the law. She'd offer him a safe house. Witness protection. Whatever it needed. No way were any of them getting away with this.

Her jaw was locked in determination and outrage as she made her way to the kitchen, knowing full well that K-Dog was not going to be in there. He was gone. He'd be in a back room somewhere, or a car on a towpath having his options explained to him by the Greenwoods. Well, Amira could play that game. Kane Lester could give evidence against Chapman or he could go down for dealing and take his chances inside. Who could say what else Amira might find if she searched this place now? Child pornography? That would ensure K-Dog was sent up to the Mansion. Oh, she had a few tricks up her sleeve yet.

The gasp that came out of her mouth was primal. A sound that conveyed the human reaction to death. K-Dog *was* in the kitchen, after all, slumped on the floor, a round wound in his forehead that looked more black than red. Behind him, the oven door was no longer visible except for the once-silver knobs that stood out from the blood and bone.

The kitchen bin had been knocked over and rubbish spilled out, K-Dog's lifeless hand among the gnawed chicken bones and ketchup-dipped fries of a half-eaten KFC.

Amira called for back-up and an ambulance although she knew there was absolutely no point.

The time spent in the cells was glacial, and after the other prisoners had been taken up, Mel and Liberty were forced to wait another hour.

'I've got to pee,' Mel announced.

'Do I need to know that?' Liberty asked.

Mel shrugged and began to unzip her paper suit. Liberty looked away but not before she'd got an eyeful of protruding ribcage and a bush that wouldn't have looked out of place in a seventies porn flick. The sound of Mel taking a leak brought a horse to mind.

At last, Raj came back.

'Oh, hello,' said Mel. 'You've remembered we exist?'

'Men and dogs, Mel, men and dogs,' Raj replied.

'What's happening?' Liberty asked.

'A lot,' he said. 'For one thing, the gun is gone.'

Liberty frowned. 'Gone?'

Raj dipped his head. 'Hassani is adamant that she saw a gun but she thought Connolly bagged it.' Liberty risked a glance at Mel, but her face was rigid. 'Connolly had no eyes on a gun.'

'Me neither,' said Mel.

'What about Lester?' said Liberty. 'He says he saw a gun.'

'Actually, he didn't,' Raj replied. 'He felt a gun. Not the same thing.'

A whoosh of adrenalin jumped inside Liberty. 'We can challenge that.'

'Well, we could have done,' said Raj.

'What do you mean?'

'Mr Lester, K-Dog, whatever his name is, can't give evidence one way or the other.'

'Because he didn't see it?' Liberty asked.

Raj nodded. 'Yep. But there's also the small issue of him being dead.'

Silence filled the cell. K-Dog was dead?

'How?' Mel asked.

'Gunshot to the head,' Raj replied.

'Well, me and Lib have cast-iron alibis,' she muttered. More silence. 'They'll have to drop the case against us.'

'Not yet,' said Raj. 'It is possible to produce a statement from someone who's dead.'

'But without the gun, what have they got?' Mel asked.

'A car full of Mr Lester's blood.'

'He had a nose bleed,' said Mel.

'Truth is, Bucky's not just going to let this go today. It's too serious.'

'But you can ask for bail while she reviews the file,' said Liberty.

Raj grinned. 'Already asked and already agreed.'

★　★　★

Dax still wasn't home. On the one hand Liberty was worried, but on the other she was grateful to have the house to herself. She needed a shower and she needed to process what had just happened.

She turned the water as hot as she could bear and stood under the stream. The burning sensation felt good as it sloughed off all the dirt. Deliberately, she turned her cheek upwards and held it to the jet of water, balling her fists against the pain.

K-Dog was dead. No, that made it sound like he'd had an accident or had succumbed to a long-term illness. K-Dog had been murdered. Someone had put a bullet through his head at close range. And that someone was very likely to have done so on Greenwood orders. Maybe Jay or Crystal had done it themselves. That way there could be no loose ends.

It seemed ridiculous that her little brother or sister could have killed anyone. The kids who had played Operation for hours, even when the batteries had run out?

But who else could it be? Who else would want K-Dog out of the way?

With her skin scalded pink, Liberty wrapped her hair in a towel and pulled on her robe. She avoided the mirror. No good was going to come of facing the horror story she knew she would find.

When the bell rang, she didn't want to answer. She wasn't quite ready to face the music. But when it rang again, she knew she would have to.

'Oh, my days,' said Crystal. 'It's Freddy Kruger's body double.'

Jay pulled a face. 'Didn't he wear a mask?'

'No, that was Michael Myers,' said Crystal.

'Who?'

'The bloke from *Halloween*.'

'I get the picture.' Liberty showed them in. 'I look like hell. And so would you if you'd spent the night in the cells thinking you were about to do a ten stretch. I'm off to bed for a week.'

Jay slid a strong arm around her shoulder. 'Sorry, Lib, but you need to get dressed. Paul Hill wants to meet.'

Liberty was gobsmacked. Surely they needed to put as much distance as they could between Paul Hill and themselves right now. 'Won't he just try to kill us?' she asked.

Crystal shrugged. 'Not unless he's the one with the death wish.'

Sol pulled up outside the bookie's. Down the road, there was no longer a younger waiting at the bus stop for a stream of punters or a succession of BMX-riding servers. After yesterday's excitement, the action would be taking place elsewhere. Probably only a few streets away, though.

He locked the car and crossed the road. At the other side was a six-foot fence, weeds and nettles poking through from the garden of a pub that had closed down over a year ago. A to-let sign listed to the right, like a drunken Friday night.

Sol grabbed a metal link in each hand and heaved himself up. At the top, he swung one leg over, then the other, and finally let himself jump. On the ground, he briefly lost his footing and put down a hand, receiving a sting for his trouble. 'Fucker.'

Sucking his thumb, he searched in the foliage, tramping it down with his boots.

The gun was here somewhere. During the arrest, there'd only been time to grab it from Mel and toss it over the fence. Fortunately, Hassani had been so busy with Liberty, she hadn't seen him. K-Dog had been too dazed to know what was going on, which left Mel, who had done nothing more than raise an eyebrow pencilled on in a colour he was pretty sure no real eyebrow had ever been.

He walked the length of the fence and found nothing. Yet it had to be there.

Out of nowhere came a snuffling sound, then a low rumble. Sol spun and was faced with a dog growling at him through the fence. It bared its teeth and Sol was glad it was on the other side.

'Come on,' said a girl's voice, and the dog was dragged away.

It tried to stand its ground but the girl was obviously strong and its paws slid along the pavement until it capitulated and trotted away.

Sol grabbed a dock leaf and rubbed it against the raised white bumps along his thumb and down the heel of his hand. The green juice left a stain but seemed to relieve the sting (was that just a placebo effect?) sufficiently to allow him to go back to his search.

'Why here?' Liberty asked, as Jay unlocked the Trap.

'We point-blank refused to meet on Hill territory,' Crystal replied.

As the door opened, the kipper smell of faulty wiring unfurled towards them and Liberty covered her nose.

'It'll be fine once we get it aired,' said Jay.

He flicked on the lights and the club was revealed. Although not yet finished, with three steel poles leaning against the stage, tables and chairs stacked in a corner, it was clear that Frankie had not done a bad job of overseeing the work thus far. A couple more weeks and the Trap would be ready to welcome the punters.

'Who's with Frankie?' Liberty asked.

Crystal fingered some mirrors piled on the bar, waiting to be fixed to the wall behind. 'Harry.'

A million questions about Crystal's husband and his other family sprang into Liberty's mind, but she pushed them aside for later. Instead, she nudged open the lid of a toolbox with her foot. Inside were pliers, saws, a hammer and lengths of cable. She wondered if Bam had managed to fix her internet. Raj's office seemed like another country. He was such a decent man and a good friend, but she no longer belonged with him.

When the sound of footsteps rang through the club as Paul Hill and two new monkeys arrived, Liberty bobbed and snatched up a screwdriver from the toolbox, then rammed it down the back of her jeans' waistband. Crystal moved from the bar to Liberty's side and Jay appeared at the other. Their physical presence made her backbone straighten. They were a wall.

'Well now.' Hill's eyes danced across them. 'The Greenwoods.'

'Not all of us,' Liberty replied.

'How is Frankie?'

'Still alive,' she said. 'Despite all your best efforts.'

Hill turned his face first to one bodyguard, then the other, as if looking for an answer. He rubbed his chin. 'And why would I want to shoot Frankie?'

'He cooked up some stupid plan to infiltrate your crew and you saw through it.' Liberty snapped her fingers, the sound echoing around the club. 'Like that.'

Hill nodded. 'It was stupid and I did see through it.' He leaned against the stage. 'But kill him over it? Don't be daft.'

Liberty watched him intently. No doubt he was armed and so were the sidekicks. But then she assumed Jay and Crystal were each carrying a gun. If anyone made the first move, there would be carnage.

'If you didn't shoot Frankie, why did you send K-Dog to finish the job?' she asked.

'I didn't,' Hill answered.

A hollow laugh escaped from Liberty's mouth. 'I can assure you that K-Dog had every intention of killing Frankie *and* me.'

Hill tapped a hand on each side of the stage beside him. 'I know, but all I can say is that I didn't give him that order.'

Though he spoke casually, it was a big thing for Hill to admit that one of his men had gone off message, and it fitted with what K-Dog himself had told Liberty: someone was playing the Greenwoods. Maybe that someone wanted to cause mayhem between the two families.

Liberty stepped forward and held out her hand to Hill. 'This stops now?'

Hill frowned at her fingers, waited with his lips parted, then at last took her hand in his own. 'I can understand why you needed to give Ozzie a pasting, but you didn't need to do away with K-Dog.' He gripped Liberty's hand tightly. 'He'd have never given evidence against you.'

She glanced down and caught sight of the gun looped under his belt. If she was quick enough she could pull out the screwdriver and take Hill out, but then one of the monkeys would shoot her in the head before Hill hit the ground.

She squeezed his hand in return. 'Does this stop now, Paul?'

They stared into one another's eyes and Liberty tried not to blink or breathe. She could feel the cold metal of the screwdriver insistent against the small of her back. At last Hill smiled and released her. 'Course. Never liked K-Dog anyway and none of us need this crap, do we?'

He wiped his hand down his thigh and moved from the stage towards the door, followed by his men. Liberty risked a quick suck of air. When he was at the exit, Hill turned to her. 'So, you're in charge now, are you?'

'No,' Liberty called back. 'This is a family business.'

After Hill had left, Jay opened a cardboard box on the floor behind the bar and extracted a bottle of vodka. He unscrewed the lid and brought the bottle to his lips. He passed it to Crystal, who took a quick gulp, then proffered it to Liberty.

She grabbed it. 'Christ, I thought he was going to kill me.'

As she held the bottle to her lips, her hands were shaking so much the glass rattled against her teeth. She took a drink, then another.

'What do you think?' Jay asked. 'Is he telling the truth?'

'No way of knowing, is there?' said Crystal.

Liberty took another mouthful of vodka and passed it back to her brother. 'I reckon he is.'

'Because?' Crystal asked.

'It's not in his interests to fight with the Greenwoods,' Liberty replied. 'He came to us in the first place, remember? He wanted the Delaney action but not enough to cause a war with another family. He was willing to go fifty-fifty to avoid that. K-Dog was double-dealing.'

'Stupid bastard.' Jay flicked the bottle with his thumbnail. 'But we still don't know who shot Frankie.'

'I'm willing to bet that whoever sent K-Dog to the hospital is behind that,' said Liberty. 'Although we won't be able to ask K-Dog any more questions now, will we?' Jay and Crystal looked back at her blankly. 'Oh, come on. I know full well you two made that happen.' They exchanged a smirk. 'Fine. Don't tell me.' She put up a hand. 'In fact, I'd rather not know.'

'Actually, it wasn't us, Lib,' said Jay. 'I mean, we talked about it, obviously, but we decided to wait and see how things played out first.'

'We knew you could hack it inside. For a while anyway.' Crystal laughed. 'What with you being so hard.'

'Then we really need to work out what's going on sharpish.' Liberty took the bottle from Jay, had a last swig and recapped it. 'Because whoever is behind all this isn't messing about.'

Chapter 21

14 April 1990

I'm still rocked by what Connor has asked me to do. I mean, I get that his mam would suggest it. She hates me anyway. But Connor? He says he loves me and that he wants us to be together. So how can he think I ought to take the rap for the drugs?

He's written me lots of letters since he's been inside. They're on thin blue pieces of paper with the prison's name and address on the top left-hand corner. He prints so hard that when I run my finger along the back I can feel the words coming through.

I love you, Lib. I need you, Lib.

I've got to talk to someone about it all, but Imbo spent yesterday in the park off his head and had to be taken off to hospital for his stomach to be pumped. I go down to Carter Street to see if I can find Vicky but there's no sign of her. A couple of working girls come out of the café and smile at me. 'New, are you?' says one, lighting up a fag. 'You won't get far in them jeans.'

I must look clueless because they screech with laughter at me. Then I realize what they're getting at and laugh too.

'You're a pretty thing though,' she says, through the smoke. 'Young as well.'

'I'm just looking for my mate,' I say. 'Vicky. From Orchard Grove. Do you know her?'

The woman gives a half-smile to her friend. 'Trouble, that one.'

'Have you seen her?' I ask.

'Not for a couple of weeks now,' she says. *'There was a big bust-up with Mel. That boyfriend of Vicky's gave her one slap too many and Mel hit him over the head with a pan, I heard.'* The women laugh. *'He needed stitches and Mel got nicked. I haven't seen hide or hair of Vicky since.'*

I don't really want to go into it with Tiny and Fat Rob because they're Connor's mates. I mean, they've always been lovely to me, but I can't put them in the middle of all this. In the end, though, I've no choice, seeing as the sad fact is that I don't actually have anyone else to talk to.

When I get to the Galaxy, I'm shocked to find the door locked and the closed sign up. It's Saturday and the shop's usually busy. I peer through the window and catch sight of a figure behind the counter so I knock.

The door finally opens and Tiny frowns at me. *'We're not open, Lib.'*

'I can see that.' I smile but she doesn't smile back. *'Can I come in?'*

She moves to one side so I can enter, then locks the door behind me. There's a smell of bleach where she's been cleaning again.

'Sorry about what happened to Connor,' she says, with a heavy sigh.

Back at the counter, as she puts a bunch of records into their sleeves, I can see she's tired.

'He wants me to say the drugs were mine,' I blurt out.

She blows on the vinyl of an EP. When that doesn't get rid of the fluff she wipes it with the sleeve of her jumper. The static crackles. *'So I heard.'*

'Do you think I should do it, Tiny?'

'Not my circus, not my monkeys,' she replies, without looking at me.

'What does that mean?'

'It means I've got a lot on my plate at the moment, Lib, okay?' she says. *'I can't be working out your problems for you. Sorry.'*

I notice then how blotchy her skin is and that she's put on some weight. *'You're pregnant,'* I say. At last she looks at me but all the sparkle has gone from her. *'Are you going to keep it?'*

'No choice.' She pats her stomach. *'Too far gone.'*

'Whose is it?'

'*Doesn't matter.*' *She carries the stack of records from the counter and starts searching for the right places in the racks.* '*I'll be fine on my own.*'

I look round the deserted shop, the sound system silent. '*Why's the Galaxy closed?*'

'*Rob's resigned.*'

'*You're kidding?*'

She's holding a copy of Chime. '*He's got himself a job in Manchester.*' *She waves the record to the left as if that's the way to the city in question.* '*Lucky bastard.*'

Present day

Sol stirred two heaped teaspoons of sugar into his tea.

'Like that, is it?' Scottish Tony asked, as he whisked away the empty sauce-smeared plate.

'And then some,' Sol replied.

Even though the air in the café was a heady mixture of bacon fat and floor cleaner, Sol could smell himself. He needed to buy some fresh clothes, then get a shower back at the nick, which left the small matter of finding somewhere to sleep tonight.

His mobile rang and he saw it was Bucky calling him. 'Hey,' he said.

'Don't hey me, Sol Connolly,' she spat. 'Do you know how close we are to losing Jackson Delaney?'

'The surveillance thing was not my idea, Bucky.'

'Never mind the surveillance, have you read those statements yet?' He hadn't. 'If you haven't read them in the next hour, I will personally come and find you and physically shove them up your arse, Sol.'

'Nice to speak to you too,' he said, but Bucky had already hung up.

He took a sip of tea, sighed and stirred in more sugar. As he opened the first PDF, he figured he was going to need all the help he could get.

'You set me up.'

He looked up and found Liberty standing at the other side of the table. Her cheek was raised and purple, the marks on her neck a less vivid brown in comparison.

'And then you took the gun,' she said. 'Do you want to explain why?'

'I've been trying to live two lives.'

'And how's that working out for you?' she asked.

'My marriage is over and I'm going to have to leave my job,' he replied. 'Oh, and Jackson Delaney's probably going to walk. So, all in all, not exactly perfect.'

She took the seat next to him, reached for his cup and had a drink. 'Christ.' She pulled a face. 'Do you not like your teeth?'

'They're the least of my worries.'

She leaned into her bag, pulled out a key and pushed it across the table towards him with one finger. He didn't look at her, too afraid that a wave of feeling would sweep over the harbour walls and drown him.

'Get a bath,' she said. 'And there are spare toothbrushes under the sink.'

'Won't your roomie have something to say about finding a naked copper in his house?'

'I'm sure he would.' She stood to leave. 'But he's on the missing list.'

Sol slid the key into his pocket. 'And what's your plan?'

'I'm going to do whatever it takes to protect my family.'

The junkie was probably the same age as the younger. Both around sixteen. One selling sex, the other selling crack.

Liberty didn't need to ask herself how both kids had got trapped. She watched the transaction take place from her car. Then the addict beetled away, rock in sweaty fist. On cue, another younger arrived on her bike and screeched to a halt.

'Oi,' Liberty called, through the open window of the Porsche. 'I want a word.'

'You want anything from us, you need to get out of the car,' said the boy.

Liberty opened the door, so they could see her properly. 'Do you know who I am?'

His cockiness evaporated. 'Shit.'

'Double shit,' replied Liberty.

The youngers glanced at one another, then up the street. The girl lifted a foot to her pedal.

'Don't even think about making me chase you,' said Liberty.

The girl sighed extravagantly but dropped her foot to the ground and laid the bike on its side. Then she murmured something to the boy and they stepped towards the Porsche. Liberty gave them a slow handclap.

'Tell me about K-Dog,' she said.

'He's dead,' said the boy.

'So I hear.' Liberty drummed her fingers against the steering wheel. 'Who did he work for?'

'The Hills,' said the boy.

'Who else?'

The boy looked puzzled, but the girl's eyes immediately fell to the pavement. These kids zipped up and down the streets night and day and the sharp ones saw things. Often things they weren't supposed to see.

'No point keeping quiet now,' said Liberty.

The kids didn't answer. Even though they presumably thought Liberty's family had murdered their boss, and they might easily be next, silence remained their default setting.

'It would be pretty stupid to annoy me and Paul Hill to protect someone with a hole in their head the size of a dinner plate.' Liberty leaned back in her seat. 'And I know you're not stupid.'

Fear crept across the boy's face but he obviously didn't know anything useful. He glanced at the girl for help but she kept her eyes steadfastly on the kerb. Liberty turned the key in the ignition and the growl of the engine made both kids jump.

'Fuck's sake, Tia,' said the boy.

The girl's head shot up and she glared at him. He opened his eyes wide at her – what? The girl made a hissing sound. Liberty reached for the door handle to close it.

'I don't know nothing for sure,' the girl said. 'I just saw someone come to the bookie's a few times.'

Liberty kept her hand on the door. 'Who?'

The girl rolled her eyes. 'I didn't ask his name, did I?'

'But you knew he didn't work for Paul Hill.'

The girl shrugged. 'Like you said, I'm not an idiot.'

The girl might not be an idiot, but she was certainly a liar.

As Liberty drove away she was convinced that the girl knew exactly who had visited K–Dog. Or at least which crew he was with.

She called Sol's mobile. 'Did you find the soap?'

'And some deodorant,' Sol replied. 'Your housemate has a fine selection of Lynx.'

'He's sixteen, what do you expect? Listen, I need a favour,' she said. Sol went quiet. They both knew that, whatever it was, it probably fell outside the police code of ethics. 'That file on people who work for Paul Hill. Did it cover the youngers?'

'Only the ones on their way up the chain.'

That was an unlikely description for the snarky BMX girl with muddy jeans. Then again.

'A girl of about sixteen,' said Liberty. 'Called Tia.'

'That rings a bell. I'll call you back.'

Liberty smiled. Underestimating girls was always a mistake. While she waited for Sol she checked her reflection in the rear-view mirror. Not a pretty sight. She had a concealer stick in her handbag, but the mess on her cheek would need a trowel and plaster.

Her phone rang and she gratefully turned away her attention.

'She's not in the Hill file,' said Sol. Liberty frowned. It had been a long shot. 'But then I remembered where I'd heard that name.'

'Go on.'

Sol took a breath. 'I don't suppose you're going to tell me why you want to know?'

'I just want to talk to her.'

'You wanted to talk to K-Dog and look how that ended.'

'Christ, Sol. I'm not going to hurt a kid, am I?'

When he didn't immediately reply, Liberty was stung. Was that what he thought of her? Of her family? That even a young girl wasn't safe?

'Hassani interviewed her,' he said at last.

'What about?'

'She was at the flat where Frankie was shot,' he said.

'Then I really do need to speak to her.'

There was another pause on the line. If Sol refused to play ball, could she blame him? A year ago, he'd met a woman who had lied to the police to protect her brother. Twelve months later, she'd been arrested for waving a gun around. Why on earth would he trust her?

'I'll mail you the statement,' he said.

It was over. As soon as the clock struck five and her shift ended, Amira received an email from the DCI asking her to come up to his office. He'd given her five days and what had she to show for it? Chapman was out on bail, pending a case review. But without the gun and K-Dog there was no case.

She punched the clear board, which flew across the room, scattering photographs like leaves in autumn. There was no way she'd be allowed to stay on the OCU now. The DCI would sideline her somewhere she couldn't cause any more embarrassment. Community Relations, maybe. And she'd be sacked if Chapman made a complaint.

Sol had stitched her up. She'd thought he'd seen the light when he told her that she'd find the lawyer with K-Dog. Instead, he was laying a trail of breadcrumbs and Amira had walked – no, she'd run – right into the gingerbread cottage.

Well, if she was about to lose everything, then so was he. The DCI might close down the surveillance on Chapman, but he couldn't ignore proof that, even now, Sol was involved with her. He'd be at her house this very second. Where else could he go? It might not be enough to get him arrested but it would end his career for sure. She ignored a second email from the DCI and set off to catch Sol Connolly.

As she arrived at Empire Rise her timing couldn't have been better. She snatched up her phone and filmed Sol leaving the house. She wanted to scream at him but instead she waited until he got into his car and put her own back in gear to follow him.

The Crosshills never improved. From time to time, the council would open a memorial garden or unveil a swanky new set of signposts. There'd even been a programme on the telly about it, where a group of award-winning architects tried to spruce the place up with new railings and jaunty colours for the doors.

Liberty almost admired the perseverance with a place so determined to remain a shithole.

When she reached the address on the statement she banged loudly. Tia tried to slam the door shut as soon as she saw who it was but Liberty jammed her foot inside and pushed. The girl was strong for her age, but no match for Liberty, who smacked the door against the wall, sending the younger backwards.

'I'm not here to hurt you, Tia,' said Liberty, forcing her way in, 'but I will if I have to.'

Tia scowled but gave up the fight. 'What do you want?'

'For one thing, I want to know why you lied to the police about who bought the drugs when Frankie was shot.'

Tia stomped into her kitchen and turned on the tap. She grabbed a chipped mug from the side and filled it. 'Does it matter who bought them?'

'It does, if you're trying to cause confusion about where you were.' Liberty watched the girl take a gulp. 'See, I think you were inside the room with my brother and you saw full well who arrived to take him out.' A dribble of water escaped from Tia's lips and the girl quickly wiped it away. 'I also think you know exactly who came to see K-Dog.'

The girl tried not to show any emotion, but Liberty noticed she was squeezing the handle of the mug so tightly her knuckles were white.

'Tell me what I need to know and I'll leave you alone,' said Liberty.

'I can't.'

'Then things are going to . . .'

The words disappeared in Liberty's throat as the girl smashed the cup into the side of her head.

Chapter 22

15 April 1990

Easter Sunday. The new foster carers had better have bought the kids lots of eggs. Our Frankie loves the ones with chocolate buttons.

Imbo's in Vicky's bed. They let him out of the hospital late last night and Carl tried to get him into his own room but gave up around midnight.

I tell him I'm off out for a bit and he grunts. His throat will be sore from all the tubes they had to shove down him.

When I get to Fat Rob's I suddenly feel a bit shy because I've never been here before. But I need to see him before he leaves for Manchester. He answers the door in a too tight Frankie Goes to Hollywood T-shirt and his pants. I have to laugh. As we walk past the kitchen a bloke looks up from a stack of bread he's buttering and waves at me. It has to be Rob's dad because they're like carbon copies, only Rob's dad hasn't any hair left.

'You must be Pretty Lib,' he says.

'Shut up, Dad,' says Rob, and pushes me up the stairs.

His bedroom is a mess and a fag is burning in an ashtray on the floor. On the bed there's a massive green rucksack, like the sort you might use for camping. Rob grabs a grey cardigan with toggles and stuffs it in. It'll be creased to high heaven in ten minutes flat.

'I gather you're leaving,' I say.

'It's all a bit mad.' He flaps his arms around the chaos of his room.

273

'I applied for this job ages ago and didn't hear back. Then they called out of the blue and said, "Can you start next week?"'

I sink onto his bed. The duvet cover is black and white checks, like a chessboard. I doubt very much that Fat Rob plays chess.

'Have you been to see Connor?' I ask him.

He crouches in front of me and puts his hands on my shoulders. 'No, and I'm not going to either.'

'Why?'

'After what he's asking you to do for him?' Rob shakes his head. 'Sorry, but that's just taking the piss.'

'He says he won't be able to stand it in prison.'

'Then he should have trained to be a plumber.'

He hugs me then. A big Fat Rob bear hug.

'I'll miss you,' I say.

'Why don't you come with me?' I laugh, but then I realize he's not joking. He shrugs. 'Why not? I've got somewhere to live. There's only one bed but I'll be working most nights.'

'I've got to finish my A levels next year,' I say.

He reaches over for his fag, takes a last drag and grinds it out. 'I know they're pretty backward over the Pennines but I hear they've got schools.'

'What about the kids?'

'I hear they have buses as well,' he says. 'They go in both directions and everything.' He stands up and tries to squash a last pair of socks into his bag. 'Seriously, Lib. Let's just get out of here while we can.'

Present day

Liberty tried to open her eyes but the right one felt as if something heavy was sitting on the lid. She reached to touch it and stickiness came away on her fingers.

Somewhere in the greyness, she could hear hissing. No, not hissing, whispering.

'What did you do that for?'

It was a familiar voice. The voice of a boy. Liberty forced open her left eye and saw two figures looming over her. The girl. Tia. And a boy. She recognized the boy. Dax.

'She knows,' the girl said. 'We need to get out of here.'

What was Dax doing here? And why were he and the girl above Liberty? She tried to ask but she couldn't form the words. When Dax's face came towards her, and she felt something solid beneath her, she realized she was lying on her back on the floor.

Dax looked into Liberty's one good eye. 'You've really mashed her up, Tia.'

'You're not listening, Dax.' The girl's voice was louder now. 'She knows everything and we need to go before we end up like K-Dog.'

'Lib would never hurt me.'

Liberty gave a grunt. She would never hurt Dax. He reached under her head with his hand and helped her to sit up. Immediately the room spun and, before she could stop it, vomit sprang from her mouth.

'Gross,' said the girl.

With her stomach contents expelled, the fog in Liberty's mind cleared a little. She'd been talking to the girl. The girl had been drinking water. Then nothing.

'She hit me with the mug,' Liberty mumbled.

'Sorry,' Dax replied. 'She panicked.'

Tia snorted. 'I was not panicking, thank you for asking. I don't do panic.'

Liberty put her hands in Dax's. 'Pull me up.'

'You might have a concussion,' he said.

The bells in Liberty's ears rang, like a church's on Easter Sunday. She'd been knocked out with a Star Wars mug. Of course she had a concussion. 'Just bloody well pull me up.'

Dax kissed his teeth but did as he was told. When she was on her feet, Liberty grabbed the side of the sink and threw up in it.

Then she turned on the tap and shoved her lips under the stream of water. She rinsed her mouth and spat.

'I thought you said she was posh,' the girl muttered.

Liberty closed her eyes for a second and steadied her breath. 'I'm from the Crosshills, the same as you.'

There was some kitchen roll on the windowsill so Liberty ripped off a couple of sheets and ran them under the tap. She then pressed the soggy wodge to her swollen eye. It all came back to her now. The girl had lied about being with Frankie when he was shot. In her statement to Hassani she'd said Ozzie had bought the drugs. But there was something else Liberty remembered about that statement. There was a new boy in the area. And he'd been there that day too.

She turned to Dax. 'You've been working for K-Dog?'

'I had to,' he replied. 'You wouldn't let me work for Jay and I needed money. Tia's mum's taken off to live with some bloke in Derby and the rent's already in arrears.'

'I told you I could sort it myself,' Tia snapped.

'You don't have to do everything on your own,' Dax snapped back.

Liberty removed the kitchen roll from her eye and found it was smeared with blood. She threw it in the sink on top of her vomit and saliva and ripped off a fresh sheet from the roll. She'd wanted to protect Dax from a life of crime but the law of unintended consequences had had other ideas.

'You were both at the flat when Frankie was shot,' she said. 'You saw who did it so just tell me.'

Dax looked at Tia, who covered her mouth with her hand. 'It was an accident,' he said. 'Frankie was giving Tia a hard time. Off his tits, putting the cash down his jeans and saying she should stick her hand down and get it.' Dax swallowed hard. 'You know what a prick he can be, Lib.'

'What are you telling me here, Dax?'

'I just meant to shut him up,' he said. 'Scare him a bit. But he grabbed the gun and it went off.'

Night had fallen by the time Sol reached the Crosshills. He checked the address again. Whatever she might think, he did trust Liberty not to hurt a kid, but the kid might well try to hurt her. Who knew what might happen then?

He didn't plan to go storming in but to wait nearby in case the shit hit the fan. Hopefully the girl would give up what she knew and Liberty would leave her alone.

He pulled a packet of Marlboro Lights from his pocket. No point in even pretending he'd given up. He flicked his lighter as he approached the stairwell but a rustling sound from behind made him start. Had it not been for the flame, he wouldn't have caught sight of the hijab (not for the first time, Sol noted that smoking could sometimes be good for you).

He lit up and shouted, 'Amira. No need to hide.' There was a pause during which Sol found himself staring at the bins, before Hassani stepped out. 'Fancied some night air, did you?' She held up her phone, obviously filming him so he threw a few shapes. 'YouTube, here I come.'

'Do you think this is a joke, Sol?'

'You're the joke here.'

She waggled her phone at him. 'You won't be laughing when I send these pictures to the DCI.'

'I won't care.'

'You'll be sacked.'

'I already resigned.' Sol took a long drag and enjoyed the look on Hassani's face. 'Emailed him earlier and funnily enough he accepted by return.'

'You'll be arrested,' she spat at him.

'For what?' He laughed at her. 'Smoking in a built-up area?'

'You made evidence disappear.'

'Well, why don't you let Dynamo know that?' Sol said. 'I'm looking for a new job.' Her eyes scorched him with a depth of hatred he'd never seen in all his years of making arrests. 'You can't touch me, Amira, because I have nothing left to lose.' He tossed the cigarette away. 'Now just go home to your son.'

Dax had shot Frankie. The thought of it made Liberty cold. Tia might claim never to panic, but something very close to it was welling in Liberty's chest.

When Jay and Crystal found out, they would kill Dax. It wouldn't matter that it had been an accident. It wouldn't matter that so much of all this was Liberty's fault. 'You have to leave,' she told him.

Tia tutted. 'Haven't I been saying that?'

'How?' Dax asked. 'K–Dog owed us a week's dollar but we ain't getting that now, are we?'

'I'll get you some money,' said Liberty. 'But you can't stay here. Frankie could wake up any second and tell everyone what went on.'

'Haven't I been saying that as well?' Tia asked.

'Get your stuff together now and go,' said Liberty. 'I'll round up as much cash as I can.'

'Shall we wait at yours?' Dax asked.

Liberty and Tia exchanged a glance. The girl was going to have her work cut out.

'Make your way over to the Trap.' Liberty dragged the keys from her pocket and handed them to Tia. 'Do you know where it is?' The girl nodded. 'Don't put the lights on, okay? Just wait for me there.'

* * *

278

Liberty ran from the flat and sped off in the Porsche. She could put her hands on a couple of grand easily enough. Then she would send Dax and Tia back to London. He knew people there who would put them up until they could sort themselves out. She'd tried to change his life and failed. Now the best she could hope for was to keep him alive.

Go home to your son.

Who did Sol Connolly think he was dismissing? Didn't he understand that everything Amira did was *for* her son, so that he could grow up in a world where right and wrong were not movable goalposts?

When Chapman's fancy car roared away, with Sol hot on her tail, Amira had almost been tempted to follow, but she knew she'd be spotted in ten seconds. And Sol was right: she couldn't prove he'd committed any crime. No amount of chasing after the two of them would change that tonight.

Instead she stayed put and tried to work out what to do next.

She didn't have to wait long before two figures charged past her, bags on their backs, plastic carriers stuffed with clothes in their arms. She knew the girl, Tia Rainsford, and she recognized the lad. Was he the one she'd seen coming out of Chapman's house? Amira scrolled through her photo roll and found him.

'There you are.'

When the pair jumped into a taxi, Amira got into her own car and followed. She wasn't done yet. Not by a long way.

Chapter 23

2 May 1990
'There's a letter for you,' says Carl.

For a second, I wonder if it's from Connor, but then I see it's in an ordinary white envelope. I'm not that surprised. Connor hasn't been in touch since I told him I wouldn't do what he wanted.

My name and address are written in pink felt tip and the postmark says Manchester.

Dear Lib

I hope you're all right. Did you get the court date yet to see your Crystal and Frankie? What about Jay? Did he get out yet?

Sorry I didn't write sooner but it's mental here. I'm working most nights in the club, then sleeping all day. The scene is banging — you would love it. The crowds we get are unbelievable. It's a massive buzz when I do a set and they're all waving their arms at me. I wish you could see it.

How's school? I still don't get why you needed until the end of term to decide what you're doing. There's nothing left for them to teach you, you chuffing little genius.

I got a letter from Connor the other day. My mam forwarded it on to me. He sounds sorry for himself but you know what? We all have to take responsibility for our own actions in this life. You can't expect

other folk to clean up the mess you've made. I can't be arsed to write
back to him.

Well I'll love you and leave you cos I need some kip.

I'm not going to nag you again about coming over here but how
about we meet up at the Stone Roses gig at Spike Island? I can get
you on the guest list no bother. Just let me know.

Take care
Your friend for ever
Fat Rob
PS I'm not that fat any more now my dad's not cooking for me!!!!

I put the letter back in the envelope and slip it into my school bag.

'I've got a travel voucher here for you to see Jay when he gets out next
Thursday,' says Carl.

'Right.'

'We don't know where he'll be placed after that so you'll want a contact visit before he goes.'

'Right.'

'Oh, and don't forget we've arranged for you to visit that halfway house
at the weekend,' he says.

I nod and leave for school.

Present day

A group of students wearing superhero costumes were making
themselves comfortable in the Cherry. They pushed three tables
together and shouted above the music, their Batman capes swishing around them. One lad, dressed as Wonder Woman, complete
with a set of plastic boobs and a tiara, was drinking beer from the
pitcher, spilling it down his leotard.

Mel watched them like a hawk, as ever waiting for the moment
when rowdy tipped into bedlam.

Liberty nodded at her as she strode past to the office. Once inside, she went straight to the mirror on the back wall, heaving it to one side to get access to the safe. Her Prada purse contained a multitude of credit cards and one for the cashpoint, but Liberty needed to get her hands on as many notes as she could muster. She tapped in the code. Even though they'd hated their father for what he'd done, Jay used his birthday. At least, no one could forget it. She reached in and grabbed a stack of cash. Using her thumb to peel through the notes, she estimated there was about four grand.

'Everything okay?'

Liberty turned and found Mel watching her. 'Yep.' She relocked the safe and put the mirror back in place. 'Just need a bit of cash.'

'Why do I assume you don't want me to tell Jay about this?'

'I'll have it back by tomorrow lunchtime,' said Liberty. Mel fingered the tangle of gold necklaces she always wore. 'You owe me some discretion, Mel. I didn't tell anyone about what you suggested to Frankie.'

'How long are you going to hold that one over me?'

'As long as it takes.'

The sound of shouts and breaking glass came from the club and Mel made for the door. 'Fine. It's your money anyway. Not my business.'

'I think we both know that's bollocks.'

A yellow glow escaped from an upstairs window of the Trap and Liberty tutted. Hadn't she told Dax and Tia not to put any lights on? The whole point was to draw no attention to themselves.

She went inside, dropping the latch, and immediately heard muffled voices from upstairs. Christ, they couldn't even keep quiet for half an hour. As she climbed the stairs, the noise became louder and there was thumping. Surely they weren't having sex.

They might be teenagers but even they must know that now was not the time.

When she reached the top, there was a shout. Should she give them five minutes? Vague memories of being sixteen told her that would be long enough. The shout turned to a scream. Then there was a smash, as if wood was breaking.

'Dax?'

She charged across the landing and reached for the door handle but it burned her hand. What was happening? On the other side, the shouts became more frantic. Liberty took a step back and kicked open the door. There was a whoosh of air and an intense heat that knocked her off balance, and for the second time in the last couple of hours she found herself flat on her back.

As she scrabbled to her feet, the air filled with an acrid black smoke that stung her eyes and filled her mouth, like cotton wool. She tried to spit it out but it came at her again and again. Then the flames were jumping from the room beyond to the landing, the ancient wallpaper going up in a firework display of oranges and reds.

'Lib.' Dax's voice came through the choking heat. 'We can't put it out.'

Liberty couldn't see him through the wall of fire and his voice was almost drowned out by the roar of the blaze.

'Is there anything in there to cover yourself with?' Liberty screamed. 'A blanket or something?'

'It's all gone up.'

Dax said something else but the words were lost as the carpet ignited. Finding herself standing in a sea of flames, Liberty staggered backwards, her arms in front of her face to shield it from the scorching heat.

She felt the top of the stairs rather than saw it as her feet lost solid ground. Her scream was sucked from her body and replaced by a suffocating ball of vapour. She windmilled her arms, desperate

283

to regain her balance, but hit the back of her head against the wall with a sickening thud. Dazed, she tried to work out which way was up and which was down but everything was hot and black. She threw out her hands. To her left she felt something hard that had to be a step. To her right there was nothing. That must be down. She tried to feel for the step below with her foot, but above her something exploded and she was showered with glass.

There was no air left. If she didn't act quickly, she'd pass out. Where was the step? Why couldn't she feel it?

Another bang above, and a wire uncoiled in a shower of blue sparks. She had to move. Eyes blinded by smoke, Liberty curled her hands over her head and let herself fall to the side. Her stomach flipped as she dropped, then pain raged through her shoulder as she landed on it. She bumped down the rest of the stairs, each landing a fresh assault until she collapsed at the bottom.

'Dax!' she screamed.

A pinball of pain ricocheted wildly through Liberty's shoulder and back, touching each nerve ending before moving on to the next. As she tried to push herself up, she cried out. Instead, she crawled away from the stairs on her hands and knees.

When she was back in the main body of the club, she gulped air and inched towards the door. Outside, someone was banging on it. She didn't think she could make it across the room and held up her fingers to it, as if to will the door open. In an eruption of wood and glass it flew wide, then Sol and Hassani burst in.

Amira shot into the club and covered her mouth against the smoke. She'd already called the fire brigade, but in the minutes it would take them to arrive, she could tell the whole place would be an inferno.

She grabbed Chapman's shoulders, and the lawyer howled. Dislocated by the look of it. 'Where are the kids?'

'Upstairs.'

Amira ran to the doorway to the stairs.

'You'll never get up there,' Chapman shouted.

Ignoring her, Amira yanked open the door and was bulldozed by the heat and dense cloud of toxic smoke. She slammed it shut and ran to Sol, who was helping Chapman to her feet.

'Give me your jacket, Sol.'

'No way,' he said.

She tried to tear it from his back. 'For fuck's sake, there are kids upstairs.'

He shook his head but relinquished it. As Amira put the jacket over her head all she could smell was Sol Connolly.

Outside, the cool air embraced Liberty's skin. Sol's mouth moved but she couldn't catch the words.

The top floor was engulfed now. No one could survive. Liberty let a tear slide down her cheek. Then a window smashed, a chair flying out into the night and crashing to the ground. A head poked out.

'There,' Liberty whispered, and Sol looked up.

'Amira,' he yelled.

She waved frantically at him, then disappeared inside. Sol and Liberty raced to stand below the window.

A face appeared, but this time it was Tia. Behind her, Hassani was gesticulating wildly.

'Jump, Tia,' Liberty screamed. Tia climbed out onto the window ledge and looked down. 'Jump.' The noise of sirens crashed towards them and blue lights flashed. 'Now.'

Tia put out her arms and let herself plummet. When she hit

the ground, there was the crack of bone as her leg went under her. The sound of her shrieks joined the sirens.

Two faces appeared now in the space where the window had been. Dax and Hassani.

'Come on,' Liberty pleaded.

Something passed between Dax and Hassani. What the hell were they doing? Deciding who should go next? Hassani was pushing Dax. His hands were reaching out to grab the top of the window frame when the fireball went off like a shell.

Liberty lost her balance as the ambulance careered around a corner and steadied herself against Tia's stretcher. The girl took off her oxygen mask. 'Do you think they made it?'

'The fire brigade were there,' Liberty answered.

The paramedic looked up from strapping Tia's leg. He exchanged a glance with Liberty. They both knew there was no way. 'Put your mask back on,' he told Tia.

Tia grabbed Liberty's hand. 'What Dax said was true, you know? The thing with Frankie, it was an accident.' Liberty nodded and went to press the oxygen mask over Tia's mouth and nose. 'He's a bit thick but he's not K–Dog crazy, you know what I mean? As soon as I saw what K–Dog was up to, I knew he'd get himself killed.' Liberty's hand froze. 'You can't work for two crews.'

'Who was it?' Liberty asked.

'Mask,' said the paramedic.

Tia panted, pain filling her, yet she held the mask away so she could speak.

'Who?' Liberty whispered.

Chapter 24

27 May 1990

The platform at Lime Street station is rammed and the staff seem to have given up checking tickets, which is lucky because I haven't got one.

A sea of people are laughing and shouting and drinking from cans as we wait for the train to Widnes. I move my rucksack from one shoulder to the other.

A lad in a white fishing hat bangs into me, his beer sloshing down my arm. He's wearing the same Stone Roses T-shirt that Connor lent me last New Year's Eve.

'Sorry, love,' he says.

I shake my head that it doesn't matter, and when he smiles I can smell the weed on him.

'On your own, then?' he asks.

Before I can answer, one of his mates smacks him across the back of the head, pushing the hat over his eyes. 'Moz, are you on the pull, soft lad?'

Moz laughs and slides his hat back. 'Can't I be a bit nice to a girl without you lot accusing me of trying to get my leg over?'

The train pulls in and the crowd surges forward. I'm just thinking I won't get on when Moz grabs me. As the train doors shut, I'm just inside.

'Thanks,' I say.

The train sets off and people start cheering.

'What's your name, then?' Moz asks me.

'Lib.'

'That short for Liberty?'

I pause. 'Yeah.'

When the train arrives at Widnes, the crowd streams off towards Spike Island, and Moz disappears with his mates. I don't know where I'm going so I just follow the flow of people. At last, I arrive at the spot I said I'd meet Fat Rob. If he doesn't show up, I'm buggered. No ticket and no money to get home.

I see him before he sees me. Thinner than before but that hair still needs a good scrub.

'Rob,' I shout.

He turns to my voice and grins when he sees me. And I run. I don't know why but I can't wait the few seconds it will take me to walk to him.

'All right, Lib?' he asks.

I throw my arms around his neck, too scared that if I try to speak I'll just end up crying.

'Come on,' he says, and shows a wristband to a bloke on the gate. 'There's loads of acts on before the Roses. Bands, DJs and that.'

'Are you doing a set?' I ask.

He laughs. 'One day, maybe.'

As we pass through the gate, a pretty lass trundles up to us, a plait jiggling on either side of her head. She kisses Rob. On the mouth. Then grabs my rucksack from me.

'Christ,' she says. 'What have you got in here? Breeze blocks?'

I laugh. What I've got in there is everything I own. My clothes, shoes and books. All the paperwork on the kids' court cases.

'Girlfriend?' I whisper in Rob's ear.

'Dunno,' he says. 'Think so.' He gives me a helpless smile. 'Just taking it one day at a time.'

'Will there be room for me back at yours in Manchester?' I ask.

He puts his arm around my shoulders. 'For as long as you like, Lib.'

BANG TO RIGHTS

A gust of cold wind blows in off the Mersey, but I don't care as a DJ takes to the decks and drops the first bars of Chime.

Present day

The funeral was an official one, with plenty of top brass in attendance. Sol had bought a new suit and tie, which itched in every crevice.

Hassani's family watched with a stoic dignity. Father, brother, son. Sol wondered if anyone had let the ex-husband know what had happened. Then again, it had been on the news and in the papers so it was unlikely he wouldn't have heard. If it had been Sol, Angie would have wanted to be there, he reckoned. Even Natasha might have turned up, if only to dance on his grave.

As Hassani's body was lowered into the ground, her brother spoke in Arabic.

'Bismillah wa ala millati rasulillah.'

Sol swallowed. Hassani had behaved like a weapons-grade bitch towards him, but she'd died trying to save a couple of street kids and you couldn't say fairer than that.

When the burial was over, Sol was about to slip away when the DCI marched over to him. 'Sol.'

'Sir.'

'Apparently it was faulty wiring,' said the chief super. 'An accident waiting to happen.'

'So I hear.'

'Any idea what she was doing there?'

'I guess she couldn't resist one last throw of the dice,' said Sol, with a smile.

The DCI didn't smile back. 'I suppose you know what's happening with Delaney?'

Sol did know. Raj Singh had made his application for the release of all details of the anonymous witnesses on the case.

Bucky was fighting it, not least because three of them had been involved in Delaney's last arrest and been found guilty of gross misconduct. Singh had also listed an application to Crown Court for bail. Delaney would probably be out by the end of the week, albeit with stringent conditions.

Liberty watched Frankie from the chair by his bed.

The doctors had removed the tube from his mouth and he was breathing for himself. They'd told her that technically he could wake up now, but there was no sign of it.

The door opened, and Sol entered. 'How is he?'

'They're going to do a brain scan tomorrow,' she replied.

Her shoes made no noise as she crossed to Sol and ran a finger down his tie. 'I could quite fancy you all suited and booted.'

'Don't blame you.' He kissed her head. 'No house, no job, a terrible track record with women. I'd say I'm quite the catch.'

Liberty smiled. She couldn't have cared less about his finances or job prospects and his previous relationships were none of her concern. What mattered was that Sol made her feel something. She couldn't put a name to it, but it was real. 'Let's put the past behind us,' she said.

Sol placed a hand on either side of her waist. 'I can't see that working out for you.'

'How do you mean?'

'You're a Greenwood, Lib. You're not going to turn your back on your family.'

'No, I'm not.' She put a finger to his mouth. 'But I'm not going to let things carry on as they are either. Dax and Hassani are dead. Frankie's like this. Things have got to change.'

'It won't be easy,' said Sol.

'I'm thinking of getting that tattooed on my arse.'

He smiled at her, and she was about to suggest they head back to her place when a horrible rasping sound came from Frankie's bed. Liberty whipped around and found Frankie awake, eyes wide, body shaking violently.

'Get a nurse,' she shouted, but Sol was already out of the room.

In two steps, Liberty was with her baby brother, a choked hiss escaping from his mouth. She grabbed his hand and found his skin was wet.

'Do not die on me, Frankie,' she screamed. 'Don't you dare die on me.'

As another shudder ran through his body, Liberty glared at the door. Where was the crash team? If they didn't come soon, it would be too late.

'It's me,' she told Frankie. 'It's Lib.'

His mouth opened and closed, and the convulsions died away. Please let this not be the end. Not like this. Just a bit more time to turn everything around. She could do it. Save them. All she needed was time.

'Lib . . .' Frankie's voice came out little more than a scratch.

'Yes, baby?'

'Tell me you're not shagging that copper.'

There were worse things than prison. And Jacko had experienced a fair few of them. The way to get through a stretch was to impose some order. Make sure that those around understood what he would and wouldn't tolerate. After that it was a matter of filling the time. Newspaper, crossword, a turn around the yard.

Still, he'd be glad to get out. His assets were officially frozen but there was plenty of cash he could lay his hands on. He fancied a trip to the football. These days, the Hoops were worse than useless but you couldn't beat the atmosphere in Celtic Park.

He picked up his soap and towel and wandered to the showers.

'Do us a favour, Jacko?' someone called.

'Depends what it is.'

The young lad walked in step. Jacko had seen him arrive, all rattling teeth and snotty nose. Smack heads were the same on the in or the out.

'I need a bit of gear, Jacko.'

Didn't they always. 'You know the terms.'

The lad nodded furiously. He'd have some poor wee lassie at home, desperate for nappies and baby food.

They entered the shower block and Jacko pulled off his shirt. 'Get the money to my people and oblivion shall be yours.' He turned on the water and the pipes gurgled. When the junkie didn't leave, he sighed. 'I've not got it on me now.'

'Right.'

When the young lad still hovered, Jacko felt annoyance bubble up. He'd always had trouble keeping a lid on things. Over the years, he'd learned to hide it but it was just an act.

'Are you wanting a look at my sack?' he asked.

He didn't see the shank before it was inside him, but the pain was searing as the junkie twisted and pulled. Then the blood gushed out of Jackson Delaney, spilling onto the tiles. As he put a hand to the wound and felt the warmth of his insides, he looked at the lad. 'Paul Hill?'

The lad gave a wee smile and shook his head. 'Liberty Greenwood says, "Fuck you."'

Acknowledgements

This novel, my ninth, was a joy to write. Lib's story flew from my head onto the page, and I'm so very grateful to all those who have helped me share it with the wider world.

To Krystyna and everyone at Constable, thank you so much. Of course the Buckman gang. When I write my tenth novel, do I get a commemorative bench? And last, but never least, my love and thanks go to my family. Your support and encouragement are never taken for granted.